A Sense of Place

Dennis Hurley

ACKNOWLEDGMENTS

A big thank you to my wife, Kathy for her support and feedback and to all my friends and family who provided both feedback and encouragement, to my Uncle, Jack Kelly who taught me to love the land and to Kelly Kimberly Brock for the cover photo.

Chapter 1

Wes Callaghan stood alone at the room's curtained arch, his eyes riveted on the casket resting in the dim light cast by a dusty chandelier. He had made all the arrangements long distance from Raleigh, North Carolina as soon as he got the word, or at least Kruckshank and Sons Funeral Home had made all the arrangements- a cheap casket, a second-rate burial plot. It had taken two days to wrap up his affairs in Raleigh.

He had left as darkness moved across the mountains. He drove north through that darkness, stopped once for gas at a tiny gas station north of Cincinnati and then drove into a foggy morning before stopping again for gas, a coffee and some greasy eggs outside of Cleveland. He crossed into Michigan before noon and for an hour and a half flowed with and then against the current of traffic heading into Detroit. North of the city the flow eased, and as he headed off the freeway and up through Lake Orion and Oxford, he felt the country settling in around him, falling into place as he remembered it until he finally crossed the county line into Lapeer county.

Now, as he stood in the funeral home entryway, he lifted his left hand and brushed self-consciously at the cowlick of black hair that stood up defiantly from the back of his head.

Black Irish, that's what his mom had called him as a young boy. He hadn't known then what it had meant, but he had come to think of it as something to be embarrassed about somehow, and some of that embarrassment still clung to him through his manhood. He stepped back into the entry hall and walked over to look at the guest register. Half a dozen names hung suspended at the top of the page. Most he recognized, a few he didn't. Probably all had come more out of curiosity than to pay their respects. It didn't really matter because as far as he could tell, the dead never look at their guest books anyway. He turned back to the viewing room without signing his own name to the list.

He sat down on a faded straight back chair at the rear of the room and watched the casket resting in the half darkness. But the watching changed nothing, he decided; no long-hidden secrets would be revealed; Cassie would still be dead and he would feel as lost as he ever had. Wes stood up and walked the length of the room to the casket, but the half-light created a strange disconnected feeling for him as he crossed the worn carpet, almost a floating sensation. The casket itself, unadorned and without flowers surrounding it, seemed the only thing grounded and of permanence in the room. That and the body it contained.

Cassie Nielson appeared smaller than Wes remembered. The Cassie he saw there seemed little more than a withered stick of a man, really, but his hands, folded on his stomach, told the truth. They were rough and callused; the arthritic knuckles pushed at the leathery skin of the thick fingers. In a room that smelt of death Cassie's hands had a living, accusing energy all their own.

A red velvet kneeler pressed against his shins as he bent to look closer at the face of the man who had played such an important role in his life, and for a moment he considered saying a prayer, but he couldn't for the life of him think what he would be praying for or to whom he would be praying. Instead, he turned away and drifted back through the darkness and out the doors into the sunshine.

He stood on the porch for a moment, stretched his arms upward and then lowered them only to hunch his shoulders up and then roll them back along his ears and down again. He stood just under six feet and seemed even taller with his lanky, sinewy frame. From every angle his body gave the impression of an athlete, strong and hard but not in the kind of artificial way that came from working out in a gym. The drive had taken its toll and he felt stiff in every joint. Since he had passed the forty mark, it seemed like everything hurt more.

Hazy sunlight backlit the red and gold of October. He let his eyes adjust to the change in light, and ran his hand once again through his hair, fingers digging against the scalp. The last time he had been in this funeral home had been when they had buried his grandpa out of it more than thirty years ago, the same year they put Cassie away for the murder. Thirty years to come to grips with it, and yet, he still didn't know for sure what he felt. Somehow though, he believed that in this burying he would find release from his last responsibility to Cassie, and maybe from that he could finally achieve a sense of peace.

He stood in the sun for a few minutes and then as if drawn by a string, he slowly started to walk west on Main Street. Partridge Creek, like Lapeer County itself, had changed since he'd left. Most of the buildings were still there, but many of the old two-story Victorian storefronts were boarded up now. What remained could only be described as utilitarian- a general store, a gas station, the mill at the edge of town, one small restaurant that served breakfast and lunch only, a few large houses set back under the shade of sugar maples. They had once housed retired farmers, wealthy merchants from a time before he had known the town, and he realized then that Partridge Creek had always been changing; he had just been too close to it growing up to see what was happening. At the end of the street he swung back along the other side, walked the raised concrete sidewalk until he stopped opposite the funeral home again.

Just then an old Lincoln angled into a parking place in front of Kruckshank's, and a tall, gaunt man, that he guessed to be in his mid-sixties, got out. The man stood beside the car for a moment, took one last drag on a cigarette and flicked it away. He wore an awkward dark suit, a high-necked white shirt-- but he was a man clearly more used to overalls and manure than dress clothes and funerals.

"Howdy." His voice sounded weaker than Wes remembered, and he punctuated his greeting with a ragged cough, but the tone sounded the same, and the shock of it stunned Wes for a moment. John Patrick Callaghan. Everybody had always called him Pat. When they were teenagers, Pat had been the epitome of the old cliché, a man among boys, two-twenty and solid muscle from years of slinging hay bales and feed sacks on Grandpa's farm. Wes had seen him pick up a three-hundred-pound heifer calf once, pick it up and hold it for a full minute while it struggled against him. Pat had been an All-State tackle on the football team at the Partridge Creek Consolidated High School his junior year, a solid, square Irishman. Now only the Irishness of his brother remained.

Wes wanted to turn away, to disappear before Pat recognized him, but instead without thinking, he called out Pat's name and immediately regretted it.

A Sense of Place

Pat squinted through the glare that separated them. "Wes? Is that you? Damn. Can't believe it." A smile split his face into two distinct parts. "Wes," he said again, like he really couldn't believe it. Neither of them moved, suspended for a moment between the separation and the connection. They stood there awkwardly. Finally, Wes crossed the street and took Pat's outstretched hand.

"How are you, Pat?"

"Oh, I get by. Hey, but look at you. It appears like you've hardly changed a bit, boy. Not even much gray in them black locks of yours, though it looks like you're wearing them a might long. You some kind of damned hippie or something?" He smiled again. "Naw, that can't be it. My little brother couldn't never be no hippie. Discracin' the family name that way. Looks like you've filled out some though, put a little muscle on that skinny frame." He stopped and looked up the street like he expected to see somebody else he knew, and then he turned his attention back to Wes. "What you doing back up here? What's it been, twenty-five years?" Wes didn't' correct him. Pat paused, gazed up and down the street distractedly, then swung his gaze back again.

"You'd hardly know the town, I'd guess. Nobody left around here from when you were here last. Well, hardly anybody." Pat smiled like he had some private joke going. "Where you headed?"

"I'm kind of between jobs." He'd been more between jobs than on jobs most of his life, so he didn't feel like he was lying there. The truth- he'd never quit when he left and probably could go back, but somehow, he knew he wouldn't, just like so many times before.

"Well then, shit. You've got to stay a couple of days. We got plenty of room up at the place. We got a whole lot of catchin' up to do. You little sonofabitch. I thought you was dead." He shook his head. "Wes," he said again. "I can't hardly believe it."   Wes frowned trying to think of some good excuse to let him just walk away, but nothing came to him quickly. Pat mistook the frown.

"Now don't you worry about imposin'. I wouldn't be askin' if I didn't mean it. You ought to know me better'n that."

"Yeah, I know you." It was all Wes could think of to say for a minute, and Pat moved away from the car and walked toward the steps of the funeral parlor. Actually, "walked" didn't really describe it. He limped badly, kind of hitching his left leg along with an awkward lift of the hip as he moved.

"I ain't taking no for an answer. You wait out here while I go in and take a look at the old boy." He climbed the steps and disappeared into the darkness just inside the door.

Wes stared after him. The man he'd guessed to be in his sixties was no more than forty-seven, two years older than him. He looked as if a stiff wind could blow him away. Wes turned and stood gazing out across the cracked blacktop of Main Street. Corn fields, neat rows of stubble now after the harvest, blended seamlessly into meadows of browning wild grasses and the dark bark of buckthorn and then beyond that into forest. The wild edge. That was Cassie. He had spent his life in this outdoor landscape in a time when the rest of the world had moved inside.

Pat was twelve, and Wes was ten when they first came to their grandparents' Lapeer county farm. They didn't come as a matter of choice or for a vacation at the farm. They came because they had no place else to go. They came because their parents had driven away one morning and crashed through the rail of an icy bridge and dropped over a hundred feet to the riverbed below. In the end they had nothing but a couple of closed caskets and an empty haunted feeling that followed them into manhood.

And so, in the damp cold of early March, 1938, they found themselves standing next to Grandpa Callaghan on the gravel drive of his Lapeer county farm while he unloaded their two bags from the trunk of the old Nash sedan. Wes stared out at the empty fields. The mud was mixed with the winter's barn cleanings, the air thick and heavy with the odor of manure and urine-soaked straw, and he wondered what he was going to do in such a lonely and empty place as this. Grandpa stood beside him for a second, looking off in the same direction as if to see what it was that he saw.

"Them's some mighty pretty fields, ain't they boy." It wasn't a question to be answered, just a statement of fact. "You work real hard around here, and one day all this'll belong to you and your brother, because family sticks together no matter what." He turned and looked down at his grandsons and a strange, sad smile passed like a cloud over his face, and then he handed them their bags, and they followed him to the house.

At the door Grandma met them. She wrapped her arms around Wes and pressed him to her. She was frail and tiny. When she let go, tears were sliding down her face. He just stood with his head down while she hugged Pat. He felt strange standing there, like he was supposed to do something, maybe cry too, but he hadn't cried when his folks died, and he didn't cry with Grandma, but he had cried more than once since.

They followed Grandma up the stairs to a tiny space under the eaves of the old farmhouse with a small window that looked out toward the barn and across to where the fields ended.

Grandma laid their things out on a pair of narrow beds covered with tattered quilts. "You must be exhausted, boys. That's a long trip from Cleveland. Whyn't you lie down for a while and I'll fix you a nice supper. I'll call you when it's ready." She turned and disappeared down the stairs.

Wes sat on the floor and stared out at the gray fields again and beyond that to the tree line. "What you looking at?" Pat asked. "They ain't out there; you know that don't you? You can stare out that window forever. They ain't coming back no matter how hard you look for them." His voice quivered, angry. He turned away and lay down on one of the beds, his face to the wall. Wes sat still and waited. In a few minutes Pat's breathing came soft and steady. From behind a clump of bare limbed tamaracks Wes watched a thin ribbon of smoke rise.

Grandma didn't wake them for dinner. In fact, she didn't wake them until after the morning milking was done. Only then did she call them down to a breakfast of pancakes and oatmeal. After eating they went outside. The day was bright and cool, and the boys stood for a minute in the sunshine while their Grandpa lit his pipe and stared out over the fields. In the distance they saw a tiny figure moving out from the trees and heading toward them. Gradually, it became clear that it was a small man dressed in bib overalls and a straw hat. He moved with a certain listless grace, like an animal casually hunting. When he reached them, Grandpa made the introductions. "Wesley, Pat, this here's Cassie Nielson."

Cassie drew his hand from his pocket. Pat turned away and stared off toward the barn, but Wes reached out to shake the hand. Cassie took only his fingertips in a delicate grip, shook once and shoved his heavy, callused hand back into his pocket.

A Sense of Place

Grandpa took out a pad and wrote a list of chores he wanted done. While he wrote, Wes studied Cassie.

He was wiry and tough, his face lined and aged beyond his years which Wes guessed at that time to be about forty, ancient to a ten-year-old boy. Cassie seldom looked up, apparently preferring to examine the circles he was making with the toe of his boot in the gravel drive. Finally, Grandpa handed Cassie the list. He studied it a minute, nodded and turned and headed toward the barn. The brothers started after him but Grandpa called them back. "You stay away from Cassie, you hear? He has work to do and don't need you hangin' around. You come with me and we'll go work on the corn planter."

For the rest of the morning they helped with the work, fetching a tool when Grandpa needed it, cleaning grease fittings with a filthy rag. Whenever there was nothing to do, Wes sat in the sun and stared at the horizon while Pat chucked stones at the large fox squirrels that darted from one small oak to another. They didn't talk.

Once, Cassie came down to where they were working. He motioned for the pad and wrote a question on it and handed it back to Grandpa. Grandpa wrote a brief answer, and Cassie nodded and turned back toward the barn. He moved through the shadows and into the sunlight. Pat stared hard at Cassie's back. Finally, he couldn't stand it any longer. "What's wrong with him? How come he don't talk?"

Grandpa gave one more turn on the wrench, and then looked off after the receding figure. "Can't," he said. "He's stone deaf." Only he pronounced it "deef." " Deaf and dumb. He's what they call a mute."

Noon came and they ate together in silence, the rich, warm smells of the kitchen mixing with the earth scents from their boots and clothing. Cassie's hands darted from plate to mouth, quick birds in flight. Afterward he shoved his chair back from the table, stood up, nodded his head in thanks and headed back to his work. Wes and Pat didn't see him the rest of the day. That evening after supper, Wes lay on the floor of their room and watched the smoke rise once again from the tamarack grove.

Chapter2

Pat shoved open the funeral parlor door and started down the steps. "He don't look all that much different, does he?" he said. He stopped in front of Wes and gave him a piercing look. "Kind of funny you showin' up here for Cassie's funeral when you didn't make it back for your own Grandma's." He paused as if waiting for Wes to respond. When he didn't, Pat went on. "But then you bein' off seein' the country and all, I guess you couldn't't've heard about it."

"I didn't know. When did she die?"

"'Bout two years after grandpa passed. I tried to find you, but didn't have no luck." He stretched his neck like a turtle peering out of its shell and turned his head to scan the street. "What are you driving?" Wes indicated the old, black, Ford pickup parked in front of an abandoned storefront. "Well, follow me, and we'll get you some supper and find a bed for you."

Wes nodded, and headed for his truck. He wanted to just get in and keep driving out of town and away from this chapter that he had avoided for so long, but somehow as he climbed into his truck, he knew that he couldn't. He had to see it through, whatever "through" meant. As Pat pulled the Lincoln by, Wes swung his truck in behind and followed.

They rolled slowly along the main street. The air had a dusty golden feel like you get sometimes in the fall in farm country, particularly Michigan farm country, Wes thought. The odor of burning leaves mixed with the smell of dry fields made the air heavy and almost palpable, and it settled over the sugar maples that cover the lawns. The road, smooth pavement as they passed the last white cluster of houses, rose gradually, curved to the north and continued up a half mile to the highest point in the township then back down into a wide valley. There the old homestead squatted a short way back off the east side of the road. The barn still stood like it had when he had last seen it, but the house presented another story. The clapboard siding showed no signs of ever being painted, pieces of it peeled back and split-dark slashes in its sides. The windows were either broken or boarded up, as if someone hadn't been able to make up their mind whether to keep on going with either its destruction or preservation. Wes watched the house in the mirror until it disappeared. He couldn't put a name to what he felt; pain, despair, sorrow- no, he decided, confusion or shock or maybe a little of both would have to be it. In the years he had been away he had always pictured Pat living on the old place, and that it would be pretty much the same as he'd left it. He turned his attention back to the road and Pat's disappearing car. He felt puzzled as to where Pat would be heading now.

The blacktop turned to dirt, and Wes found himself swallowed up in Pat's dust, following the cloud rather than the car. Finally, through the haze he saw him swing into a familiar drive and pull up through the tall firs to what had been the next-door neighbor's farmhouse. Pat's best friend, John Brody had lived there with his Mom and Dad. John had been a rarity for that time and place, an only child.

The farmhouse like so many across southern Michigan, sat on a low hill, always the highest point near the road. A

A Sense of Place

Michigan farmhouse, a one-story wing connected to a two-story main section with a long, screened porch across the front, clapboard siding painted white, an occasional bit of scrollwork or an imitation Greek column to give it character. Wes took it in. Here they had used the Greek motif, and the columns served as anchor points for the rusty screen on the porch. It looked nearly as rough as their old home place, he decided. About the only thing that set it up a notch- the windows were all intact, the original wavy glass still predominant. The paint, where it still existed, sloughed off like dead skin, and the grass grew in scruffy, wild patches. Pat pulled up along the side of the house, got out of the Lincoln and stood waiting. Wes pulled in behind him, turned the engine off and sat for a moment. He still wanted to make an excuse, to pull out, to drive on, head back south to North Carolina, but instead, he sat frozen, unable to move. October poured in through the open window, swirled about and settled all around him.

...

All that first summer of 1938 and into the fall Pat and Wes spent their free time exploring every inch of the farm, all one hundred-sixty acres of it. The wildest parts drew them most strongly and it became their vocation to know what they could of that wildness.

One October afternoon they lay in an open field watching a red-tailed hawk circle overhead, both of them drowsy in the warm autumn sun. Suddenly, Pat rolled over onto his stomach. "What's that?" he whispered. Wes lay still and listened. He could hear it too, a kind of low moaning sound coming from the other side of the hill. "I don't know," he whispered back.

He rolled over too, and they both inched forward, their bellies rubbing softly against the dry grass. At the top of the hill they could look down into the valley and out through the trees to the marshy top end of the mill pond. For a moment everything settled into stillness. The breeze carried the brittle smells of dry leaves and field corn up the hill. They lay there watching, like animals, part of it all.

Finally, Wes saw a movement in the cattails at the pond's edge. Something struggled; dark fur, a black tail, bare and gleaming, wet. A muskrat caught in a trap. He started to get up, to go down to it, but Pat grabbed his arm. "No, wait. Look down there." He pointed to a movement about 100 yards to their left, a figure moving from shadow to light to shadow, working the bank, hunting. Then they heard it again, the low moaning sound. It drifted eerily up to them. It came from the man as he moved, and they could see now that it was Cassie. It seemed almost as if he was singing, singing a song of his own device, and yet it felt deeper than singing, more plaintive than any song they'd ever heard. He carried a woven splint pack basket on his back, and he bent ever so slightly under its load. They watched him, fascinated as he appeared to float through the wind driven swirl of marsh grass, drawing closer to the trap.

Out of the corner of his eye Wes caught another movement as the red tail dropped out of the sky like it had been shot, plummeting straight down onto the muskrat. Its talons sank deep and it struggled to take off, but the trap chain anchored the muskrat and the hawk firmly to the ground. Over and over the red tail beat its powerful wings, tried to rise, only to come to the end of the tether. Then Cassie was running, covering the distance to the trap in short, quick steps, a stick clutched in his hand, a Stone Age man. The hawk rose again, still clutching the muskrat, and as it reached the limit of the chain, Cassie swung the stick and knocked the bird down. Immediately, he pounced on it, pinned it to the ground under his knees, its talons grasping, desperate to grip something, anything to pull it up, to help it escape.

Cassie grabbed the neck and picked the hawk up, held it for a moment looking at it like it was some fine work of art, a piece to be lovingly studied, and then spun the bird with a quick twist of his wrist and broke its neck. Wes drew in his breath and felt a wave of nausea sweep over him.

The hawk thrashed for a while and then hung lifeless and limp in Cassie's hand. He looked it over once again and then stuffed it into the pack basket. With the same quick motion, he swung the stick down hard on the muskrat's head, and it lay still.

That night, Wes slept fitfully and dreamed of a car careening off an icy bridge and in slow motion flipping and twisting toward the rocks below.

...

Pat waited for Wes. He stood on the porch now, beckoning, and Wes obediently opened the truck door and stood in the dust. "Come on up, now, Wes. Don't hang back. You remember this place? John's daddy's old place. You remember it?" He was smiling that crazy smile like he took pleasure in the very possibility that Wes might remember something that had been like a second home to him growing up. "Hasn't changed all that much, has it?" he said.

"Nope." Wes lied. "You're right about that. Nothing's changed. Except, how is it that you're here and not on the home place?"

"Long story. I'll tell you about it when we've had a chance to set a while."

Wes climbed the porch steps and edged forward, almost afraid to go inside. Pat held the door, and Wes stepped again into the past. In this kitchen for sure nothing had changed -- same linoleum floor, more yellowed and worn than before. Same chipped enamel sink, faucets, gray, protruding like the heads of ancient birds, but everything appeared clean just the way John's mom had kept it. The only thing different, a bouquet of dried flowers and weeds, stuffed into an earth-toned vase, afternoon sunlight catching in the heads of goldenrod. Not like John's mother but a woman's touch none-the-less. Even as he thought it, he heard the voice from the front room.

"Pat, that you?"

"Yeah. it's me, honey. Brought someone along with me. You'll never guess who." He was smiling again, that crazy face-splitting smile.

Even though he had known nothing of Pat's life since he left, Wes thought he had prepared himself for anything that might happen if he returned. He'd always thought there'd be the possibility that he'd run into Pat if he was still around. He'd thought about the scenarios, rehearsed them in his head enough times so that he wouldn't show surprise, give himself away, but no amount of rehearsal prepared him for the rush of emotion he felt when Nora walked into the kitchen.

"Wes? Is that you?"

Thirty years had changed her, but it hadn't dulled her beauty any, he thought. The tall, thin teenaged gawkiness was gone now, but what had replaced it seemed more her, or maybe just more what he had expected she would be like, had envisioned her to be through the years. Slender and tall, auburn hair cascading to her shoulders, she stepped further into the kitchen and stopped to look at him. She wore a light blue shirtwaist dress, faded, missing a button, but it showed off her still narrow waist, the curve of her breasts. Her legs, tanned and long, still appeared smooth and fit as if she worked out, but more likely it was from just working hard around the farm. Her hair longer now than when he had seen her last, the auburn faded, and cut with thin ribbons of gray, set off a face that still drew him in, her blue-gray eyes riveting him as they once had a million years ago. The one memory for which he hadn't prepared. He struggled for words.

"Hi, Nora." The heat spread across his face. "Hope you don't mind. Pat here kind of insisted I come back with him. He didn't say anything about you being here though. I guess I never got the wedding invitation." He wanted it to be a joke, but it came out stiff, accusing. "Good to see you."

"Good to see you too." Her eyes were locked on Wes' for a moment, and then she turned away, headed for the sink. She touched her hair, smoothed it a bit, and then turned on the water and washed her hands. "You'll be staying for supper, I hope. I'll have to think of something special to celebrate," she said. "Pat, I'll get dinner started before I head out to help you with the milking."

"Maybe Wes'll help me out tonight. That all right with you, Wes? You think you remember which end of the cow the milk comes out of?" Pat clapped him hard on the shoulder.

"I suppose. You can always point it out to me if I make a mistake. You always liked to do that as I remember. I'll have to dig out some work clothes to wear out there." He pointed his thumb in the general direction of the barn.

"No problem, son. Got a set of coveralls just made for you. And a fine pair of rubber boots to go along with them. The perfect outfit for wading through cow shit. Follow me."

The barn was a timber framed affair from a time when building a barn was both one man's art and a community's responsibility. The red paint had faded to weathered gray; the sheet metal covering the old shake roof, showed rust in places. The lean-to section of the building was sagging badly. Inside though, it smelled of fresh hay and the warm, rich, surprisingly comforting smell of fifty cows. Outside the thick black and white bodies of a herd of Holsteins crowded up against one of the doors, each cow in its own place in the pecking order. Occasionally, one would try to mount another and there would be a small commotion, but generally, they stood quiet, patient. Pat nodded toward the herd.

"All Holsteins now. Used to keep some Jerseys and Guernseys to keep the butterfat content up, but it don't pay no more. All that matters is production today. Ship lots of milk. Seems like all anybody thinks now is more is better." He broke into a severe coughing fit and doubled over with the violence of it. When he finally got it under control, he shook his head.

"Man, I can't seem to shake that thing. Been with me for months now." He took out a bandana and wiped his mouth. "Hey, there is something I want you to see here before we get started. I had this built a few years back. The very latest in automated milking parlors, or at least it was then. It ain't quite so up to date as it used to be." Wes followed Pat into a whitewashed room. "She's a beaut', ain't she? So damned clean and shiny, I sometimes come out here just to sit. Cleaner than the house I'd have to say." He smiled. "But don't be saying that to Nora now. I'd get my ass in a sling, and then I'd have to whip yours for telling, just like I did when we was kids." He smiled again.

The milking parlor. Wes hadn't heard the term in years. He mainly thought of a parlor in a more traditional sense now. It brought back thoughts of the soft light of kerosene lamps, formal furniture, old farm houses. It was a place to retreat to on Sunday afternoons, a haven from the sweat and grime of everyday living. That image contrasted starkly with the stainless steel and rubber that presented itself before him now. Here in the dirt and darkness of the old barn, it appeared to Wes as if Pat had tried to create his own bright, unsoiled spot.

Wes turned toward him. "Real nice. Not much like the milk operation I remember from when we were kids." He hesitated, not sure what else to say. Finally, "What do you want me to do?"

"How about you go up in the mow and throw down about a dozen of them bales. Get the ones up in the southeast corner, the ones that have a little more timothy in them. I want to get that fed out while they're still on a little pasture. Then you can start flaking it out in the mangers. When you're done with that, I'll tell you how to grain them. I'll get them in here and into the stanchions and then get the parlor set up." He grinned. "Just like old times, ain't it?"

"Not quite," Wes said. "In the old times you and John would be looking for a chance to get me in trouble or beat the living shit out of me."

Pat laughed. "You're sure right about that. You was always an easy mark too." He turned and disappeared into the milking parlor.

Wes paused at the bottom of the chute and looked up into the dark shaft above. His palms were sweating, and he felt his stomach knot up. It took a while before he could force himself to climb onto the first step. Finally, he willed himself to do it as he had so many other times in his life, and he climbed the worn wooden rungs to the loft, the warm air, a dusty cloud, rising around him. The chute insinuated itself up into the darkness, narrow and claustrophobic, and with each step he fought the waves of nausea sweeping over him.

When he got to the top, he stepped across the shaft and onto the hay. He bent over and let the dizziness pass. When it did, he reached out and felt for the light switch he knew was there. He flipped it on, and the power went to two small bulbs which cast a dim light from high up on each wall. Stillness. The sounds of the cattle below muffled by tons of hay.

...

"See, I told you I wasn't scared to climb up here," Wes said. Truth was he was fighting a desire to bend over and throw up as he stood there. He wondered how he was going to get down.

"You little shit. You was too scared. I see it in your face." Pat grabbed his shoulders and stared into his eyes. Wes tried to look away, but every time he did, Pat would reach up and grab his chin and force his face around to look at him. Finally, Wes twisted away.

"Leave me alone." He was crying now, and, embarrassed. He threw himself face down into the hay.

"Come on, you little baby. Stop crying. You're such a baby." Pat watched him for a while and then, "It's all right. You can stop now. I'll leave you alone."

Wes heard him moving away from him, and turned his head to look. Pat lay down on a bale and stared at the ceiling. It was quiet for a while, and then, "What did you make of that thing with the dummy. I mean the way he killed that hawk and all. It was so fast- bam, whop and the thing was dead. I bet he's killed a lot of things. Hey, maybe even a person." He paused for a minute and then, "You know how grandpa's always trying to keep us away from the guy. Maybe it's because he killed somebody sometime, and grandpa knows it or something. Yeah,

I'll bet that's it." Pat sat up and looked at Wes with a new interest.

"Hey, I got it. Instead of tagging after me and John all the time, whyn't you make friends with him? You can pal around with him and find out whether he's a killer or not. What do you think, huh? You could be the killer's best friend." Pat laughed and started to climb up the side of the loft. Like a cat, he moved from one rough beam to the next until he stood at the top.

Wes watched Pat as he leaned out from the wall and grabbed one of the mow ropes. He balanced for one brief second and then swung out in a long dizzying arc and then dropped as he reached its apex. Wes watched him fall, and drew in his breath in the anticipation of the landing.

...

"When's that hay comin' down?" He could hear Pat calling from below now. He called back down to him.

"I'll be done in a minute." Wes pulled bales to the chute, pushed each one over the edge and listened to the rush of dry grass as it brushed the steps, hurtled toward the barn floor below and finally landed with a soft thud. When he had a dozen, he stepped across the open shaft and started down. On the third rung his foot slipped off the worn surface, and for an instant he hung suspended by his fingers, his breath coming quick and short, his hands sweating, slippery, and then in almost the same instant his feet found the rungs, and he climbed down. Pat was waiting for him when he stepped onto the pile of bales.

"What you been up to, buddy? Sure took you long enough. Thought you took your girl up there for a roll or something." He laughed, coughed again, and then turned toward Wes. Pat eyed him carefully. "Hey, what's up with you? You look a little shook. You ain't still afraid of heights like when you was a kid?"

Wes didn't answer, didn't want his voice to give him away. Pat moved off toward the milking parlor and called over his shoulder, "Hurry up now with that hay. Otherwise Nora's dinner is going to get cold."

He took out a worn knife and cut the twine from the bales one at a time and began flaking the timothy out into the mangers. The cows, muzzles deep in the automatic waterers, eyed him with that stolid curiosity cattle seem to have. He moved slowly, shaky fingers sliding through silken stalks; a radio playing in the background.

When they finished the milking and the cleanup, it was dark. A sliver of moon cut a bright wound across the sky, and they made their way through the shadows by its feeble light. The house itself was dark except for the kitchen which was lit by the golden glow of a single bare light bulb suspended like a spider from its wire web. Nora sat at the table, an open National Geographic magazine in front of her, her head down, the hollows of her eye sockets in deep shadow. Three pots steamed on the stove, and the warm smells of meat and vegetables filled the kitchen in a way that Wes hadn't known for a long time.

Nora looked up. Her face seemed tired, and Wes could have almost sworn that she had been crying, but she smiled as they came in. "Renewed your acquaintance with the business end of a cow, eh, Wes? Pleasant things, aren't they."

"Never minded them much myself. They seem to have life pretty much on their terms when you think of it. We provide for their every need, and all they have to do is what comes more or less naturally anyway. Sometimes wish I had it so good."

"What's the matter, Wes. Your wife not taking care of you the way she should?" She smiled a little mocking smile, but there was an unsettling urgency to it.

He went to the sink, rolled up his sleeves and began to wash his hands. "Not married, Nora. Wouldn't know what it's like for a woman to take care of me." He didn't look at her when he said it, so he didn't see her reaction, but a palpable silence fell across the room for a minute. As he finished washing, He heard her at the stove stirring one of the pots.

"Pat, how about you wash up too and set the table. Use the good china from the sideboard, and get out the real silver, your ma's old set. It's the prodigal son back to the fold."

"Yes, ma'am. You see, Wes, the secret of a happy marriage is that you always do exactly what your wife tells you. Keeps them thinking they're in control, you know. Come to think on it, I guess that actually means they are in control." He laughed and went to the sink. Nora turned and took serving bowls from off some shelves hidden behind a faded piece of drape. She ladled the pale yellow of canned, creamed corn into one of the bowls and then drained the potato pan into the sink. Steam rose up around her, enveloped her and then drifted away.

"How about you mash these potatoes, Wes. Pat'll be all day finding the utensils. There's milk in that pitcher in the fridge, and butter on the table. Salt and pepper are there on the stove. I'll be back in a minute." She spun away and disappeared into the darkness of the front room.

"Fine woman, ain't she," Pat said. "I try not to let her know it. Don't want it goin' to her head, you know. Truth be told it's the only control we actually have over them, keeping them in the dark about how we feel and all." He set the plates on the table and came over to stand next to Wes. "Whyn't you sit down over there. I'll finish them taters up. After all, you're the guest here. Got to treat you right."

"That's OK. I can get it."

"No, now I insist," he said. "'Sides, I'm softening you up for a little proposal I'm goin' to hit you with right after supper."

Wes handed him the masher and settled into one of the painted, straight-back chairs at the table. Nora came back now and busied herself with setting the table, never looking up from what she was doing. "Made us some nice steaks, Wes. Thought you might like a little down-home food for your homecoming and all."

"It's not really a homecoming," he said. "I'm not planning to stay beyond tomorrow. Thought I'd see Cassie into the grave and then head out."

Pat started to say something, but it caught in his throat, and he had a short coughing spell. When he got it under control, he said, "Now don't be making them decisions too fast, boy. You wait until after supper to hear what I have to say first." Pat's voice had the same urgent tone Wes had sensed in Nora's earlier. It felt uncomfortable, like there was something he was going to have to do whether he wanted to or not.

Dinner was eaten mainly in silence, except for the click of forks on the plates. Pat wolfed his food down and then got up and started a pot of coffee. Nora ate slowly, more picking at her food than eating it. Every now and again Wes would look up and catch her watching him, but she would turn away as soon as he caught her eye.

Finally, Pat came back with the coffee and poured each of them a cup, sat down and leaned his elbows on the table. "So, Wes. I'm mighty surprised to see you back here for Cassie's funeral. Thought after all that happened, you'd as soon not have anything to do with him, even at the end."

Pat waited for a response, but Wes couldn't really think

of one, so he continued to eat. He didn't really want to even think about it, but Pat had put it right out there now where he couldn't ignore it. Finally, he settled on the truth for an answer. "I don't know for sure. Might have been a mistake, I don't know. It just seemed like something I had to do." He pushed his plate away. "Thanks for that, Nora. Been a while since I had anything homemade, or at least homemade by somebody besides me."

She smiled. "Sorry I don't have anything for dessert. I tell Pat now, he either gets dinner or dessert. Tonight, it was the dinner. Can't do both anymore."

"Don't really need it. What I do need is some exercise though. I think I'll take a walk." He started to push away from the table, but Pat stopped him.

"How about listenin' here for a minute before you go. I'd like to give you something to think about while you're walkin'."

Wes sat back down.

Pat leaned forward in his chair again, his hands gripping the edge of the table as if he needed it for support. "First off, where you headed? I mean do you have job waiting for you or what?"

Hard to know how to answer that, Wes thought. He could see where Pat was going with this, and one part of him wanted nothing to do with it, but he had to admit that something nagged at him, had drawn him here. "I'm headed back down toward Georgia. There's quite a bit of work there right now."

"And what kind of work is that?"

Wes studied his hands clasped before him, square, solid hands, the palms callused and split. "I'm a carpenter. Rough and finish work, but I'm leaning more to finish nowadays. A little bit easier as I get older."

"Now there you go. No need to go all the way down and

work with them southern red necks. I got work for you right here. Yes siree, plenty of work. You seen that barn lean-to, didn't you? Well, that for sure has to be taken care of before she falls down. I'd appreciate it if you'd consider it." Pat looked at him with an eager intensity.

It seemed to Wes that Pat had ignored the fact that he was leaning more toward the finish work now. "Well, I don't know, Pat. I'd have to find some place to stay around here. I'm not sure it makes sense. Isn't there somebody local who could do it for you?"

"Nobody as I'd trust. Besides, you could stay right here with us. We got that hired hand's place out back. It ain't much, but it stays toasty in the winter, and with a little cleaning up it ought to be downright comfortable. Hell, truth be told, I've spent a night or two there myself over the years." He gave a conspiratorial wink and glanced at Nora working at the sink. He hurried on. "Now I couldn't pay all that much, but there'd be plenty to eat, and you know Nora's a good cook. Hell, be almost like a vacation for you." He smiled and leaned back.

Wes looked at him smiling there, glanced at Nora. "What about that, Nora? This all right with you? Cooking for an extra mouth and all?"

She continued scrubbing a pot, her shoulders hunched over with the effort. "One more won't change things. You're welcome if you want." Her flat tone left him unsure of what she felt.

He stood up, pushed his chair back under the table and picked up his plate. "I'll think about it, Pat. I'll take a look at the job while I'm out walking, and I'll let you know." He carried the plate to the sink and set it down on the drain board. As he did, his arm brushed against Nora's, and she turned toward him. She

looked like she wanted to say something, but she glanced at Pat
and turned back to her dishes.

Wes hesitated for a moment and then headed for the
door. Nora's voice stopped him. "I've got a bed made up for you
upstairs. I'll show you where when you get back."

"I appreciate it. Didn't mean to put you out though. I
know you weren't expecting company."

"No trouble," she said. "You go on and enjoy your walk."

"Thanks," and he pushed the door open and stepped out
from the warm pool of light into the clear, cold darkness. He
breathed in deeply for a minute, felt the bite of the first frost in
the air, a certain smell to it like ammonia. Not that it smelled like
ammonia, he thought, but like ammonia, it cuts away the dirt and
dust in a piercing way and leaves everything clean in its wake.
He closed his eyes and savored it for a while before he finally
stepped off the porch and headed once again toward the barn.

Even in the darkness it was clear that the lean-to off the
west side of the barn needed immediate attention. It sagged
badly. The wood shingles, missing in places, had obviously let in
the weather for a long time and weakened the underlying
structure, a big job to repair. He flipped the metal hook out of its
latch, and swung the lean-to door open. Inside, the darkness was
complete. He reached around the corner and slid his hand across
the rough boards feeling for the light switch. Finally, he found it
and flicked it on.

The effect was less than dazzling, a series of three dim amber
bulbs glowed along the whitewashed ceiling and cast a soft light
into the deep shadows of the sides and corners. The cows
stanchioned in this section of the barn raised their heads in
unison, some old herd instinct, to check out the intruder, jaws
still moving as they munched on the last strands of timothy in

the mangers, or just chewed their cuds. He turned his attention to the rotted ceiling. His eyes were becoming accustomed to the low light, and soon he could get a fairly clear picture of the structure. The moonlight filtered through a large, gaping hole in the mid-section; the peeled oak poles that had been used as rafters had a definite sway to them, and the ones where the hole was were rotted through and broken, the only thing holding them, the downward arch of the roof boards. As a result of the stress from the decaying roof the whole lean-to had a slight list to it. Like most things, it was repairable, but not without at least a month's worth of work for one man, he thought. He sat down on a pile of feed sacks in a corner and looked closely at the structure of the place.

The work was not as closely fitted as the older timber framed section of the barn, but still he recognized the care and skill of the builder. If Pat hadn't let it go like this, it would have stood as long as the rest of the barn. The rafters were carefully flattened and pegged to the girts that ran along the wall of the main barn, all hand done with an ax from the look of it. He knew the maker from his work. Cassie had done this. Obviously from before Wes' time, but he knew the workmanship, the style. He had watched it played out on their own farm a long time ago. He could picture Cassie clearly now as he worked at it. It had come out at dinner one August night when he was twelve.

...

"Cassie's going to start on the machine shed next week." Gramps was talking to grandma, but Wes was all ears. Cassie interested him more than he wanted to even admit to himself. More than once Wes had shadowed him as he ran his trap line in the late afternoon or the early morning after the milking. He had even had the nerve to spy on him at his cabin one night, lying in the darkness as Cassie went about making his supper and then later as he produced a dark bottle of liquor and proceeded to get falling down drunk.

Despite his observations, he knew really no more about Cassie now after two years than he had when he first met him. Gramps didn't seem to know much about him either except approximately when he came to Partridge Creek back in the late twenties, and that he was a good worker when he was sober. None of which satisfied Wes' curiosity. He couldn't even say what he was curious about. Maybe the way he kind of lived off the land. Or maybe the difference that his deafness represented. He guessed maybe the difference attracted him because he identified with that. Cassie moved through the world with everyone else but isolated from them.

Unlike Pat, a popular guy, a good athlete, always the center of things, Wes was quiet, more interested in reading, in nature. He spent most of his time alone. Whatever the reason, Wes decided that day that he wanted to make some contact with Cassie while he worked on their barn.

...

Wes looked up again at the lean-to. Not too high. That was important. He had done what he had to do working as a carpenter all these years, but he never felt comfortable with the heights. The ranch homes were all right, but when they started building more two-story places in the late sixties, he got into the finish work. But now this low, lean-to he figured he could handle. He rose now and stretched. The dinner sat heavily in his stomach, and he needed the walk. He stood there in the dim light for a minute trying to figure out what he would tell Pat when he went in. Finally, he decided to put him off until tomorrow. He felt too confused by everything right now. Thirty years gone by and Pat hadn't really asked him about any of it. All he seemed to be interested in was him staying on, a puzzling response that Wes felt too tired to dissect for now. He looked once again at the roof of the lean to. Not too high for him to handle. He walked to the door, switched off the lights and stepped out into the darkness.

Chapter 3

When Wes first heard stirrings in the next room, he rolled over and took hold of the clock. He moved it to where a tiny sliver of moonlight caught its face. Five a.m. He rolled back and stared up at the dark ceiling, hands behind his head. He heard Pat and Nora's door open and Pat shuffled into the bathroom. He didn't know if Nora had gone down to the kitchen already or whether she still lay in bed. He realized that he didn't know anything about the way they lived their lives, these two people that he had known and not known his entire life.

...

"Time to rise and shine, boys." Grandfather at the door, head stuck in, light from the bare bulb in the hall slicing the darkness. "Cows can't wait. Gotta be milked on time, so get a move on." His head disappeared, but the door remained partly open. Wes closed his eyes, opened them and then swung his legs out from under the blankets, feet onto the cold, pine floor. "Pat. Come on. Let's go. Gramp'll be mad if you don't get moving." Nothing. Wes stood up and felt for his overalls. They were clammy and cold from lying on the floor. He pulled them on and grabbed the clean denim work shirt he had set out the night before. It smelled fresh and good as he slipped it on and flipped the suspenders of the overalls onto his shoulders. He was twelve now and the routine was as familiar to him as putting on his shoes. He walked over and shook Pat's bed a little. "Come on.

It's late. You're going to get us both in trouble."

"Get the hell out of here." The threat muffled by the blankets.

"Come on. Gramp'll yell at you." Wes didn't want to be part of that. Pat and Gramp had gone head to head almost since they'd come there. Gramp once said it was because they were too much alike, both headstrong, hot tempered Irishman, and that never was a good combination. Gramp wasn't a big man, five-seven at most, but even at the age of sixty the muscles in his arms and shoulders were thick and defined from years of physical labor. Pat himself at thirteen had begun to develop the strength that later on would make him such a force on the football field, already big enough that the confrontations between him and Gramp held a real feeling of danger.

Wes put his socks and boots on and walked over to the door. He looked back, Pat lifted his head. "Tell him I'm sick."

For some reason Gramp accepted the excuse. Maybe he was just tired of the constant wrangling, but whatever the reason, he and Wes did the milking that morning. While they worked, the rich smells of newly turned earth filled the air, and a May Saturday stretched out ahead like an invitation. As Gramp finished up the last of the milking, Wes stood in the barn door and watched the barn swallows darting in and out, dark moving silhouettes against the half-light. A figure took shape out of the morning mist, and he could see Cassie coming across the fields, his tool pouch slung over his shoulder. He had started on the machine shed three days ago and was working on the stone foundation now.

Wes went back into the barn and helped Gramp turn out the herd. When they were all out and milling about in the barnyard, Gramp turned to him. "You think you can drive them back to pasture by yourself?"

"Sure. Where do you want them today?"

"Put them out on that open forty that backs up to the tamaracks near the pond. You know where I mean?" he asked.

Wes nodded and moved in behind the herd to get them started. Slowly, they edged toward the end of the barnyard. He ran ahead to open the gate to the lane. They knew the routine as well as he did. This was one of his favorite parts of the day, the slow movement of the herd heading back to pasture, the dew wetting the bottoms of his pants, sliding off his rubber boots. It was as peaceful as he ever felt. The herd was moving now, steadily for the most part, stopping only occasionally to rip off a clump of grass to work on like chewing gum as they ambled along the lane.

They crested the first hill and the tamarack grove came into view, the light yellowish green of the needles just starting to lend color to their dark frames. Mist rose around them like ghost smoke as it drifted in off the pond. The sun was a hand's breadth above the horizon now and the silhouetted trees cast long dark shadows toward him. He ran alongside the herd to turn them into the open gate to the pasture, and as the leaders crowded through the gate, the others poured in behind, a jam up that turned into a spreading wave as they moved out onto the fresh grass. He swung the gate shut behind them and then climbed it, straddled its top rail and stood looking out across the field.

The mist was beginning to burn off, and from behind the trees a trail of smoke drifted up and flattened out against the sky. In that grove sat Cassie's cabin, a shack really, nothing but tarpaper and boards with one tiny window facing east. He swung his leg over the top of the gate and dropped to the ground on the other side. The cows ranged out across the field, all eating, moving in the same direction with their heads pointed to the west. Wes kicked at a loose stone, bent to pick it up and flipped it toward the last cow in the herd. It caught her on the flank, but she hardly seemed to notice; one quick step and she was back into the routine of moving and eating.

He turned toward the tree line now, hardly thinking about what he was doing. It was maybe a hundred yards to the edge and then fifty or so yards into the trees. At that point the trees gave way reluctantly to a clearing at the edge of the pond, a clearing so small that it seemed that the forest would force the cabin into the water. He started to jog toward it. Even though he wasn't sure what he was going to do, he felt some urgency. He knew Cassie was at the barn now, but soon Wes would be expected back for breakfast, and he didn't want to explain what had kept him so long.

Inside the tamarack grove the ground felt spongy and damp, not the dampness of dew, but rather a permanent dampness that clung to the place like a pall. He didn't follow the narrow trail, but instead walked parallel to it, bushwhacking until he pushed into the open and stood staring at the cabin. Smoke came from a black chimney pipe which stuck out the side of the shack and then rose like some crazy top hat to two or three feet above the roof line. It was wired in place with rusty pieces of baling wire. The door was made from pieces of old barn siding, but it hung straight and true in its opening and had a handle fashioned from a bent piece of a tree limb, smooth and polished from use.

He moved across the clearing cautiously, half expecting something to come jumping out at him at any moment. When he got to the door, he could see that it was slightly ajar. Even if it weren't, it appeared to have no form of lock. Tentatively, he pushed it open and peered into the interior. The single four pane window let in a steady stream of sunlight which seemed suspended between floor and ceiling, the beam filled with drifting dust particles. He stood in the doorway for what seemed like a long time, more than a little frightened by his boldness. Finally, he stepped inside and closed the door behind him.

The room was tiny but incredibly orderly. A narrow bed ran along one wall, neatly made with a red and black Hudson's Bay blanket, A black stove, ornate with its silver trim, stood along the opposite wall, and it was obvious it served both for heat and for cooking. Wes walked over to the table in the far corner and sat down in the only chair in the room, a straight-back wooden side chair with a homemade cushion fashioned from a piece of old quilt stuffed with something for padding. It felt strange to sit there, like for a moment he had entered into another person's life.

The hairs on the back of his neck stiffened, and he instinctively looked over his shoulder to see if someone was in the room with him. There was no one. Whether out of guilt or fear, he felt that he had to get out of there right away. He stood up, and as he did, almost knocked over the tiny table that stood next to the chair. He grabbed it and steadied it. As he started toward the door again, he noticed a long shelf running the length of the bed wall, a shelf swaybacked from the weight of the books stored there, all of them old and well worn. He looked at the door again. No movement or sound, no one coming. He could take another moment. He stepped closer to the shelf.

There, carefully placed in order by the authors' last names, rested a collection of books by authors whose names even he had heard-- Shakespeare, Plato, Dante-- at least twenty of them he guessed. He picked one, and took it from the shelf.

The cover showed the wear of heavy use, but the book was still in good shape. It was <u>The Republic</u> by Plato. He flipped it open, and the pages fell into a natural break in the book. He quickly skimmed it to see what it was about. It was the section that most people know as "The Cave" a description of an imaginary world where the inhabitants live underground in darkness and can only see the world above by means of the shadows of the people and things passing in front of the opening to the cavern.

...

Wes could hear Pat open the bathroom door and pad out into the hall in his stocking feet. A fit of coughing followed. When it stopped, he heard him continue down the hall. He paused momentarily in front of Wes' door as if considering whether to wake him or not, and then he started down the stairs. Wes swung his legs out from under the covers and slipped into his pants.

When Wes came into the kitchen, Nora stood at the stove and Pat was already at the door, a cup of coffee in his hand. "So, you decided to join the living, eh sleepyhead." He grinned.

"Knew you'd need a hand, old man, so here I am ready to help you out." There was more of a nasty edge to his voice, more emphasis on the "old man" than he had intended. A look of hurt showed briefly on Pat's thin face. Just as quickly, it disappeared. He turned, swung the door open and was gone. Wes turned to Nora. She stood watching him.

"What'll you have, Wes? I've got coffee or milk." She hesitated for a moment. "I might even have a little cocoa left. What's your pleasure?"

"I guess I could do with a cup of that black stuff you have in that pot." She turned away. "Help yourself. Cups are in the cupboard to the right of the stove."

He walked over to the cupboard, opened it and pulled out

a flowered mug. The coffee smell was rich and thick as he poured the dark liquid. "It seems like I need this jolt more and more to get going in the morning. Couldn't be old age setting in, could it?"

Nora smiled. "I'm sure I don't know. Never have that problem myself. Besides, you look like you're holding up pretty well, still pretty much the same tall, skinny-strong, handsome fellow you were as a kid. Just an older, somewhat grayer version is all."

"Can't complain, I guess. Still can read without glasses or extra-long arms." He took a deep drink and walked over to the table and sat down. "I'll just finish this cup and then head out and give Pat a hand. How've you been, Nora? I haven't really had a chance to talk with you since I got here."

"I get by." She stood staring out the window toward the barn.

"How about Pat. He doesn't seem all that well to me."

She looked at him, started to say something and then seemed to think better of it. "You'll have to ask him," she said.

Wes finished the last of the cup, and Nora turned around. "You going to stay?" she asked.

"I don't know. I'm still not sure it's the right thing to do. I probably ought to just move on with my life. Leave all this behind me now. Putting Cassie in the ground today ought to finish it once and for all." He said it, but he knew that he didn't really believe it. He thought it probably never would be finished for him. Too many questions with no answers, but he wasn't sure that staying around would make it any better. Nora turned away from the window and walked over to the table. She sat down next to him and laid her hand on his arm.

"Wes. He needs you. He won't come right out and say it. There's too much pride in him, but there's something about you being here that's changed him. I don't know what it is, but I felt it right away when he walked in with you. It's like something he had been hoping for had just come true." She took her hand off his arm, and he immediately missed the warmth of it. "I know you have other plans, and I don't want to beg, but if you could stay for even a little while, I'd appreciate it."

Wes looked at her now, her hair pulled back in a single braid. At first glance she still looked far younger than her forty-six years, but the work in the sun had taken its toll in small wrinkles around the eyes. And the eyes, the tired, maybe even haunted eyes, really were what told the story. They revealed more of what he guessed her life had really been about. Wes pushed his chair back, stood up and looked down at her. He fought the urge to reach out and touch her face. "I guess I could stay on for a while. At least as long as it takes to repair that lean-to. Couldn't hurt anything anyway."

He walked over to the door and turned back toward her. He wanted to make some joke, lighten up the situation, or maybe cover up his own feelings, but nothing came to him. He had started out when he heard her call out behind him.

"Wes." A pause and then, "Thanks."

Chapter 4

The cemetery, heavily shaded by oaks and a smattering of maples, crawled up and across a knoll high above the millpond. As a kid, Wes used to come here often in the late afternoons. He'd sit with his back against the warm stone of a large, angel monument and watch the sun set across the valley below. He didn't know why he had liked it there. Seemed kind of morbid now when he thought back on it, a kid spending time in a cemetery. The only thing he could make of it now was that maybe it made him feel closer to his parents, kind of a transitional place between the living and the dead. It sure seemed like that kind of place to him right now. The leaden sky, and the cold rain that had started to fall almost as soon as they got out of the cars masked the remaining fall colors and obscured the view, made the landscape seem otherworldly.

There weren't many there to appreciate it anyway; Pat and Nora, the preacher, Mrs. Pritchett and her son. Wes looked at Mrs. Pritchett, a short stocky woman with dyed red hair. He thought about how she used to have Cassie over for Christmas dinner every year. She used to say that she saw it as an opportunity to do her Christian duty. Wes guessed Cassie saw it as an opportunity to get drunk on somebody else's liquor because every year produced that result.

The casket rested on a rack covered by a carpet of fake grass to disguise the hole underneath it. They crowded under a temporary canopy and stayed more or less dry while the minister said his piece. He was young, not more than thirty, and as Wes listened to him speak in generalities about Cassie, he came to resent him. The man hadn't known Cassie and so he distilled the man down to a wisp of air, meaningless and empty. Wes hunched his shoulders against the cold and tried to ignore the words.

Finally, it ended. The coffin rested there, moisture beading on the too-polished wood surface. Wes waited for them to take away the hideous carpet, to expose the hole, to lower him in, but everyone was backing away, saying their good-byes, heading toward the cars. He wanted to see the whole thing through. He had been preparing himself for it since the prison official had telephoned him about Cassie's death, but unless he came back later and caught the grave diggers at it, he wasn't going to see that final act.

The lack of finality left him uncomfortable. He didn't want to remember some vision of fake mahogany on artificial grass. He reached out and wiped a streak across the moisture with his bare hand. While the minister spoke, he had wanted to say something, but now he could think of nothing. Finally, he turned to go back to his truck.

Pat and Nora waited for him beside their car. Before they left the house, they had wanted him to ride with them, but he had begged off, hadn't wanted to make small talk. Nora stepped forward and laid her hand on his arm.

"Are you alright?" she asked.

He nodded.

"You look like hell. You are coming back, aren't you?"

He didn't know if she meant to the house or from wherever she thought his head was. Maybe she just expected he was going to bolt and run. What the hell. He wasn't sure himself at this point. He felt her hand squeezing his forearm.

"Yeah. I'll be there in a while. There's someplace I need to go first. "He caught the look she gave him. "I'm OK. Don't worry." He sought to reassure her, but it came out too quickly, sounded rehearsed. Pat didn't say anything. His shoulders were bent forward and he stared across the cemetery at the casket. He seemed almost to be melting in the rain.

Their car pulled out of its parking space and turned onto the main road. The windows were steamed, and Wes could barely make out the blur of their faces inside. He climbed into the pickup. The heavy rain had almost stopped now, but the air felt thick, filled with gray moisture. He started the engine and headed out into the main road.

Fifteen minutes later he pulled into the drive of his grandfather's old place. In thirty years, he hadn't ever figured to come back here. But here he was, and here was the farm, so there went all that figuring.

The house appeared to be in pretty sad shape, maybe not even salvageable, although the roof line was still straight. The front porch, which stretched across the whole one-story wing, sagged badly, a heavy load of Norway spruce needles weighing the roof down, absorbing water, rotting it through. On two of the shutters the slats were all but gone, and the rest of the shutters hung at odd angles. The gingerbread at the top of each porch pillar dangled loose and broken. It surprised him that someone some time ago had gone to the trouble to add such a frivolous decorative touch to an otherwise no-nonsense sort of structure.

He opened the truck door and stepped out into the drizzle, then reached back and grabbed his canvas work coat. Worn and faded to the color of dry beach sand, it didn't shed water all that well, but it would take a while for it to absorb the moisture, so he slipped it on. He wanted his boots, but remembered they were back at Pat's place. He made do with his dress shoes. He started across the fields toward the pond. The wild had pretty well taken over now. Lots of scrub brush and medium sized hardwoods rose up from what had been well tended fields in his grandfather's day. The wildness confused and disoriented him until he crested the hill. From there he could see the tamaracks, soft golden needles tracing the outlines of the spidery limbs, all of it blurred by the drizzle and the bank of mist rising from the pond. In five more minutes, he stood in front of what had been Cassie's cabin.

The roof had disappeared on one side, and the door sagged at a crazy angle. The stove pipe was gone. He shoved at the door, and slowly, it dozed the pile of trash behind it. He ducked inside and stood under the portion of roof that was still intact. Most of the place was trashed, some of it by time and the elements, some by vandals who seemed to have started the job and then lost interest. The stove lay on its side as did the table, but the bed that Cassie had pieced together out of salvaged pine boards still stood straight along the back wall. There was no mattress now, just some bare springs with the remnants of a blanket bunched at one end. One side of the blanket cascaded through the springs and onto the bed frame in a fuzzy avalanche where a mouse had done its handiwork. Wes turned to survey the rest of the room. On the east wall a red and black mackinaw coat still hung on a spike as if Cassie would be back any time to slip it on and go out for wood. He felt a chill run down his spine. He knew it was totally unrelated to the damp cold that blanketed this place. What he felt rose not out of the autumn mists but, instead out of the mists of the past. He had felt the same that first time he had stolen into Cassie's cabin.

...

He never heard his approach. Plato's Republic had caught his attention so thoroughly that until the door swung open, he didn't realize that he had put himself in a place with no way out. He slammed the book shut and tried to put it back on the shelf, but the cover caught on the edge and the book fell back and onto the bed. He wanted to run, but the only way out was through the door, and he turned now to see Cassie standing there, a dark silhouette against the gathering light. Deep shadow darkened his face, so Wes couldn't read his expression, but instinctively he backed away until his spine pressed against the far wall.

Cassie stepped into the cabin, and small as he was, his shape seemed to fill the room completely. Wes' body shook trying to retreat into itself. He waited for the anger to explode, to feel the hands at his throat, maybe spinning him like they had spun the hawk. Instead, Cassie bent and picked up the book from the bed. He smoothed the pages almost reverently, and carefully closed the cover. He turned it over, and examined the title. Wes slid slowly down the wall and crouched in a protective ball on the floor.

Finally, Cassie looked at him. His face, divided into light and shadow by the sunlight streaming through the window, gave no hint of what he thought. He stared down at Wes for what felt like forever, and then he moved toward him. Wes' heart felt like it would explode with fear. He waited for the blow that would end it, but nothing happened. Instead, Cassie squatted down and held the book out. Wes hesitated, not sure what he wanted, even half expecting some kind of trick, but Cassie nodded toward him, as if to say, "Take it." Finally, Wes reached out a shaking hand, and took the book from him. Cassie stood, and Wes could see that he was smiling. He turned, took something from a shelf beside the door and disappeared into the sunlight.

···

The drizzle had tapered off by the time Wes got back to the truck. He took off the canvas coat, now heavy and dark with rain, and slipped into a dry, hooded sweatshirt that he had stuffed behind the seat. He hung the coat from a cord hook in the camper top, climbed in the cab and started the engine. A last burst of rain showered the windshield as he pulled out of the drive and onto the main road back into town. He didn't bother with the wipers, just peered through the spreading patterns of water at the road ahead. Out of the blur, the town appeared, empty of traffic this late on a Saturday. He drove slowly past the Mobil gas station, its winged horse perpetually flashing skyward, past the restaurant, closed now, and pulled into an angled parking spot in front of the general store. The title, Partridge Creek General Store, insinuated itself across the inside of the front window in yellow paint, faded and chipped. The rain had stopped again and a stillness engulfed him for a moment after he got out. A farm stake truck with a bad muffler crested the ridge to the east and broke the spell. He went in.

A line of neon tubes cast a greenish light over the half empty shelves of Wheaties and corn flakes, potato chips and pretzels. The store itself hadn't changed all that much since he'd left. The shelves were still arranged in pretty much the same way. Things were a little shabbier now, the gray wood floor a little more worn and stained, but at least no fly paper strips hung from the ceiling with their loads of deceased specimens. The sales clerk was new though and she seemed to be growing out of a tall wooden stool she sat on behind the front counter. She might have been fifteen or twenty-five with her straight hair, her loose, peasant shirt, bell bottom jeans and layers of neck beads. She didn't look up from the magazine she was reading. Wes wandered over by the packaged cereals, studied the brands, the labels.

Once, when his grandmother had gone to help her sick sister, his grandfather had bought packaged cereal from this same store. Thought it would save some time and some work in the morning. The first day when they sat down to eat it, Wes thought the cereal was moving, and said so. "It's just your imagination," his grandfather said. "Go on and eat that now, and quit wasting time." He did eat most of it, but when his grandfather started to eat his cereal, he saw that it was moving, loaded with some kind of bug. It was the last of the cereal experiments around there. Wes thought it was kind of funny now as he thought about it, but he also remembered he hadn't trusted his grandfather so much for quite a while after that.

Finally, he went over to the counter. The girl barely looked up at first, then stared at him intently. "Give me two pints of the cheapest whiskey you've got," he said. She seemed to be assessing his age and then spun on the stool and took down two bottles of some no-name brand, spun back and set them on the counter. It seemed like a remarkably efficient maneuver for someone who gave no indication of any real interest in her job.

"Six bucks," she said, and held out her hand.

He extracted his wallet from his hip pocket, drew out the exact change and offered it to her. With the same practiced economy of motion, she took the bills, placed them in the till and snapped it shut. "You're not from around here, are you?" she said. "Where are you from?"

"Oh, from lots of places, I guess, and maybe from none."

"You been to San Francisco?" she asked.

"Yeah. I worked there for a year or so."

"What's it like?" She seemed eager now, intent. "My boyfriend and I are going there just as soon as we get out of school."

"It's cold, and it's wet, just a somewhat warmer cold and wet than what you get here in Michigan." She looked disappointed.

"We hear stories about how cool it is. Not dead and godawful boring like this place. Anything else you can tell me? Any tips about where to go?" she asked.

He felt the sudden urge to try to talk her out of it, to discourage her completely from going, but he understood her need, her suffocation. He could think of nothing to say. He shook his head, picked up the bottles and made his way to the door. "You go. You'll probably like it." He could feel her eyes on him as he opened the door and stepped out into the cold.

He didn't remember much about that afternoon after that. He knew he went back to the home place and pulled into the drive and parked the truck. He got out and carried the bottles up onto the rotting porch and sat on the remnants of an arched back kitchen chair that was tucked back into the one corner of the porch that didn't leak. He remembered thinking it kind of odd at the time that the chair would be there, like somebody had been using it regularly, but he didn't think much about it. He just started drinking.

The next thing he knew he found himself in a warm bed with the rough texture of air-dried sheets against his face. He awoke with a panicky feeling, the absolute darkness leaving him confused and unsure. He sat up and the sheets and blankets slid away from his bare shoulders and down around his hips. He had only gotten drunk twice in his life and the two times were more than twenty years apart. It took him that long to forget how bad the hangover was. He remembered it clearly now as pain shot across his eyeballs and then ringed his head like a clamp. He guessed anybody who has ever been drunk knew the feeling in the mouth, like a number of barnyard animals had spent the night there. In this case it felt like they had been there for a month. He drew his knees up to his chest as a wave of nausea swept over him. A cold draft flitted intermittently across the room and swept across his shoulders, cooled his neck. He shivered, but it felt good, and he wanted it to pour steadily across him, to wash away the ache in his head. He stood up, and walked to the window.

The rain had disappeared now. A breeze came out of the west and the huge white pine outside the window swayed back and forth interrupting the pattern of moonlight across the ground below. He tried to open the window more, but as he did, the metal slides ground against each other and let out a high-pitched squeal. He stopped and listened. Nothing for a moment except the night sounds of small creatures rustling around in the bushes and leaves, and then, a creak from the bed in the next room, the sound of a door opening and then very carefully closing. He stood up and felt the breeze pick up again, slide across his bare torso, drift into the room and pick up speed as it found the now open door. He turned, and there in the dim moonlight stood Nora. She wore a long, light blue night gown, her hair in a thick braid over one shoulder. She leaned in.

"You OK?" she whispered.

"Yeah. Good as can be expected, I guess." He was suddenly aware that he was wearing nothing but his underpants. He walked back to the bed, sat down and drew the covers over his legs. She came over to the bed and squatted in front of him, looked at him closely.

"You don't look too great. How about we go downstairs and I make you some coffee?"

He looked at her there in front of him, her face pale and beautiful in the moonlight, and he wanted to reach out and touch her, to feel her skin, to know she existed and that this was real and not just some hangover induced dream. Instead, he nodded his head and reached for his pants at the end of the bed.

"I'll be down in a minute," he said.

By the time he stepped into the pool of light from the kitchen, the smell of coffee already had started to fill the air. Nora set two chipped blue metal ware cups on the table and filled a small pitcher with thick cream. She looked tired, and he felt guilty for waking her.

"Are you sure you want to have coffee at this time of night?" he asked. "It probably is going to keep you awake."

"I haven't been sleeping much lately anyway, so what's one more night."

He slid a chair out from under the table. "Sit down. I'll get it when it's ready," he said. She didn't protest. Instead, she sank down like a weight had been lifted off her. While they waited, he stood by the sink and looked out the window at the moonlight glowing across the yard. Neither spoke. He couldn't really think how to start. It seemed obvious that she wanted to talk, but he wasn't sure he wanted to hear what she had to say.

He didn't know why for sure. Maybe it was just that he had always avoided anything that might complicate his life, and this seemed to him to be another one of those things.

He took the coffee pot off the stove, walked over to the table, poured the two cups full and set the pot on a charred potholder in the center of the table. Nora took her cup in both hands and sipped tentatively watching him over the rim. Finally, he felt like he had to say something. "Pat looked like he took the funeral pretty hard. Never figured on that. He didn't even know Cassie all that well. What do you make of that?" he asked.

She looked past him out the window into the darkness for a moment before answering. "I'm not really sure. Might not have been Cassie at all he was thinking about." She paused again and then turned back to look at him. "This seems kind of strange to say, but he seems to be thinking more and more lately about his own mortality. He brings it up all the time anymore. Not that it's changed him much."

"What do you mean?"

"Oh, I don't know. You'd think if somebody was concerned about dying, they'd start going to church or make peace with themselves or something. He just talks about what's in store for him after he dies and then just goes on like always."

Once again, he wanted to reach out and take her hand, but instead, he just took another sip of coffee. "You want to talk about it? I'm not going anywhere."

"Aren't you? I mean, are you really going to stay around for a while?"

"Do you want me to?"

Nora hesitated, stared back at him. Finally, she whispered, "Yes." She hesitated again as if not sure whether to go on or not and then she laid her hand on his arm. "Please stay, Wes. I'm not sure I can go through this winter alone."

He wasn't sure what she meant by alone, and didn't really want to ask, but somehow the intimacy of the moment caught him off guard, left him wanting something that he didn't know he was still capable of. He laid his hand on top of hers. "Yes. I'll stay through the winter if Pat can find enough work for me." The tiredness seemed to lift from her face. She smiled back at him as she stood up. "I've missed you, Wes." She took her cup to the sink and then walked to the kitchen door. "I'd better get upstairs. He knows if I'm gone for any length of time." She turned and started into the dark hall and then turned so only her face caught the light. "It's good to have you back." Wes watched her disappear into the darkness and for an instant he felt himself roll back thirty years to when she was his best friend and his first love and a bittersweet sensation coursed through him.

Chapter 5

Wes slept fitfully for a couple of hours and the next morning he rose at the first sound of Pat moving about in the bedroom next door. During the night, his mind had raced with thoughts that he hardly wanted to consider, and when he did fall asleep, the same nightmare that had plagued him repeatedly since his parents deaths came back to haunt him- the picture of their car going off that bridge and tumbling in slow motion toward the rocks below.

The brothers worked together in silence through all the chores and while Pat finished up in the barn, Wes stood at the barn door and watched as the last of the cows filed out and stood expectantly at the lane gate. The sun stood low and cold in the sky's southern quadrant, one of those Michigan late October suns which casts a surreal light through the filter of the few remaining leaves. The cow breath came in steamy clouds and rose around their faces until they were headless creatures. The strong smell of urine and manure permeated everything, but Wes had always found the odor rich and comforting somehow, sensory memories-- smells and sights and textures of a happy time. For him that time came during the days from his boyhood when he could be outdoors. It made him happy to feel firsthand the changes that each new day brought. He owed a lot of that to Cassie.

...

After the encounter in his cabin, Wes didn't see much of Cassie for quite a while. Cassie worked on the new barn, and Wes had his own chores to do. Besides, Grandpa still didn't want them hanging around with Cassie, and Wes never openly questioned that. Then one day Cassie completely disappeared. Grandpa didn't say anything about it until several days had passed, and they went into town with ten bags of field corn to have it ground into feed.

"You seen Cassie anywheres?" Grandpa yelled over the sound of the machinery as the miller dropped the corn into one of the hoppers and watched it slide away into the bowels of the building. The miller, Ben Fraser, a big man perpetually covered in a fine white dust, peered out from under the overhang of his brow. His dark eyes didn't seem a part of him, seemed instead to belong to some small animal that lived inside his head. Ben and his grandfather had known each other since they were boys.

Ben looked up at the spinning belts as if searching his memory before he finally answered. "Can't say as I have," he finally shouted back. "Last thing I heard tell was that he was on one hell of a toot over in Otter Lake. Haven't seen hide nor hair of him since. Why? You need him?"

"No, things are pretty slow right now, but he was working on that new building for me. I'd kind of like to see him keep after it and all." Grandpa paused and slid open a tiny door in one of the chutes and watched the feed fly by for a minute. When he slid it shut, he turned back to Ben. "Damn. He's such a good worker when he's sober. I wonder what goes through that head of his when he runs off and does this kind of thing?"

"Probably nothing. Anyhow, he's got no way of telling you if there was. I swear he's a frustrating son of a bitch. I hate writing them notes all the time to tell him what to do."

A Sense of Place

For the first time Wes wanted to say something in Cassie's favor, to stick up for him, but he thought better of it and held his tongue. It started him thinking though, and he wondered if there wasn't some other way to talk with Cassie.

Cassie came back two days later, and started work on the barn as if he'd never left. Grandpa had a few choice words for him which he didn't bother to write down. Cassie just stood there and hung his head and took it and then went back to work.

School started about that time, Wes' eighth-grade year, and so his days were tied up with classes and chores and homework in pretty much that order. The school was one of the last of the one room schools in the county, but he liked it, partly for the family quality it had and partly because with thirty kids in the school from grades four to eight, he always had plenty of time to himself. He spent that time reading mostly. Pat had started his first year at the high school, and so Wes walked the mile each way by himself and got there early enough to help the teacher, Mrs. Randolph, with the set up. One morning in late September as he came in, he noticed three big cardboard boxes sitting on a table to the side of the room. Mrs. Randolph was working at her desk, and didn't see him at first. He got a pan and a sponge and started to wash the board before she looked up.

"Oh, Wes. I'm glad to see you. When you finish with that, you can help me unpack those boxes over there." She pointed to the table. "There's something in there that I think you'll find interesting."

"Yes, Mam. Is that the book order you said you were getting from the Ladies' Library?"

"It surely is. And I know what a bookworm you are, so you're the perfect one to help me unpack it. That way you'll get first choice." She winked at him and went back to her paper correcting.

He set a new record for getting the boards washed, and when he had put away the pan and rinsed out the sponge he went up to the desk and stood in front of her until she looked up at him again. "Where would you like me to put the books, Mam?" She smiled. "Why don't you arrange them on the table along the wall there. Maybe you could sort them out by fiction and non-fiction titles. Here. Let me help you get started." She stood up, though she was so tiny that it appeared that she was still sitting. She came around the desk and walked to the table. He followed close behind. She opened the boxes carefully, and he helped her lift out the stacks of books and pile them on the table. When the boxes were empty, she thumbed through the stack until she came upon a large book bound in black leather with gold lettering on the cover.

"Here it is! I hoped that they had this there." She turned and held it up with both hands like some Old Testament prophet.

American Sign Language. Wes had a strong interest in Indians and Indian lore, and he immediately thought the book dealt with the sign language the Indians used between tribes. She held it out to him, still smiling. He took the book, and flipped open the cover. Inside he found the sub-title, A Guide to Hand Signs for the Deaf.

"I know that Cassie Nielson lives out on your place. And since you see him all the time, I thought maybe you would like to try learning this so that you could communicate with him."

"Yes, Mam. I guess I could give it a try." He wondered why she had thought of it. Not many people paid much attention to Cassie, and Mrs. Randolph probably almost never saw him unless maybe her husband hired him once in a while to do odd jobs around their place. He decided to risk a question.

"Mam."

"Yes, Wes."

"Do you know anything about Cassie? I mean like where'd he come from or how he came to be deaf."

"Well, I don't know much about him really. He worked out on our place a while last summer doing a little logging for my husband, so I got to know a bit about him then. I was curious about his name. Not a real common one."

"I wonder about that myself sometimes.".

"Well, I asked him about it one day. Wrote him a long note to explain why I wanted to know. It seems he was born in Cassopolis way over on the west side of the state. His father was already dead, killed by a runaway team of draft horses a month before Cassie was born. His momma had been a teacher before she was married, and she was a reader, and, I suspect, a bit of a dreamer too. She felt that names shape your destiny, so she wanted a name that would shape her son, a name with strength. Actually, her first choice was to name him after the town where he was born and where his daddy died. She thought Cassopolis had an important sound to it."

"So, is that his real name?"

"No. She got to thinking about what people would really call him and figured it would be Cassie. She decided that he would be fighting a girl's name all his life if she did that. Still, she didn't want to just give him something common like Bill or Harry or Charles. Her mother's maiden name was Truman. She decided to call him Truman, a name that everybody would call him and give him the middle name of Cassopolis. So, his given name became Truman, a name with the dignified quality she wanted, but middle names get found out and so his nickname became Cassie and it did have the character shaping qualities she believed in."

"What about his deafness?"

"All he knows about that is that he was deaf from birth, profoundly deaf. He really hears nothing in the way that we understand hearing. Sometimes, though, I got the feeling while he was with us, that he does hear things, just differently from you or me."

Wes nodded. He had felt the same way around him sometimes. What really amazed him right now was that Mrs. Randolph knew more about Cassie after he had worked for her only one summer, than he knew after three years of him living and working on their farm. And all she had done was ask.

There was one more thing he wanted to know right then. "How'd he end up all the way over here?" he asked.

"I wondered that too. His mother had relatives over near Flint, so they stayed with them. I don't think it was a really happy time for him. He didn't seem to want to explain it at all." She took out a handkerchief and wiped her hands as she returned to her desk. "And that's all I know about him. It did make me curious though, and I got to thinking that you might be the perfect person to learn a little sign language and try talking more with him. I think he's a lot more interesting than people around here know. You're so quick to pick things up in class, I thought you could easily learn sign language. And somehow, I think Cassie would like to talk with you. Are you interested in trying?"

"Sure," he said. He didn't know whether he was truly interested or just flattered because Mrs. Randolph thought he could do it, but he sure would give it a try.

"Great. I'll be curious about your progress. You finish sorting those books, now, if you will, while I get these papers done." She sat down and opened another of the small black tablets on her desk and began to circle the errors.

He had a vague notion that people in other countries spoke other languages, but he'd never heard any, so for the first time he began to explore what it would be like to try to cross over into another culture's way of thinking. When it came time to head home, he shoved the black book into his bag. When he got done with his chores, he would read it in his room by the light of a kerosene lamp.

They were a year away from getting the results of the Rural Electrification Act, so it meant kerosene lamps and an outhouse or the chamber pot on really cold nights. That night he sat on his bed and opened the book, and in that moment, he felt like he had walked through a door into another world he hadn't known existed. The text was brief but the book was packed with drawings of hands forming signs of words and phrases. The signs were interpreted under each picture. He practiced finger spelling his name until he could do it quickly. Then he worked on the other letters of the alphabet. He continued practicing the letters until by the time he fell asleep, he had learned them all. The only question that came up in his mind over and over was whether Cassie knew this language or not. Wes wanted to find out as soon as possible.

Cold and rain settled in in the morning. He watched for Cassie to make his way across the misty fields as they finished the milking, but by the time they had turned the cattle out to pasture and headed up to the house for breakfast, he still hadn't showed up. Rain didn't normally make a difference. They would still work outdoors if something needed doing, but today his Grandpa decided on an indoor job. The barn walls had to be whitewashed with a DDT mixture. Twice a year, each spring and fall, they would clean everything thoroughly and spray on the new, deadly whitewash. The spring always made some sense to Wes. The fly time always brought a host of the pests into the barn, speckling the windows with their excrement, leaving their bodies struggling and suspended from the long, half-living strips of fly paper, so anything that they could do to cut down on the pests seemed like a good idea. Now, in the fall though Wes thought it seemed kind of silly to include the mix of poison with the whitewash, but Grandpa insisted on it. "Can't hurt," he'd say.

Grandpa, Pat and Wes started by sweeping the dark cobwebs that hung like veils from every beam and corner. They floated down around them, streamers mixed with flakes of whitewash, like the confetti from some bizarre parade. He hated it. Before long, his clothes and hair were covered with dried bits of whitewash and streaked with cobwebs. Suddenly, Cassie appeared, broom in hand. He motioned for Wes to start sweeping up the debris and he took over sweeping the beams and walls. Relieved, Wes moved away from the falling dust and began to sweep the debris into the corner. He wanted to say something to Cassie, to thank him for taking over for him, but he couldn't get up the nerve to try it. "Thanks" was an easy sign, a simple touch of the hand to the chin and away. If Cassie didn't know sign language it could easily be missed as some kind of a tick on Wes' part, so it could save him the embarrassment of having to try to explain anything to either him or his brother or Grandpa. And above all he wanted to avoid having to explain anything to Grandpa and Pat.

By noon they had swept everything clean. They washed up and sat down to a lunch of baloney sandwiches and milk with a thick layer of cream floating on top. As always, they ate in silence, grandma standing in the background watching, filling the glasses when they were empty, putting out more bread. Wes never knew if she actually ate at noon because she never sat down with them. Breakfast either. The only time she sat down to eat with them was at supper. She seemed always to be in the background, quiet and increasingly frail and somehow distant.

The rain came down more heavily as they headed back to the barn. Pat and Grandpa went to the tool shed to mix up the whitewash and get the sprayer. Cassie and Wes went to the barn with buckets of soap and water and began washing the windows. They were alone now, and Wes itched to try out his new skill, limited as it was. He balanced on a small milk stool and scrubbed away at the fly specks, gradually stripping away the dirt until the wavy glass clearly showed the rain streaking down the outside. Still looking at his handiwork, he started to step off the stool, but lost his balance and began to fall. Suddenly, a hand grabbed his shoulder and steadied him. Cassie took the bucket from Wes' hand and set it down. Wes turned toward him, and without thinking, signed, "Thank you."

A rare smile cracked Cassie's face and he signed, "You're welcome." There was no mistaking it. They had each understood the other. The problem was that from there Wes was stumped. He wanted to say more, to ask him a million questions, but he couldn't think of one and he couldn't really say anything else anyway unless he finger spelled it. Finally, he settled for spelling out his name and pointing to himself. Just as he did, Pat and Grandpa walked into the barn with the whitewash and sprayer.

•••

Just as they finished with breakfast Pat had a fit of coughing which left him doubled up and clutching his chest in pain. When he finally got his breath and stood up, he looked drawn and pale.

"I'm goin' to lay myself down for a little while," he said. "Didn't sleep worth horse shit last night, nothin' but tossin' and turnin' the whole night."

"Something bothering you?" Wes asked.

"Well, truth be told, I been thinkin' about you and whether you're goin' to stay or not. I still ain't gotten your answer." He tried to smile, make a joke of it, but Wes knew he was serious. The smile came out as more of a grimace.

Nora obviously hadn't told him, and Wes almost said something about that before he thought better of it. Maybe she hadn't wanted him to know they had talked during the night or that she had asked him to stay and that he had said yes. Wes glanced at her before he answered, but she turned away and started clearing the table.

"Well, if you think you can keep me busy for a while, I might as well be here as someplace else. Yeah, I'll stay, Pat. You better take care of that cough though. I don't want you dying on me just to keep from paying me what you owe."

Pat smiled kind of sheepishly. "I'll try not to do that." He started toward the stairs and then turned around. "Wes, thanks. I sure appreciate it."

"You get some rest, and I'll head out and take a look-see at what I'm up against."

Pat turned and disappeared up the stairs. He sure appeared different from what he had been as a kid. Wes knew people changed, but the cocky, inconsiderate Pat that he had known then would never have said thanks for anything, ever. Wes sat and sipped his coffee until he could hear the creak of the bedsprings as Pat lay down upstairs. Nora stood at the sink washing the breakfast dishes.

"How long has he had that cough?"

"For months. I know it's something more serious than some chest cold, but he won't go to the doctor. All he takes are some over-the-counter remedies that he's sworn by for years. He's so stubborn. Maybe you can convince him, Wes. He has to get to a doctor soon. I know it has to be pneumonia or something."

"Don't know that I'd have much influence on him. He never listened to anybody except John when he was a kid. I'll give it a try though. As I remember it, our daddy'd never have anything to do with doctors either. Used to say, if you needed a doctor, you might as well get hold of the undertaker." As soon as he said it, he wanted to take it back because Nora turned with a stricken look on her face.

"I'm sure it's nothing, Nora. Just a bad cold," he tried to reassure her. "We'll get him in if we have to hog tie him and drag him."

She smiled a weak smile. "You do that. I want to see it. He may be skinny, but he's still tough enough to give us a scuffle, you can be sure of that."

"There you go. Anybody that tough is going to make it come hell or high water."

He stood up and took his coffee cup to the sink for her to wash. "I better get out and take a look at that roof. I'd like to work on it while we still have a little bit of decent weather left. I'll move my stuff into the shack and get myself set up out there, and then I'll take my tools around to the barn. I'll see you at lunch."

"You don't have to move into the shack if you don't want to. There's no reason you can't stay here in the house with us."

"I don't think so. It would probably be better for me to be out of here." He paused and looked sideways at her. Then, uncomfortable, he stepped away from the sink. He could feel his face starting to redden. "You don't need me under foot any more than necessary."

She turned, drying her hands on her apron, "Suit yourself, but you're really no trouble." She smiled, brushed a stray bit of hair back over her ear and waved him out the door. "You take care now. If you get tired, come in for a cup of coffee. The pot's always on. I'm going to put on some soup for lunch. Good old family cold remedy."

He pulled the truck around to the shack. They always called it the shack when they were growing up, but looking at it now, he guessed he'd have to say it was proportioned more like a miniature house. It had a covered porch across the front, clapboard siding, a couple of small windows and a handmade door. Like everything else around the farm, the clapboards were in serious need of paint, but otherwise it seemed sound. He pushed the door open and switched on the overhead light. The cold air smelled of mold and dust, but he knew that a little cleaning would take care of that. The furniture consisted of a small steel framed bed, the mattress covered by a quilt whose stitching lay in loose, curling loops over most of it, two straight backed chairs and an old kitchen table that showed the possibility that the wood underneath all that white paint was cherry. A small woodstove stood along the west wall, and he bent and opened the door. Someone had laid the makings for a fire in the firepot. In the corner he found and old broom and did a cursory sweeping of the place then brought in his suitcases.

"Home." He jumped at the sound. Nora stood in the door behind him.

"Well, as near as anything has come in the last thirty years," he said. "What brings you down here? I thought you were working on soup, our local pharmacist, so to speak." He turned away and tried to busy himself with opening the suitcases.

"It's already on the stove. I just wanted to see what condition this place was in and if you needed anything. Pretty dirty, isn't it. I'll clean it up while you're working. By tonight you won't recognize it."

"Thanks, but you don't really have to. In fact, I'm a little insulted that you didn't notice that I already have cleaned it," he said.

She smiled. "Like I said, I'll get back down here and clean it." She walked into the room, and sat down in one of the chairs. "Wes, where have you been living all this time? I heard something about you being over in Pittsburgh for a while, but that's all."

He walked over to the other chair and stood with his hands on its top. "Where have I been? That's a good question. Physically, I've been all over, probably in twenty of the states at least. I even spent a small chunk of time in Alaska right after it became a state. Never really long anywhere though. Nothing ever felt right. I had none of what Cassie used to call a 'sense of place.'

"What does that mean?" she asked.

"I can't really put into words. Cassie's mother used to tell him that each person had a place they were supposed to be and that they would know it when they were there because they would have a sense of that place, that you would really know it in a way you couldn't really express with words. You know what I mean, all its colors and moods." He walked over to the window and looked out toward the fields behind the barn.

"Well, I never found that place while I was on the road. I'd wake up somewhere I'd been for almost a year and it would be like waking up in some dream. I couldn't even tell what time of year it was. A weird feeling."

She leaned forward, her elbows on the table. "What about this place, Wes? Do you feel it here? Did you feel it before you left?"

"What do you mean? This farm, this shack?"

"Don't play with me, Wes. You know what I mean. This place-- Partridge Creek, Lapeer county. Is this the place? Is this why you're back?"

"I don't know, Nora. I've been away so long, I don't remember what I thought before. And I haven't been here long enough to feel much of anything right now." He ignored the last question. He couldn't answer that for himself yet, so he didn't even want to try to answer it for her.

"What about you, Nora? Before I left here all you could talk about was how you wanted to get out of here, travel, see the world. Now here you are thirty years later and still in Michigan. I never expected that somehow. Thought sure you would be long gone when I came back and I sure as hell never thought you would be married to Pat." The last part came out harder than he meant. "I mean, I know you got swept up in the fact that he was a star on the football team, Mr. Popular, but marry him? I just couldn't picture that."

She hesitated a moment head down as if weighing her response. "Wes, when they convicted Cassie of killing your Grandpa, Pat seemed to kind of fall apart even more than he had that season he blew out his knee in the homecoming game and was laid up for a couple months. I just couldn't leave him. He needed me and even more so when your Grandma died. Here he was just out of high school and he had to take over the farm completely."

A Sense of Place

"Were you in love with him?" the question came out before he even thought about it,

Nora stood and turned away. "I don't know. I was a kid. I didn't have any specific plans and I think it was more that I felt sorry for him. I don't know, Wes. I am not sure that is a fair question to ask me. You left! You left me here to figure it out by myself. What was I going to do? I never even knew where you were for all those years. The fact of the matter is I felt kind of trapped. I held him off as long as I could. I really expected you would come back, but when the months slipped by and I didn't hear anything from you, I really didn't know what else to do"

"Nora." The call came from the house.

"I'm coming, Pat," she called back. "I'll be right there." She stood up and walked to the door.

"Wes. There's still a lot that I want to ask you. There are just some things I need to know." And then she disappeared out the door, running; her legs, beneath the hem of her skirt, bare and red from the cold.

An hour later a raw wind cut through even his canvas coat as he unloaded his tools into the relative warmth of the barn lean to. Most of the tools were old and well worn, maybe worn to the point where another carpenter would get rid of them, but he couldn't do that. They were like old friends. They had their own special peculiarities, their own tendencies, and since he knew them so well, he knew what to expect from them. No surprises. He kept his tool kit simple like his life. Cassie used to tell him, "The right tools in the right hands can build anything." He believed him then because he had seen what Cassie could do with a small set of hand tools, believed him now even more after thirty years of doing the same himself.

The only power tool that he owned was an old circular saw from which he'd stripped the blade guard. The rest of the tools fit into two small wooden tool chests he built himself out of red oak- a set of carefully honed chisels, a block plane, a bigger jack plane, a short crosscut saw, a coping saw, a rawhide mallet, a long handled framing hammer and a shorter finishing hammer, a seriously worn leather tool belt, a miter box and miter saw and various nailsets, punches, tapes and folding rules. Hanging in the truck's camper were the cords for the circular saw. More than Cassie had when he was working, but just the right number of tools for the kind of work Wes did now. Cassie taught him that too. Each man has a tool kit which is right for him.

...

All that first winter after he started to learn how to sign, he used every excuse he could get to hang around Cassie while he worked on the barn. Grandpa didn't like it much whenever he caught him, but Wes kept a lookout for him and took off whenever he saw him coming. The signing progress was slow at first. His hands felt awkward and clumsy, but he persisted and Cassie was patient. When he got a new sign right, Cassie would grin and clap Wes on the back. He learned that signing was more than just the hand signs. It involved your facial expressions, your whole body. Wes did everything Cassie told him to do.

By February they could carry on regular conversations on a limited basis. By this time the barn framework was up and the roof on. Part of the siding on the north side was up, but they had run out of boards to complete the outside. Now Cassie spent his days in the forty-acre woodlot selecting trees to be cut for the lumber they needed. The second Saturday that month after the morning chores and breakfast, Wes found himself free to do pretty much what he wanted. He layered long johns and overalls with a heavy sweater and his chore coat. Finally, he put on a thick wool hunting cap and a pair of mittens and went out into the snow. He headed immediately south to the woodlot.

When he entered the edge of the woods, he could see Cassie staring up at a large elm about one hundred yards in. He was leaning his weight against the handle of a double bit ax and steam rose from his clothes and enveloped him, blurred his image. As Wes approached, he looked up and waved.

"Hi," he signed. "What are you doing here?"

Wes took off his gloves. "Thought I might help."

Cassie smiled. "You help, and you won't need all those clothes."

He could see that Cassie had made the undercut with the ax. The back side of the cut would be made with the two-man cross cut saw. He held the ax up to the tree, the handle suspended between his fingers the head hanging down.

Wes kept his now bare hands in his armpits and watched. Finally, he had to ask. "What are you doing?"

Cassie leaned the ax against his leg. "You know what a plumb bob is?" He finger spelled plumb bob.

"Sure. It's a pointed weight on a string. You use it to find a straight up and down line." Wes' hands were cold, and he blew on them before putting them back into his armpits.

"That's right, boy. You a quick learner. This axe like a plumb bob. It tells me where the center line of the tree is. That way I know if I make my undercut right so it falls where I want it."

He moved around the tree sizing up the cut and finally set the ax aside.

"You want to learn cutting? You grab the other end." He picked up the saw and started to work the long teeth across the back side of the tree until he had a kerf started. Then he pointed at the other handle and motioned for Wes to grab hold. Wes pulled on his mittens and gripped the worn wood handle. Suddenly, the saw flew back and he lost his grip as Cassie pulled it toward him. Cassie laughed and lifted one hand and then squeezed it shut to tell Wes he needed to grip it tight. Wes reached forward and took hold of it again. He pulled hard, and the blade slid toward him, slicing deeper into the wood. As soon as he reached the end of his stroke, he tried to push the saw back. The blade bent slightly, and bound up in the kerf. Cassie let go and held up a finger to get his attention.

"You pull. Then I pull. Do not push. Smooth, smooth. Each person does his share."

Wes nodded and took the saw handle once again. Cassie pulled the blade to him, and when he paused, Wes pulled it back. The teeth ripped aggressively through the fibers, pouring out sawdust with each stroke. Once the saw disappeared inside the kerf, Cassie took a wooden wedge and pounded it into the kerf to open it slightly. The sawing became immediately easier. In a few more strokes Wes signaled that he needed to take off his jacket. Cassie had been right. He didn't need all those clothes. While he stripped off his jacket, Cassie drove another wedge into the kerf.

Now the saw flew through the wood, and Wes could see the undercut less than three inches away. Cassie stopped.

"When the tree cracks, you let go the saw and run that way." He indicated a direction back and to the side of the tree. "Don't wait too long."

"How do you know when it cracks?" Wes asked, pointing to him.

He smiled. "I hear it," he signed. Wes looked back at him, puzzled. Cassie laughed a kind of hollow, discordant laugh.

"I feel the cracking through the saw," he said.

Before they started to saw again Cassie tapped one of the wedges lightly. They began the smooth back and forth motion, and suddenly, a loud pop exploded from the cut on Wes' pull stroke. He looked up and the tree shuddered almost imperceptibly. Now a second, louder crack and he let go of the handle and began to back up, all the time looking up at the swaying mass above him. Out of the corner of his eye he watched Cassie pull the saw free and start to run toward him. Cassie waved his free hand at Wes, but he couldn't understand what Cassie meant, what he wanted him to do. The tree started its rush to the ground, and Cassie grabbed Wes around the waist as he reached him and dragged him several feet back before falling on top of him. Above them Wes could see the tree as it ripped through the branches of a small hickory, caught the trunk and then rocketed back off the stump and shot directly at the spot where he had been standing when Cassie grabbed him.

They lay there for a moment not moving as the sounds settled all around them, and then Wes heard Pat calling from the edge of the woodlot. "Hey, what are you two doin' out there? You ain't cuddling are you?"

Cassie continued to lie on top of him while Wes struggled to get free, to stand up. Then he looked up and saw Pat's large, square form standing above them and rolled away and stood up.

"It's not what you might be thinking, Pat." "Cassie just saved my ass."

"Yeah, sure he did. He saved it for himself from the looks of it. Hey, ain't Grandpa going to love hearing about this. Maybe he'll even appreciate it, you know. Now maybe Cassie'll leave them sheep alone."

Wes tackled him before the last word was out. "Shut up, you son of a bitch. Take it back. Cassie, ain't like that and you know it."

They rolled back and forth in the snow neither one able to get enough of a purchase on the slippery ground to land a meaningful punch. Even though Pat with his extra two years of growth outweighed him by a good thirty pounds, Wes' anger, kept him in the fight longer than either of them expected. Finally, Pat broke loose enough to catch Wes with a right uppercut to the jaw and he sank back into the snow, stunned. By now Cassie stood between them, wagging a finger at Pat and signing for Wes to stay down. Pat hadn't quit.

"You know it's Cassie. He's an old queer, and now you're queer too, and I'm telling Grandpa. Wait until we get back up to the house."

"Cassie's not that way. Take it back." Wes struggle to get up, to get back into the fight, but Cassie held him back with his outstretched hand. He seemed confused, but he knew that the fighting was wrong. Finally, Pat shrugged loose, brushed the snow from his clothes and started toward the house.

"Don't tell grandpa," Wes called. "It wasn't nothing, I'm telling you. He just saved me."

Pat didn't say anything. He just shook his head and kept walking.

"He saved me." Wes' voice trailed off in the thin cold.

Chapter 6

Wes spent four hours working in the cold with little to show for it. At least ten feet of rafters would have to be replaced and new roof boards added to make the repair. Not that much really, but the tear out would be difficult and then there were new rafters which he would have to pick out of the woodlot if any were to be had out there. Otherwise he would have to make arrangements to buy some off somebody else's woodlot. He always liked for a repair job to blend in as seamlessly as possible with the original builder's work. Somehow, he thought he owed it to the builder as a sign of respect for his craft. It was a weird feeling sometimes when he opened up a wall or tied into a roof. It was like he could feel the carpenter's hands in the old work that he saw there. It was as if the builder's spirit stayed in the wood and now told Wes what the man was like and what he tried to do in this piece of the construction.

Sometimes he felt a beginner's hands in the work, lots of excitement and enthusiasm, and sometimes he could feel the hands of a master, all smoothness and flow, but the energy was always there. He felt the master's hand in this roof and this time the master had been his teacher, and so, he couldn't just throw in some new, planed lumber in the middle of the old hand-hewn rafters. It would be an insult to Cassie's work. So even though it would go more quickly and be more practical to go to the lumberyard and pick up pre-cut, pre-planed lumber, he knew that he would have to hunt out raw timber and hew the rafters himself to honor the work that came before.

Instead of starting the tear out though, he spent most of his time building a scaffold out of scrap lumber so that he could work along under where the lean to connected to the main barn. At the lower end he wouldn't need any scaffold because he planned to work off a step ladder, but the upper end was high enough that it intimidated him.

At the end of the day, all he had to show for his time was a twelve foot by three-foot platform running along under the top end of the rotting structure. He stood on it for the first time and tested its strength. No give. He had braced it and cross braced it until it could easily have supported an elephant, yet he still felt mildly shaky as he stood there.

He focused on the pegged ends of the rafters to take his mind off the height and the darkness below. He would have to take a handsaw and cut through to each of the oak pegs, then drive them free with a mallet and bolt to free the rafter end. After that he planned to cut the roof boards on both sides of each rafter and pull out the section. Dirty, nasty work, but the safest way to take it down. The only problem would be that all of the debris would fall inside the barn and have to be carted out to be hauled away. The dust floating around also worried him. DDT might have been an acceptable chemical back in the forties, but residue floating around now and possibly contaminating Pat's herd, probably wouldn't go over that big. He made a mental note to talk with him about how he wanted to handle that. He climbed down and stood in the cold and darkness.

Pat would be in any time now to start the milking, so he gathered up his tools and moved them to a corner behind the feed boxes. he could hear the cows milling around outside the door, mooing impatiently to be let in, and suddenly the door swung open and Pat swept in with a cold burst of air and a gut-wrenching coughing fit. He bent double for close to a minute before he got it under control and stood up. His voice sounded thin and hollow when it came out.

"How we doin', Wes? You got her all rebuilt for me?" He looked up at the scaffold structure. "Appears like you got yourself a place to stand anyways," he said.

"It's a tough spot to work, but now I can get right to it. You don't by any chance have any poles cut that we could use for rafters up there, do you? I'd kind of like to match everything in so that it looks like the original."

"Can't say as I do. There might be a few young trees down along the edge of the woodlot, but I've been letting the cows graze in there the past couple of years, and they pretty much take care of any new growth. Mrs. Randolph has a woodlot that's pretty much untouched. You might get down and see her about buying what you need off of her."

"She's still around here? That surprises the hell out of me. I thought she'd be either dead or long gone. She must be, what-seventy, seventy-five?"

Pat smiled. "As hard a time as John and I gave the old gal, I'm surprised she made it this long too. She taught up at the high school for a few years after they closed the one room, and then retired ten or so years ago. Her husband up and died that fall. Guess she didn't have the heart to pick up and start someplace else after that. She rents the land now. Stays pretty much on her own up there. She'd be glad to see you, I'm sure. As I remember it, you was one of her favorites."

"Yeah, I guess so. I never gave her any crap anyway." He took his cap off and ran his fingers through his hair. I'll go over there tomorrow and see her about the poles."

Pat started coughing again. When he stopped, he leaned back against one of the barn posts, took a bandanna out of his pocket and wiped his face.

"Pat. You better haul yourself into a doctor and get that cough checked out."

Pat shook his head and waved him off. "It's all under control," he said.

"No, I'm serious. Nora's worried sick about you. She says this has been going on for months."

"I'm fine, I'm tellin' you. Just shut the fuck up. It's just a smoker's cough, that's all. You drag in enough of them coffin nails, you're bound to have to pay some way or another. Besides, Nora's got you around now."

"What the hell is that supposed to mean?"

"Nothin'. Just leave me alone, little brother."

Wes shook his head. "Hey. it's your business, but it seems like you better try explaining it to Nora. You owe her that."

"You're right. It is my business." Pat's voice tense, tight. "Now you goin' to help with the milkin' or are you just goin' to stand around jawin' all afternoon?"

After the milking and dinner Wes helped Nora with the dishes while Pat worked on the farm books. The kitchen's thick warmth enveloped him as he stood next to her drying the plates, and fatigue from working in the cold all day began to sink in.

"You look pretty whipped," she said as she rinsed the last of the soap suds out of the sink. "I went out just before you boys came in from the barn and lit the fire in your stove. It ought to be pretty cozy in there by now, so you can turn in whenever you like."

A Sense of Place

A picture of Nora in his room, the intimacy of it, touched him. He could hardly understand his response. Maybe being this tired had drained his defenses he thought, but he wanted to see her there, to sit and have a cup of coffee, to talk, to touch her hand. He let the feeling pass through him, let it ease away into some unknown place.

"Thanks, Nora. I think maybe the travel, the weather, it's all taken its toll. I really do feel like I should turn in early so I'm rested for tomorrow."

"You mean you don't want to sit and watch the tube with us. We offer pretty high-class entertainment here you know." She smiled.

"Tempting, but I think I'll pass on it tonight." He draped the towel over the oven door handle to dry. "You and Pat take it easy, and I'll see you in the morning."

Just as Nora had said, the shack was warm and comfortable when he opened the door. He slipped out of his coat, took off his boots and stretched out on the bed. He didn't bother with a light. Instead, he just lay on his side and watched the moonlight pool on the floor next to the stove, a contrast of cool light and warm glow.

...

Pat never said anything to their grandpa after the incident in the woodlot. Wes was never sure whether Pat felt embarrassed that he hadn't been able to beat him easily or if he had something else in mind, but he let it slide. Pat never missed a chance to zing him, after that though. He just never let Grandpa hear. As much as Gramps didn't want them hanging around Cassie, he still wouldn't stand for any insults or mockery toward him. He said it was a matter of respect, plain and simple.

Pat never put respect high on his list of virtues though.

There were constant reminders of that when he got to high school. Together with John he was a terror. One young teacher found out the hard way. A first-year teacher just out of one of the state teachers' colleges, he made the mistake of confronting Pat on the first day of the first semester of Pat's sophomore year. By that time Pat had grown into a man. Not as big as John, but thick and well-muscled, he presented a pretty intimidating force as he stood over the slender little English teacher.

"You want me to what? Go to the office? What are you, nuts? I go to the office and they suspend me. They suspend me, and I don't play in the game on Friday. I don't play, and we lose. You want that responsibility?" He looked around and smiled at the circle of students that had started to gather around them, playing to the crowd. John stepped up beside him.

"Hey, Mr. Bannon. What're you thinkin'. Pat here is the key to our offense. He's not goin' to the office, you get that?" Pat looked down at the teacher, a full head shorter than he was.

Mr. Bannon got really pale, and his hands shook as he tried to take Pat's arm to get him started to the office. Pat pulled loose. "Take your damn hands off me, you little creep. You touch me again and I'll beat the crap out of you, you get that?"

Mr. Bannon started to look desperately around for some help, but all he saw were student faces pressing closer all the time. Finally, he turned back to Pat. "Listen to me, Mr. Callaghan. You are getting yourself deeper into trouble than you were before. You might not just find yourself suspended. You could be expelled."

At that point Pat moved in on one side of the teacher, and John moved to the other as if it were a well drilled football play. Each grabbed one of the teacher's arms, and in a single movement they lifted him off the floor and carried him around the corner into a narrow hall that led to a utility closet. Mr. Bannon was either too scared or too stunned to say anything.

Pat bragged about it later. He said he told Bannon that if he got him expelled, that one day he would wake up and his house would be in flames. Bannon walked out after that and never came back. The principal called Pat down to the office to ask what he knew about the situation, but he denied knowing anything and since nobody was willing to step forward to tell what they had seen, nothing ever happened to either John or Pat. They pretty much ran the school from that point on. Most of the time it was an us versus them situation with the us being the majority of the student body. You didn't dare go into the bathrooms between classes if one or both of them were in there because you would come out with your head soaked from a swirly where you got it flushed in the toilet. For a while, lookouts would stand outside the lavatories and let people know when they were in there so that nobody made the mistake of going in. That didn't last long. When Pat and John discovered it, the lookout got it twice as bad as anybody else.

Even Wes felt somewhat afraid of them. They pretty much left him alone physically, but they took every chance they got to embarrass him, especially in front of girls.

In the spring of his eighth-grade year he developed a crush on the most popular girl in the school, a delicately beautiful, blonde seventh grader by the name of Becky Rogers. She had all the boys chasing her around like flies after honey, so Wes was sure she never really noticed him, skinny and shy as he was. Nevertheless, he mooned around after her all the time, always on the fringes, always daydreaming about her.

One night he got it into his head to write her a letter and tell her just how much he loved her. He decided he would send it to her and not sign it. It seemed like a great idea, a way to make contact without actually exposing himself. He could find out through the grapevine what she thought of it, and, if she liked it, maybe get up the courage to reveal his identity to her afterward. He made several attempts before he finally felt satisfied with the result. The next day he got to school early as usual, and when Mrs. Randolph left the room to do something, he slipped the letter into Becky's desk.

He watched her all that morning and finally around eleven, she spotted the letter in her desk. As she read it, she smiled and afterward she carefully folded it up and looked around the room. Wes quickly averted his eyes and bent as if reading a book that he had open on his desk. He could feel the glow of embarrassment flooding across his face. At the noon recess he sat as close to Becky's group as he could, once again pretending to read a book. She had the letter and read parts to her friends. They giggled and looked around as if assessing the boys, trying to figure out who could have sent it. Finally, the emissaries went out to check with key boy leaders to determine the author of the letter. Nothing. No one knew anything. Wes had the feeling of being inside a room with a one-way window looking out at the world, observing everything without them knowing. It made him both excited and depressed. Here he was again on the outside looking in. He decided to take a chance. The next day he would reveal to Becky that he was the author of the letter.

He made one mistake. He left the rough drafts of the letter on his desk, and that night Pat found them.

"What's this, lover boy? You got yourself a girlfriend? What's your friend Cassie, going to think? You abandoning him and all."

"Get away from me asshole." His heart sank even as he said it. "It's none of your business."

"Oh, I think it is my business. I'm your big brother. I'm supposed to take care of you, initiate you into this kind of thing. You know, teach you about the birds and the bees."

"Get out of the room. I don't need any of your help." Wes pushed against his chest. "Get out of here. I mean it."

"Oooh, ' I mean it.' I am really scared." He deflected Wes' hands and spun him around until he pinned his arms and head in a Full Nelson. "I'm sorry if I've neglected your education little brother. But I'm about to rectify that."

"What do you mean?" He struggled as best he could to break loose.

"I mean from now on I'm going to take a close interest in your romantic escapades. You wait. You'll see how well your big brother takes care of you."

"And I'm telling you to leave me alone. I don't need your help." He struggled again to break loose.

"I just want to get you off on the right foot, little brother, make sure you get some on your first try. I plan to make you instantly popular with all the girls, but first I need to know this one's name." He put more pressure against the back of Wes' neck, until he felt like it would snap.

Finally, Wes couldn't bear it any longer. "Becky," he said. "Her name's Becky."
Pat eased the pressure.

"OK little brother. I'll see to it that Becky will really love you back. You take care now, and get yourself ready for a hot time." Pat released him, and Wes took a wild swing at him as he stepped back out of the room. It missed and Pat laughed as he shut the door.

Wes worried all that night, both about revealing to Becky that he was the mystery writer and that Pat would find some way to embarrass him. He tried to dismiss Pat's threats as just more of his show. He didn't really figure that Pat would go out of his way to get to him, but it did worry him nevertheless. By morning he felt like a wreck and had pretty much decided to not say anything to Becky, to let the whole thing slide.

Since the high school started earlier than the one room school, Pat always left before Wes did. Because he had to leave early, he also didn't have to help with the morning chores, so Wes hadn't seen him since the night before. Not seeing him helped to ease his second worry, that Pat would pull some stunt which would make him look like a freak in front of Becky. It was a worry he should have taken more seriously.

He didn't know if it was the exhaustion from not getting enough sleep, or what, but he seemed to be moving in slow motion that morning, and as a result, he would have to run the mile to school in order to keep from being late. As it was, he knew that he would be cutting it close. The cold seared his lungs as he ran through Art Dinkhaus's woodlot where it backed up to the school property. He concentrated on breathing deeply through his nose to try to warm the air as he took it in, but it didn't help much. All he could think about was getting to the warmth of the classroom and sitting once again anonymously in the back row with the other eighth graders. As he approached the edge of the woodlot where it opened onto the school grounds, he had one of those weird feelings where you feel like someone is watching you. He slowed and looked around, but saw nothing. The playground stood snow covered and empty. Everyone was already inside. He started to jog once again when a figure stepped out from behind a large Beech and grabbed him around the waist. Another stepped in and grabbed him around the neck with one arm and covered his mouth with his other hand. He struggled to tear loose, but they were both strong, and he quickly found himself, pinned face down on the ground.

"Easy, little brother. We don't want to hurt you. We just want to get you ready for your big introduction to Becky. Isn't that right, John?"

"That's it. Now hold still, Squirt, while we get you set up."

Wes tried to bite through the gloves around his mouth, but Pat's big hand had his jaw locked together like a clamp. Suddenly, he felt his pants being tugged toward his ankles. He fought to get a hand free to hold them up, but they had him wrapped so tightly, he couldn't break free. The pants broke over his hips, the long john bottoms, coming with them until he lay half naked against the snow. Then they picked him up and carried him, still struggling, toward the playground at the back of the school. The wind cut icy rivers of air across his exposed privates. He wanted to cry, but he wouldn't give them the satisfaction.

When they got to the swing set, John slung Wes' pants up over the top bar a good ten feet up. Then he came around behind him and looped a piece of bailing twine around his hand and wrist and bound it to the other hand. All this time Pat kept a firm grip on Wes' mouth and neck so that he couldn't yell or break free. They shoved him up against the steel leg of the swing and then he felt the tugging on his hands as John tied him to the swing set.

"There. That ought to hold you until Becky can get a good look at what she's getting. Good luck, little brother. Let's go John."

Their hands set him free, and he looked up to see John and his brother running for the cover of the trees.

"I'll get you for this, you son of a bitch," he whispered after them as he struggled to free his hands. They entered the woods, and then he heard them start to shout, the surreal sound of their voices cutting through the still cold air like a razor.

"Hey, Becky. Becky, come out and play with your boyfriend. You know the letter writing one. Come on out Becky." He watched them in silent fascination, and then they were gone, hidden in the trees, invisible, and he knew that behind him, Becky and his classmates were staring out the window at his naked ass.

Mrs. Randolph sent out Albert Stewart to cut him loose and help him retrieve his pants from the swing set. Albert was a serious student, not a popular guy, but a generally nice guy. Even he had a kind of smirk on his face as he sliced through the twine with his pocket knife and then shinnied up the pole to retrieve Wes' pants. When he pulled the pants loose and dropped them back down, Wes grabbed them and ran for the woods. He struggled to get them on over his boots, wondering detachedly how his brother had managed to pull the pants off so easily. When he finally got them on again, he wasn't really sure what to do. He couldn't go back to school. He wasn't sure he could ever go back to school, and he couldn't go home and tell Grampa what happened either, but he sure as hell couldn't stay out in the cold all day. Finally, he thought of Cassie's cabin. Cassie would be up working all day. He wouldn't know the difference.

Wes' feet and hands felt like blocks of wood as he stumbled half running half walking through the woodlot back towards the farm and the pond. At times he felt like he wouldn't make it. He felt the cold really taking over to the point that all he wanted to do was lie down and go to sleep. He knew that would be a mistake. Finally, he saw the cabin through the filter of the snow-covered tamaracks around it. He staggered the last few steps, pushed the door open and fell inside. The roaring stove comforted him. Cassie must have built the fire up before he left rather than banking it to last. His mind felt slow and as numb as his hands, but somehow, he figured that meant that he planned to come home around noon or before to rebuild the fire. At that point it didn't matter much to him. The hypothermia consumed his body and clouded his mind. All he could do was lie on the floor and shiver violently.

At some point he fell asleep, and the next thing he knew, he woke up on the bunk with Cassie covering him with a blanket. He looked down at Wes frowning.

"Why are you not in school?" he signed.

"I had a problem at school. I could not stay." Wes tried to look away, to not let him see the tears welling up in his eyes, but Cassie took Wes' chin in his rough hand and made him look at him.

"Tell me." His fingers flashed the now familiar signs.

Wes looked at him, his face reddened by the wind, skin coarse and thick as he bent over him. Wes wanted to tell him what had happened; He really did, but he didn't know if he could. He didn't know if he had the skill with sign language, and he wasn't sure if he could reveal something so painful and personal to him. How would he take it, and what would be the point after all? Highly unlikely that he had ever had anything like that kind of experience, so what could he tell Wes that he didn't already know himself. Wes turned toward the wall, but Cassie put a hand on his shoulder and with a surprising strength for a small man, he rolled Wes back toward him.

"Tell me. My mother always say, 'Tell and you feel better.' " he signed. Wes didn't get the last part, and he had to sign for him to repeat it. This time Cassie's fingers moved slowly, spelling words when he could see the puzzled look on Wes' face.

"Your mother still alive?" he signed.

"No. Dead a long time."

"Mine too." His fingers stumbled over the words, and he felt tears form in the corners of his eyes, but he fought them back. He lay still and stared at the roof boards of the cabin for a while until he felt he had himself under control, and then he looked up at Cassie once again.

"I'll tell you, but you got to promise to not tell anyone." He knew it would be slow and that He would have to finger spell much of it, but he didn't have anyone else to talk with then.

Cassie looked a little dubious at first, but finally he nodded his head and pulled up a chair beside the bed. Over the next hour, he told Cassie everything. He told him about his crush on Becky. Cassie smiled and nodded as if to say he really understood although Wes didn't see how. He told him about the letter and Becky's reaction, his plan, the ambush and his total embarrassment. Finally, he stopped and waited for Cassie to respond in some way. Instead, he just sat there looking out the window for the longest time. At last, he looked down at Wes. His eyes were a clear pale blue, almost faded looking and for the first time as Wes looked into them, he felt like he looked directly into Cassie's soul, a weird sensation that stayed with him for a long time.

"Something like that happen to me four times." His thick fingers counted the numbers out one at a time for emphasis. "Each time I want to die. I so ashamed. I young like you. In school. Everywhere I go one boy try to beat me or take my pants down. I fight sometimes, but I small and he big, so I get beaten anyway." He got up and opened the stove, put in two more small logs, shut it and sat back down.

"Then I decide they do what they want. I'm still me. They can't take that away. My brain, my thoughts, they are who I am, so embarrassment does not matter. I always will be different from most people. Different isn't bad, so I shouldn't feel bad. Easier then." He dropped his hands to his sides like the weight of telling something so personal had been too heavy for them. Wes waited for him to say more, but he pulled the chair over to the window and sat looking out at the pond. Finally, Wes sat up and waved for Cassie's attention.

"How can I go back to school," Wes signed. "Becky will think I stupid, weak."

"It takes courage. If Becky is good person, she sees that." He went from the last sign to a full stretch of his arms, then he stood up. He smiled and then began to move his fingers slowly through the signs so that Wes would be sure to understand.

"You stay today as long as you want. I not tell anybody. Tomorrow you go to school like nothing happen. You see then who is good and who is not." He slipped into his mackinaw and took a wool cap from a peg beside the door. He waved, stepped out into the cold and shut the door behind himself.

Chapter 7

Cassie had pegged it perfectly. After the naked embarrassment on the playground, he did find out who his real friends were. For sure Becky wasn't one of them, though he could hardly blame her now. He felt terrible for her because she became the butt of as many of the jokes as he did because now, she was associated with him. Neither of them could even look at the other in class the rest of the year. The only one who seemed to intuitively understand and reach out to him was Nora Stamps.

Two days after the event Wes sat down to eat his lunch outside on the lee side of the school in order to be away from the passed notes and whispered comments. He squatted in the cold with his back against the wall and with gloved hands clumsily unwrapped the waxed paper from his egg sandwich. By that time, he felt pretty sorry for himself.

Suddenly, he felt another person next to him, and looked up. Nora stood looking down at him, her lunch in her hand. She was tall and skinny and awkward then. Not the most popular girl by any means but smart and always nice to everybody. He'd known her pretty much since they'd come to the farm. Her father owned a small piece of mucky bottom land on the far side of the pond from their grandpa's farm where he raised mint and had a mint press. The operation was marginal at best, but somehow, they managed to survive from year to year, and each summer the thick richness of pressed mint came like a sweet cloud across the pond on the hot summer breezes. Something about the mint fields made them the perfect breeding ground for Massasauga rattlers, and during those hot summer days Pat and Nora and Wes would carefully pick their way through the thick mat of mint, long, forked sticks at the ready, and catch and kill rattlers for a nickel apiece. Pat teased Nora mercilessly during that time, and because of their often-shared misery, Nora and Wes became friends.

"OK if I eat with you?"

"Are you sure you want to?"

"Listen, Wes. What happened wasn't your fault you know. That was just your brother's mean little trick. Before long everybody will have forgotten about it."

"I doubt it. Who's going to forget my frozen red butt hanging out there on the playground for everybody to see? No one's likely to forget that for a long time, least of all me." He could feel his voice cracking, and he buried his face in his arms. He felt her squat down beside him and rest her hand on his shoulder.

"It's going to be all right, Wes Callaghan." She stayed that way for what seemed a long time and the warmth of her touch even through her gloves and his jacket gave him a sense of comfort like he hadn't felt since his mother died. Finally, he looked up at her, her face inches from his.

"Thanks, Nora," he said, and she reached over and took his hand.

"You're welcome, Wes."

...

Now as he drove slowly down Livingston Road looking

for the turn off to the Randolph property, he felt sorry for himself all over again, and though he didn't want to admit it, he wanted Nora's comforting touch. Finally, he spotted the Randolph house. It sat back a quarter of a mile from the road at the end of a lane lined on each side by dark Norway spruce. Mr. Randolph had been a good farmer all his life- first in dairy and later in beef, some of the finest Black Angus in the state. They had won year after year at the State Fair and even now after his death the farm showed the evidence of his success. The house appeared to grow right out of the earth, a rich dark fieldstone layered up from a heavy base until it grew into the curves and arches forming the broad porch which extended across the entire front of the house. The shrubs which lined the walk were wrapped in shrouds of burlap, their pointed tops bent forward like so many hooded monks in prayer. As he stepped out of the truck, the wind came around the corner of the house to greet him, sweeping up a pile of leaves on its way, swirling them into the air in a mini tornado and sending them skidding across the brick walk. Mrs. Randolph stood at the door waiting as he came up onto the porch.

"Wes Callaghan. Land sakes. You've hardly changed since I saw you last. I knew you were in town and I hoped you'd stop by." She held the door for him as he stepped in.

"Hello, Mrs. Randolph. You haven't changed either." And she hadn't changed much from the picture he had of her when he was a kid. Maybe a little smaller was all. Her tiny frame hardly seemed like that of an adult, more like an old child. Her eyes were still a clear faded grey and still showed the sharpness that he had always admired about her. She wore a flowered apron over a dark blue dress and the apron was dusted in flour. She brushed it away with quick hand sweeps and then gave him a warm hug. Then she stepped back and held him at arm's length.

"Let me take a look at you," she said. "Some of my students come back and they've changed so much I can't tell who they are unless they give me their name, but you I recognized immediately. Gosh almighty. Life must be treating you pretty well to keep you looking so young."

He took off his cap and scratched his head. "I don't know about that," he said. "There are some mighty gray hairs cropping up on this head for a young fellow." He smiled down at her. "But I guess I can't complain all that much. I've had work all these years. Never went hungry."

"Well, take your coat off and come sit here in the parlor with me for a while. I'll get us a cup of coffee. Cream and sugar?"

"No, Mam. I take it black." He slipped out of his coat and walked down the hall a few feet to a small, dark very formal room on his left. The chairs and settee were from another time, curved dark wood with seats and backs of a pinkish brocade of some type stuffed to form elegant curves. He sat down on the edge of one of the chairs and waited. In a minute she returned with two delicate cups and a plate of freshly baked oatmeal raisin cookies on a small silver tray.

"I'm sure these aren't the size cups you're used to, so don't hesitate to let me know if you want more." She handed him a cup, set the tray on a mahogany side table and sat across from him on the settee.

"I was surprised to hear you were in town, Wes. So, tell me, why did you come back for Cassie's funeral?"

Wes smiled. She always had a way of getting right to the heart of the matter. And as always there was no way he could lie to her.

"It's a long story, Mrs. Randolph."

"You're not my student anymore, Wes. You can call me Emma, and I have all the time in the world if you feel like telling me about it."

"Well, Emma." He tried the sound of it, but it didn't feel right somehow even after all those years. "I kept track of Cassie ever since they sent him away. I never went to see him or anything, but I sent him things, books and such, without saying who they were from. He had been a friend to me all through my growing up years, and despite everything, I never could forget that. I let them know at the prison that if anything happened to him, to let me know. When he died, I figured he had to be buried here, so I made the arrangements."

"You mean his feeling about place and all. You told me how he felt about each person having a sense of a particular place for them. Yes, I believe you were right in that. You don't see it as any sign of disrespect for your grandfather?"

Wes took a sip of coffee and rubbed his hand through his hair. "I never thought of it that way. Until the murder I always thought that he and my grandfather were," he hesitated. He wanted to say friends, but he knew that wasn't really the word he was looking for. "I guess I would say that they had a mutual respect." He hesitated again because the speculation about someone else's feelings weighed heavily on him, especially two men he'd cared about and who were now dead.

"Somehow I don't think my grandfather would mind. He had a hot Irish temper sometimes but he seemed to forgive just about everything about someone if he got enough time to think about it." As if to punctuate the thought, the grandfather clock in the corner began to chime loudly the ten o'clock hour. They sat silently, surrounded by the sound. Mrs. Randolph stared intently over the rim of her coffee cup. Finally, the chiming stopped.

"I wanted to go to the funeral, but I came down with the flu that week, and there was no way that I could go out." She lifted her coffee cup as if to take a drink then hesitated and set it down. "Wes, there's something I've wanted to ask you since the trial, but I didn't think it was appropriate then and I'm not sure if it is now, but I'm going to ask anyway and you can answer or not as you see fit." She paused for a moment as if trying to think of a way to frame the question and then, "Do you think Cassie did it?"

He leaned over and set the coffee cup on the tray, and then stayed leaning forward, his elbows on his knees, hands hanging down limp and lifeless.

"I don't know, Mrs. Randolph." Not Emma. Too hard to break old habits. "In a way I'd like to think so because it keeps everything simpler. It sure appeared that way. The jury didn't have any doubts."

"But what about you?"

"Well, when it happened, I couldn't believe it. I thought there must be some mistake. That wasn't the man I had come to know. But now after seeing all that I've seen over the past thirty years, I know that things happen, and people do things that don't seem at all to fit with their character. Back about twenty years ago I was working on a subdivision of big houses in New Orleans. There was a fellow working on the crew named Jack LeBlanc, a big guy and a good carpenter. He worked as the saw man on the crew."

"What's that mean?" Mrs. Randolph asked.

"The saw man precuts all the small pieces for the job-- bridging to go between the floor joists, the window headers, sills

-- those kinds of things. Anyway, he always seemed quiet, polite, you know. Never aggressive or pushy like so many of the guys on the crew. In general carpentry crews are about speed and yelling. If you're not running all the time, somebody is sure as hell... OOPS, sorry about that." She smiled and nodded her head in acceptance... "Sure as heck going to be yelling at you. Well, this Jack LeBlanc never seemed to get upset, as easy going as you could ever expect from somebody. Never raised his voice or got mad when somebody yelled at him to work faster. He just smiled and took it and kept working. One night after we had just finished up a big complex house, we all went out drinking at a bar down on Bourbon Street. Jack kind of insisted we go there because I was new in town and, according to him, nobody should be living in New Orleans and not be familiar with, as he put it, 'the pleasures and perils of Bourbon Street'."

"I've always wanted to go to New Orleans," Mrs. Randolph said. "I saw a program on the Mardi Gras once, and it looked so exciting. Frank and I never could get away from the farm long enough for that though."

"I can't say as you're missing all that much. It's a lot seamier than you might expect. Anyway, that's the way it appeared to me even back then when I was young and more into the excitement of it." He paused and took another sip of coffee, set the cup down and ran his hand through his hair again before continuing.

"The bar itself appeared about as rough as any I've ever been in. Sawdust on the floor, dark and filthy. The clientele pretty much matched the place. Jack bought us all a beer and then started drinking on his own and playing a pinball machine in the corner.

Before long he was pretty roaring drunk and one of the other drunks in the room, a big longshoreman with huge arms and no neck, started giving Jack a hard time because he wanted to use the pinball machine himself. Jack wasn't about to let him, and the friction between them which started out verbal got more and more heated until there was some drunken pushing going on. Finally, Jack just seemed to lose it. He shoved the guy hard and he crashed into a table on the other side of the room. When he got up, he broke a beer bottle and came at Jack full tilt. But as he charged, I saw that Jack had a knife and as the longshoreman got in close, Jack laid the man's belly wide open."

"But that was self-defense, wasn't it," Mrs. Randolph said.

"Might have been if Jack had left it at that, but the guy went down and before anybody could stop him, Jack grabbed the guy's hair, pulled his head up and cut his throat." He stopped and suddenly became aware of the stricken look on Mrs. Randolph's face.

"I'm sorry. I shouldn't have filled in all the details. I just wanted to make the point that I thought I knew this guy. I thought that there couldn't be a gentler soul than Jack, and yet he proved me totally wrong. So, if Jack could do that, why not Cassie? I saw his violent side when he trapped. He lived alone. Who knows for sure what went through his head? I guess I sure didn't." He shook his head.

"Well, you knew him better than probably anybody around here, but I still can't believe it. He always seemed a little distant with everybody, but never mean or violent. If anything, he was the one who got the violence directed at him. Seems like there frequently was somebody harassing him just because he was different."

"Which maybe proves my point. He was harassed. Maybe Grampa said or did something to him that brought that all back, and he just snapped. You never know what will trigger something like that."

"Well, whatever happened we'll probably never know for sure, so I guess you have to just let the past be the past and move on. Speaking of which, how long are you planning to stay here in Partridge Creek?" She took a sip from her cup and peered at him over the rim as she did.

"I don't really know for sure. I was headed back down south for the winter, Georgia probably, but Pat has some work out on his place that I agreed to finish up first. By the time I get that done it will be full winter and by then most of the finish carpentry work will be sewed up until the late spring."

For the first time he admitted to himself that he might be spending the winter there. It shook him to hear himself say it. He thought that he had pretty much made up his mind to be on his way as soon as he finished the barn. Now he would have to decide what to do after that. Not that he ever minded uncertainty much. He had picked up and moved so often without any idea of where he was going that it was like second nature to him. This was different. Here he had a plan that he hadn't even seen develop, didn't even consciously know existed. It made him realize that there was a lot running around the back of his mind that he didn't really recognize, and that for sure scared him.

Mrs. Randolph leaned forward on her chair and took his hand, hers delicate and brittle, the scent of her both clean and old. "It'll be nice to have you around Wes. It's good to see you again. You probably know this already, but you were always one of my favorites. Teachers aren't supposed to have favorite students, you know, but we're only human, and when you have a student as bright and pleasant as you were, it's hard not to like that person a bit more than the ones that give you a hard time. I always tried to be fair to all my students, but I'm sure my favoritism showed through every now and then." She let go of his hand and sat back. Her feet dangled a couple of inches from the floor.

"Now I'm sure you didn't come just to chat with an old lady, Wes, so why don't you tell me what brings you out here."

"Well, I did want to see you, Mrs. Randolph, sorry, Emma." She smiled. "The feeling was mutual. You were my favorite teacher, but you're right. I do have a business deal for you. I'm looking for some oak poles for this barn repair I'm working on. Pat said you might have some cut that you'd be willing to let go or else that you might let me get into your wood lot for a while and thin out a few."

"Well I don't really know what's out there for sure. Since Frank died, I haven't been out and around the farm that much. I do know that he at one time was cutting some poles for rafters for a loafing shed for out in the west forty. He might have set them aside somewhere to season, I don't know. You're more than welcome to look around. If there's something there, take what you need."

Wes stood up. "I'll do that, Mrs. Randolph. I'll stop back up at the house and tell you if there's anything we can use before I haul it away. Thanks. It's been good to see you. If there's anything I can do for you, let me know." He slipped on his coat and started for the door.

"Wes."

He stopped and looked back at the tiny little figure perched now on the edge of her chair. "Take what you need, and don't worry about paying me for it. I don't have any use for oak poles anymore. Pat's always been a good neighbor, and right now I don't think he's doing all that well. I'm glad you're here to help him."

He thanked her and left. He drove the pickup out over a stubble field to the west of the barn. The poles were stacked vertically in a teepee shape in a corner of the stubble field which backed up to the west forty. Tall and straight, uniform in diameter, the few limbs carefully trimmed away, they were perfect rafters. He selected a dozen of the best and stacked them carefully beside the pickup. He had taken the camper cap off the truck to carry them and now he loaded them into the bed, the ends up over the cab, the tails jammed against the tailgate. A little rope to tie them off and he climbed into the cab once again.

He sat there for a minute and thought about his conversation with Mrs. Randolph. So, it was common knowledge that Pat wasn't doing all that well. His impression of the general deterioration of the place was right. Yet there had been a spark at one time in Pat, enough of one to have him build the new milking parlor. He wondered if it could be brought back. He wondered why he cared. He started the truck and drove carefully back to Pat and Nora's place.

The rest of the day he spent up on the roof tearing out the old roof boards carefully, saving what he could, pulling nails and dropping them into a rusty coffee can. On job sites that he worked on across the country they never spent time pulling or saving nails, never worth it in terms of time and money, but here it was both an economy, and a safety issue. Cows would eat anything if it was mixed with their feed. A lot of farmers fed their cattle magnets so that they would attract any stray metal to one spot and not tear through the digestive system, but there was no need to add any more metal to their diets than necessary, so he tried to account for every loose nail.

As a result, the going was slow but by the end of the day

he still had managed to tear away most of the roof over the rotted rafters. At sunset he climbed down and looked off toward the west. A heavy cloud bank rolled up over the horizon and began to spread across the sky. He pulled down his ladder, and headed for the house, his collar turned up against the cold dampness that had begun to settle in.

Chapter 8

Wes had tried to avoid Nora as best he could after their discussion in the shack. For the first time in many years he felt confused and vulnerable and it made him uncomfortable. He worked on the lean-to during a spell of typically bad November weather and when he wasn't able to work, he left and went into Lapeer to walk the streets or eat lunch. Anything to not be alone with her again.

Pat had wanted to get the corn picked, but heavy and constant rains made it impossible to get into the fields. The rains lasted a week and then a hard freeze hit which made it imperative that they get the corn picked and into the cribs. With Pat's help he had draped an old canvas tarp over the gash in the barn roof and put the project on hold while they answered to the unyielding rhythms of the farm. For a week they harvested corn, Pat ran the picker while Wes hauled the hard, golden ears to the cribs and emptied the wagons by hand until well after dark each day. Corn harvesting, like much of what Pat did on the farm, contained an element of the primitive in it.

The only thing that even remotely resembled a modern dairy operation on the farm was the milking parlor, and, truth be known, Pat wouldn't have any choice in that matter. The milk dealers had stopped buying from anybody who hadn't automated their operations. The only thing you could do with your milk if it wasn't stored in bulk tanks, was sell it for cheese at a lower rate. So, the milking operation became a more or less modern system on a farm which seemed to struggle desperately against change. While other farmers combined their corn, the shelled kernels pouring golden from the steel snouts of the huge John Deere or McCormick harvesters into high sided wagons and trucks inching like pilot fish alongside their sleek steel bodies, Pat harvested with a picker, the whole ear loaded into wagons from which Wes shoveled it onto a conveyor belt that took it to the tops of the wire cribs. Replace the tractor with two teams of Belgian horses, and their grandfather could have stepped into the operation without missing a beat. It had hardly changed since the way they did it as boys.

On the seventh day of the harvest Wes made the mistake of commenting on the backwardness of the methods Pat favored. For the month he had been back, their conversations had been short, generally polite, but Wes guessed looking back on it, he'd have to say they were also guarded, as if neither of them wanted the other to glimpse any of their shared truths. Something about either what Wes said or the way he said it when he commented on Pat's farming, touched a raw nerve that maybe neither of them knew was there. Nevertheless, for the first time since Wes had returned, Pat's response let Wes once again glimpse the boy he had known.

"What the livin' fuck are you talkin' about? You don't know from shit about farmin'; never did as near as I remember. So, who are you to tell me how it should be done?"

Pat turned away and went back to greasing the picker. Suddenly, he whipped around, his face red and angry. "You left me here to take over on my own when we put Grandpa in the ground. Eighteen and nobody else to do what had to be done so what I didn't know, I figured out on my own. So, you got no place criticizin' what I do here! You got that?" He turned back to the picker.

When they were young Wes had feared these outbursts, the vindictiveness of Pat's anger. Now Pat seemed more pathetic than anything else. Despite that for the first time since he was a boy, Wes wanted to strike back, to not take it.

"Look around you," he said, his hand sweeping the horizon. "Everywhere you look the place is in rough shape. You've even let the old homestead start to fall apart. So, don't be trying to fool me or yourself with what an expert farmer you are."

"You leave that alone," Pat's voice, high and cracked now. "You don't know nothin' about that, so you just leave it alone." His face contorted into a black scowl.

Wes did leave it alone, and they worked in silence for the rest of the day. They said nothing more about it that day, and by Sunday they had put up all the corn, and both returned to their usual superficial conversation.

At dawn on Monday the sun managed only to momentarily crack the horizon before it disappeared behind the heavy shade of clouds. By seven-thirty the rain had returned, a steady rain that blew out of the west and worked hard to strip the trees of their last leaves as if to prepare them for winter. Pat and Wes did the morning milking in silence, the cold and damp settling over them like a pall. The tarps weren't enough, and the open lean-to roof let the cold and rain pour into the normally warm barn, adding to the sense of depression and discomfort they both felt. Not until they finished and were walking from the barn to the house did Pat finally say something.

"Looks like it's going to blow like stink all day. I think I'll head into the mill and get some feed ground. You want to ride along? Not likely you're going to want to be out workin' on that roof in this shit."

"I don't think so, Pat. I'm going to peel those new rafters and I can do that out of the weather. That should keep me busy most of the day. I'll help you get loaded up though."

"Suit yourself. I figure to take a little nap when I get back. This is about the only time of year a farmer can do that sort of thing. Might even try to drag Nora in there with me." He laughed.

As much as he didn't want to admit it, it made him uncomfortable to hear Pat talk about her that way. He had no idea what their relationship was, but somehow the less concrete the details, the better as far as he was concerned.

After breakfast Pat backed an old Ford pickup into position and they stood in the cold and damp once again, this time loading ear corn into burlap bags with a large bladed coal shovel and loading the bags into the truck. The smallest wire crib was down to the last of the corn from the year before, and what was left was mostly broken, deformed ears and loose grain but they scraped up what was left and filled nine bags. By the time they finished, steam rose steadily off their coats, and mixed with their visible breaths

"That ought to do 'er. You sure you don't want to go along. Get a chance to say hello to Tommy. Ben retired, you know. Went down to Florida, I heard. His son runs it now. You remember Tommy? That skinny little runt used to hang around the millrace fishin' most of the time?"

Wes nodded his head.

"Well, you'd hardly recognize him now. Big son of a

bitch. Hefts them grain sacks like they was nothin'."

"I'll get down there soon enough. I'll see him the next time I'm in town. You hit the road now, so you can get back and get some rest. Help that cough maybe. Why don't you see the doctor while you're in town? "

"There ain't no doctor in town no more. Have to go into Lapeer if I wanted to see somebody. Naw. I'll just come back and take a rest. That's all I really need."

He climbed into the pickup and shut the door. He slid his hat off, set it on the seat beside him and took out a pack of cigarettes, tapped one loose, put it to his lips and waited for the cigarette lighter to heat up in the truck. Wes stood watching. Pat started the truck, lit his cigarette and pulled slowly away without looking back.

The rain came down harder now. "Rain before seven, quit before eleven." The old adage went through his mind as he headed for the barn. Well, what about seven-thirty. Would it be, "rain before seven-thirty, quit before eleven-thirty?" Whatever, it really didn't matter. He had enough indoor work to keep him busy for most of the day anyway, even though he wouldn't have minded climbing back into bed right about then himself. He had almost forgotten how a Michigan November did that to you. Despite the fact that he had tried to spend the winters in warm and sunny places since he left, bleak is still the only word that really came to mind for him when he thought about November because Michigan weather got into your blood and interpreted the seasons for you no matter where you went afterward. It seemed like it was always the same. Usually October bursts like a golden dream out of the promise of September. The trees and sky stand in brilliant, dense contrast to one another. But by that last week of October, the leaves are well stripped from the trees, and the air seldom warms past the forties during the daytime. He always thought of it as a transitional week to prepare people psychologically for what was to come.

Then November makes you remember what winter has in store. Gray dominates the landscape in the most oppressive way, and the cold really starts to get a grip. By Thanksgiving the ground frequently freezes solid and they had their first snow. All of it depressed him and made him want to hole up until spring. The only redeeming factor was that with the leaves all stripped away, as he looked through the trees, he felt like he was looking through the skeleton of the earth. Everything revealed itself- the roll of the land, the hidden fox den, its bare earth excavation cascading out into the open, a bare boulder, its sharp, pink form contrasting with the gray-brown of dead grass and weeds. He felt that he got to know the land in November. The rest of the year it hid itself like a secret, but in November, there was no place left to hide.

He dragged the poles inside the lean-to and laid them alongside each other on the concrete floor. Each one was twenty feet or longer, and straight and dense as only young oak can be. He quickly built a set of saw horses roughly three feet high and slid the first of the poles across them. A draw knife was the only way to really do the de-barking job. It has two handles which point back at the user connected by a thick, sharp blade. The one he had carried in his toolbox for years had roughly a ten-inch blade and handles worn and polished to a dark, rich patina from years of sweaty hands. He stood beside the pole and drew the first strokes along its top. Long curls of bark peeled away with each stroke and he quickly fell into the rhythm of the work, losing himself in the mindless repetition.

He had been working maybe a half hour when the door

opened and Nora came in, the rain and wind swirling along with her. She wore a denim barn coat and had a man's felt hat pulled down low across her forehead, her hair, damp and curly, pouring out from underneath.

"Hi, Wes. I just came out to see how it's going, and..." She paused and drew a thermos out of her jacket pocket. "I thought you might like a cup of coffee to warm things up a bit out here."

"I'd say that would go down pretty well. There enough for both of us?"

"Sure. I wouldn't want you to drink alone. That's the beginning of the end, you know. How about we pick out our table. That one over there looks to be about perfect." She pointed to two bales of timothy at the far end of the lean-to. "Not too close to the kitchen and just dark enough to be intimate but still allow us to see what we're drinking." She smiled at her own wit.

"Shall we?" He offered her his arm and they walked the length of the barn and sat down facing each other on the bales, the stiff cut ends of the hay against their legs, pushing sharply against denim. Nora loosened her coat at the neck, removed her gloves and pulled the battered thermos from her pocket once again. She unscrewed the cap, set it on the bale beside her and poured it full, the coffee, rich black and steaming in the cold barn. She held it out and he took it from her.

"How about you?" he asked. "No cup?"

"I had some before I came out. I'll have a little from your cup when you're finished."

He shivered as the heat traced its way down to his stomach, as if the warmth inside him had intensified the exterior cold.

"You OK," she asked. "You look like you're chilled."

"I'm fine, just thrilled to be sitting so close to such a beautiful woman."

Nora blushed and tried to hide it by rearranging herself on the bale seat. Finally, she looked at him. "You think I'm beautiful, Wes? I mean after all the wear and tear these years have taken their toll. I know it seems vain to even care about that, but I never hear that from Pat. It's almost like I am invisible most of the time."

He took another long sip of the coffee, felt its warmth settle into him before he answered. "More than beautiful, Nora. I can't imagine anybody not seeing that right off," he said.

She smiled. "That's nice to know. I guess it may seem kind of shallow, but it's still nice to think that somewhere in the world someone finds me beautiful."

"I'm sure Pat does too, so that's at least two of us."

"Pat's in his own world most of the time. As long as we've been married, I'm not sure what to think of him or what he's thinking most of the time. I always thought that when two people lived together for most of their lives, they would almost intuitively know one another, but I now know it's not true. Large parts of Pat are still a mystery to me."

"It sure doesn't seem like it. You seem to know what to expect from him most of the time, at least a hell of a lot more than I do. He's so different from when I left here, I hardly recognize him, so I never know what he's going to do or say."

"Oh, I don't mean the superficial things that we know about each other, the tendencies, the habits," she said. "I mean the core of him. He keeps that locked up tight, and I've never been able to touch it. When we were kids, like it or not, we all knew who Pat was. Right after your grandpa's funeral he started to change. I'm not sure how, really. Kinder maybe. Not as brash or cocky, but more locked up."

"I guess I've felt that to some degree since I got back, although I couldn't really put my finger on it."

"It was like the funeral took something out of him," she said.

"What do you mean?"

"It was like some of his spirit disappeared. I've thought that maybe the realization just hit him that now he was the man of the family, and the responsibility for you and your grandma and the farm rested on his shoulders. Then too, there was what happened to his knee that football season." She stretched her legs out and put her feet up next to me.

"The limp. I've wanted to ask him, but he's never offered anything about it, so I've just let it ride. I always thought that limp would eventually go away, but clearly it hasn't."

"You men. No curiosity." She shook her head in mock disgust. " He never walked right after the football injury and any plans he might have had for doing something else with his life were pretty well shot."

Wes thought back to those days, and he knew what Pat had wanted to do more than anything. "He wanted to join the Marines. We both did really, even though I never talked about it with him, " he said. "From the time they bombed Pearl until I left in '43, that's all he talked about though. His only worry was that the war wouldn't last long enough for him to get there. At night after chores and homework, we'd be glued to the radio listening to the news. I guess if he was like me, he re-fought every battle over and over in his imagination where he was the hero. War, glorious war. What a joke, eh."

"Vietnam has pretty much been changing that attitude," Nora said. "I doubt you'd find too many teen age boys looking forward to their turn to get themselves killed today."

"Yeah. A lot has changed in thirty years." He stood up and stretched. "I guess I should get back at it. I have seven more of those rafters to peel, and they're not getting done with me sitting around soaking up coffee."

Nora screwed the cap back on the thermos and stood facing him, a thin shaft of grayish light, like a faulty spotlight brightened the left side of her face. "What about your attitude toward Pat? Has that changed?"

"What do you mean?" he said.

"I mean I don't think there was any love lost at any time between the two of you, and after I started going with him, I'd say there was downright hostility."

"I guess you've got that right. The thing is, it's like a lot of things in my life right now. I'm not sure how I feel about him or about much of anything else. I'm just going to have to sort it out in my own time. Until then, I guess we'll be polite to each other and let it go at that."

Nora smiled and reached out and took his hand. "You take as long as you need just so you stay around here while you're doing it." She squeezed his hand, turned and left. He stood still for a minute staring at the spot where she had been, and it was almost as if he could see the warm shape of her melting into the cold.

Chapter 9

By the time they got to high school Nora had become Wes' best friend. From the moment that she ate lunch with him and he realized she understood his great, bare-naked embarrassment, he knew that he could trust her with anything including friendship. They signed up for most of the same classes as freshmen and did the homework together either in her kitchen or his, the smell of the evening meal still clinging to the warm air. Afterward, if they had worked together at his grandparents' farm, he would walk her across the dark fields to her dad's farmyard, and then stand and watch as she made her way into the pool of light from the kerosene lamp hanging on the porch. Whether they had worked at her place or his, the walk home was always the same for him, a time of warmth and contentment that came from the connection he had made with her.

Gradually, the total innocence of their relationship began to grow into an awareness that a bond had grown there which was much stronger than something just between buddies. At first, he wasn't sure either of them knew it. He just knew for him, the awareness crept across his consciousness with a delicate, subtle warmth. He found himself thinking of Nora all the time--what he would tell her about his day, what he thought they might do after school. He also thought about the essence of her, the smell, the touch that he had become so accustomed to but never aware of in the first few months of their friendship. By late winter he knew that he wanted more from their relationship than friendship, but he had no idea how to take it to a new level. Nora helped him get past that obstacle.

Near the end of February, a fierce snowstorm hit Lapeer county. Each hour as they looked out the school windows, they could see the intensity of the storm building, matched only by the excitement among their classmates as they anticipated some time off from classes. Wind-driven snow piled in long drifts. The storm swept the football field, the frozen grass stiff and brittle like some aggressive brush-cut on an oversized head. The snow that should have piled up there, edged through the snow fence at the southeast side of the field and gradually grew into a wind curled mound creeping out onto the county road. The sheer beauty and strength of the storm filled him with a sense of the true uncontrollable power of Nature like he had never felt before.

Nora and Wes watched the wind whip past the building, the snow almost horizontal in its driven fury, and they exchange smiles across the room. The unsaid something began to grow between them, the knowledge that the feelings they shared about the storm and its wild excitement were identical. They both wanted to be in it, to feel its fury pounding against them first hand.

The announcement came soon after lunch that classes would be ending at one o'clock, and the busses would be there to take them home. After the announcement students began to gather up their things even though there was a long time yet to wait. Nora and Wes were in Biology 1, and the teacher, Mr. McCaffrey, a middle- aged balding man who never let them get away with anything, seemed to be caught up in the storm himself, because he ceased teaching and began to tell them stories of other storms he had seen in the county since he had lived there. In general, everyone felt a little like they were on the brink of a holiday of the most precious kind--the unexpected.

When the bell finally rang, they walked with each other to their lockers. They normally took the bus to and from school together, but on nice days they often opted to walk the four miles home across the fields and through the woodlots. Their lockers were next to each other, and as they pulled on their coats and chose what books they needed to take home, neither of them spoke. Finally, Nora shut her locker and turned to him. "Wes, let's walk home."

"Are you serious?" he asked. "I mean it will be freezing if we really do it." At that moment he probably would have walked through Antarctica if she had wanted to.

"What do you think? That I can't take a little cold. I'm as tough as you, and don't you forget it," she said as she lightly socked him in the shoulder. Her eyes flashed with a bit of righteous indignation, but also with humor.

"OK. You're on. We'll cut across the football fields and then stick mainly to the woodlots to keep out of the wind. It's a little longer that way, but it should be warmer." His schoolbooks were caught tightly in an old leather belt that bound them together. He slung them over his shoulder and headed for the door.

"Hey, would you wait just a minute? I need to put on this babushka," she said. "I can't have my hair getting all messed, now can I?" She smiled and flipped the white scarf over her long auburn hair and snugged it under her chin. "There. I guess I'm ready to weather any old storm now. OK Nanook. It's just you and me."

The white scarf set off the shining beauty of her hair, and he caught himself staring at her, his mouth, he was sure, open.

"What's the problem? Is there something wrong with the way I look? Too much like an old lady?"

"N-n-n no," he managed to get out. "You look perfect." He could feel the heat of embarrassment spread across his face like a wildfire. To hide it he turned away and made once again for the door. "Let's go," he said.

The rest of the school stood in ragged lines loading onto the busses idling in front of the school, the exhaust swirling and mixing with the snow. Once into the full, raw force of the storm, he began to have some second thoughts and wondered if they shouldn't just join the rest, but Nora already had begun to move purposely toward the football field, her books clutched to her chest, her head bent to the wind. Wes plunged through the ever-deepening snow after her. When he finally caught up and walked along beside her, she turned her wind-reddened face to him, and he felt her pure pleasure in the wildness that surrounded them.

"Isn't this great?" The wind took her words and slammed them past them so that he felt like he caught a glimpse of them instead of heard them.

"I love storms," he said. "I love all kinds of storms-winter or summer. They make me feel more..." he searched for the right word. Finally, "Like I'm really here," he said.

Nora nodded and bent back into the wind. "I know what you mean. I feel the same way This is like an adventure."

It took them nearly a half hour of battling deep drifts and wind-driven snow to reach the edge of the first woodlot. Inside the tree line the wind dropped, and the snow came down more vertically, but the intensity of the snowfall seemed to grow. He could hardly see ten feet in front of him, and time and space took on a new reality as he tried to keep familiar landmarks in mind. He knew that the woodlots connected one to another most of the way to Nora's daddy's place, but everything blurred before them as they began to make their way through the first trees. His eyes watered with the cold, and the tears rolled down his cheeks and froze. He looked over at Nora. She still clutched her books tightly to her chest and kept her eyes focused on the ground right in front of her. She depended on him to lead the way, and he had no idea if he had headed in the right direction.

"Maybe this wasn't such a good idea," he called back to her, his voice louder than it needed to be now that the wind didn't carry his words away.

"It's a fine idea. We'll be there before you know it." She reached out and took his hand and gave it a strong squeeze. He smiled at her and squeezed hers back.

"OK. I think we need to bear more to the left. I'm a little confused right now. Everything looks so different in the snow, but I think we have been moving more east than we should." He looked at her again. "Are you alright?" he asked. "You're not too cold, are you?" She shook her head. "OK. Let's go then." He turned what he thought was more to the north and west and set out once again.

The trees took on new forms in the blizzard. The elms and oaks of Otto Hermann's woodlot drooped and bent under their snow load. At the edges of the woodlot where the wind blew strongest, the trees had stood bare and bleak against the snowscape. In the depths of the woodlot the tree outlines blurred into the background creating an otherworldly quality all around them. He walked with a confidence that he didn't feel in order to make Nora think that he knew where he was going. In reality, he had no idea when he passed from the Hermann woodlot into the Woodburg lot or even if they had made that transition. Nothing looked familiar. At least an hour passed, and by that time he knew that he had to be totally lost. He kept glancing at Nora, but she always appeared the same, head bent, following his lead. Each time the guilt and responsibility of it made him redouble his efforts to find their way out of the mess he felt he had gotten them into.

By the time they stumbled onto Art Vanborn's sugar shack, cold and fatigue had taken its toll on them both. The shack appeared as a dim shape in the woods ahead and gradually formed into a squat metal roofed shed with sides made from split logs standing upright. It wasn't much, but Wes knew it would shelter them for a while and give them a chance to get warmed up a bit before they tried to make it the rest of the way home. He pulled open the door and stepped in out of the driving snow. Nora followed. He shut the door and turned to her. She brushed at the snow on her coat and looked up at him.

"I'm sorry, Nora. I got us into a big mess here. I had no idea we were this far west. We're going to have to stay here for a while until we can get warmed up. Otherwise we aren't going to make it."

She set her books on a rough bench and taking his from him, placed them next to hers, then she took his hands in hers and looked into his eyes.

"Not your fault, Wes. I chose this with you. We just didn't know how confusing it would be walking in a blizzard, although..." she laughed, "the very words 'walking in a blizzard' should have been enough to give us a hint."

He laughed too and the pure relief of it felt like a weight had lifted from him. "I know what my grandfather will say. He'll say, ' For such smart kids you don't have a lick of practical sense between you'."

"I could care less. What a great adventure we're having. I mean everything in my life is boring. Everything predictable, routine. I want my life to be one adventure after another, don't you, Wes? I mean don't you just die sometimes for something to happen?"

As he looked down at her, her tanned face framed by that incredible hair, He'd have said anything if he thought it would please her. "Sure," he said. " I love a good adventure." Truthfully, he liked the quiet routine of the farm. It represented a kind of serenity and stability that he cherished more than anything. He'd have been perfectly happy to never see it end.

"Oh, I knew we felt the same about it," she said. It seems like we feel the same about most everything, don't you think?"

He didn't say to her that it seemed that way only because he always told her what she wanted to hear. Now he just nodded. She squeezed his hands tight, and as he looked down at her, all he could think was how much he wanted to kiss her. He felt it rising in him like the rush of water over the mill pond dam. He didn't know if she sensed his discomfort or not, but he knew he had to step away from her or lose control. Suddenly, it came to him. "The stove," he said.

"What?"

"There's a stove in here for boiling the sap. We can really get warm. "His eyes had become accustomed to the dim light, and he turned to look for the boiler that he knew had to be there.

"There at the far end. See it. And there's some dry wood in the corner." She looked past him in the direction he indicated, and they moved together to the other end of the shack. In one corner an old green painted cabinet leaned awkwardly against the wall. The rusted catch made it difficult to open, but once he broke it loose, he found a box of wooden kitchen matches and some newspaper.

"Great," he said. "It'll be warm in here in no time."

She nodded. "I'll get the wood." She went to the corner and gathered up a big armload as he opened the stove door and began to lay the paper and kindling in place at the back of the fire chamber. In a few minutes he had the fire roaring, and as the dry wood disappeared behind a wall of flame, it immediately gave the impression, if not the reality, of great heat. He added a couple more logs and then closed the stove door. Nora sat down on the bench closest to the stove and stretched her legs out toward the fire.

"Come sit with me," she said, and patted the bench beside her.

He both wanted to sit with her and feared it. Being so close to her, he felt, would break down whatever control he might have left. Nevertheless, he sat down beside her. The fire quickly began to do its work, the warmth rolling in hot waves from the stove toward them, heating their fronts, leaving their backs still bathed in cold.

They sat for several minutes staring silently at the snapping, hissing blackness of the old stove, the only light shooting like a sunbeam through a small crack in the side near the chimney pipe. The darkness, the growing warmth and the fatigue of their struggle in the snow, combined to create an almost dreamlike atmosphere. He rubbed his hands across his eyes and when he took them away, he turned to look at Nora. To his surprise she sat cross legged on the bench staring at him.

"Wes, I really like you."

He felt like his heart stopped for a minute. No one had

ever said anything even remotely like that to him before. He came from an Irish- Catholic family. No words were ever used to communicate how you felt about anyone else, that was for damned sure, he thought. He wanted to say something back, but he had nothing to draw on, and so he reached out and laid his hand against the warmth of her cheek. Nora leaned toward him and her warm breath passed along his cheek, and then they kissed-- not probably much of a kiss as he later remembered it, awkward and brief really, but life-changing for him. For the first time he knew that he wanted something, and maybe, by some miracle he could have it.

They sat head to head until the warmth and tiredness took over and they fell asleep, on the bench, Nora's head resting in his lap, his leaning against the shack wall, until Nora's dad found them. He didn't remember much of what her dad said, but he did remember he yelled a lot, and it was quite a while before he'd let Wes see Nora outside of school time, but none of that really mattered. He knew now how she felt, and with the little time they could steal to be together, they grew closer than he could have ever hoped.

Chapter 10

Wes struggled to come to when he heard the knock on his door. He could hear the sounds, but they seemed to come from far away slowly penetrating his consciousness. Finally, it sank in enough for him to rouse himself. "Who is it?" The words came out in puffs of visible breath. The stove had burned out during the night, and the cold had settled into the room like some uninvited guest.

"It's me, Wes." Nora's voice, unmistakable through the thin door.

"Door's unlocked," he called back. "Come on in."

The door swung open and an even colder flow of air rushed across the floor. Nora stepped in and the door swung closed behind her. "Phew. Cold in here." She rubbed her hands together.

"I was getting concerned," she said. "We missed you at supper last night. Pat knocked and called for you a couple of times this morning, but finally figured you were out somewhere already and gave up. When you didn't come up for breakfast though, I got worried. Never knew you to miss a meal." She smiled down at him, and he felt awkward and sheepish as a schoolboy lying there. "Pretty tired, eh fella?"

A Sense of Place

He sat up and drew the blanket around his shoulders. " I went into Lapeer last night and got supper at a restaurant. When I got home, it was late and I didn't want to disturb you so I just went to bed. I don't think I dropped off until well after midnight though. Bunch of stuff going through my head, and I just couldn't get it turned off."

"Like what?"

"Oh, I don't know. Just stuff. Nothing important really." Too much to tell, not enough reason to tell it. When I went over to see Mrs. Randolph the other day, it brought up a lot of old feelings. I guess I was thinking about that mainly. We talked for quite a while, and it brought back a lot of memories and brought up even more questions that I have avoided for a really long time. My mind just got going and I couldn't turn it off when I went to bed."

Nora, nodded. "I know those nights well." She pulled her sweater tighter around her neck. "I haven't seen her much over the years. She keeps pretty much to herself. I am sure you found out, her husband has been dead for a while now, but she still manages out there. Pat and the Kunzler boys help out every now and then when she needs something. She rents the land out, and she seems to get along pretty well on her own." Nora sat down on the bed next to him and the rich scent of her settled down with her. She had on a thick home-knit sweater over her blouse and bib overalls, but the cold had to be cutting through even that.

Dennis Hurley

"Whyn't you turn around for a minute, while I slip into some pants," he said. "I want to kick that fire on before we turn completely to ice."

"Like I haven't seen that skinny butt of yours naked before. A little late to start getting a case of modesty, isn't it?"

"Maybe so, but things are different now. As I remember it, that was your choice." He didn't mean it to come out the way it did, meaner spirited and more bitter than he really thought he felt now, but maybe it was like a lot of other things about his life, one of the layers which had worn a little thin, so if you looked closely, you could see the original feelings just there below the surface. He kept those thin spots covered up mostly, so he wasn't happy to see that one jump right out that way. She stood up, and the scent rose with her like her shadow.

"I guess if you're going to stay here, we're going to have to talk about that sooner or later, aren't we?" She stood staring down at him.

"That's up to you, I guess. I don't really care. I let it go a long time ago," he said.

"Oh, I can see that. You're just totally over it, aren't you." Her voice quivered slightly and the wrinkles at the corners of her eyes deepened as she squinted to keep back the tears that began to form. He reached up and touched her hand, but she drew it away and turned toward the window. He stood up and pulled on his pants, the floor cold against his bare feet. He reached out again and touched her shoulder, and she spun toward him suddenly, her cheeks tear stained but now her eyes flashed with anger. "You think you're the only one who's suffered because of what happened? I didn't go anywhere thirty years ago. I've been here all along while you were off wandering the world."

The fierceness of it shocked him. He couldn't even think what she meant by it all. She wasn't through yet.

"What have you been doing all that time? Where have you been? How many women have you been with? I'm sure you haven't been some monk lying on your pallet all this time."

"Why does it matter?" he said softly, not sure why this conversation was taking place.

"While you were gone, I tried not to think about it. And then after the first few years I guess I never really expected to see you again." Her face softened now, the features blurred in the morning grayness. "The problem is since you came back, stupid as it seems, I can't stop thinking about you with other women?"

The revelation stunned him. He wanted to grab her and hold her tight, but he fought it back, stood looking at her there, inches from him after he thought she was completely gone from his life.

"Do you really want to know what my life was like?"

"Yes, I think I do."

"Do you want to know how many, or at least how many meant a damned thing to me, because that number is exactly zero. You spoiled me for anybody else, Nora. I never ran into another woman I cared to spend any more than a night with." He hesitated, afraid to go on, afraid he had already said too much.

"Look. All this doesn't mean a thing anyway. We've both made our choices, and we both are going to have to live with them." The cold had really sunk into him now as he stood there shirtless in front of her. He began to shiver uncontrollably.

"Oh, Wes." She bent and took the blanket from the bed and draped it carefully over his shoulders, and her touch went through him like a shockwave. "Sit down there while I get the fire started." She motioned to the chair near the stove. He pulled the blanket tighter around himself and sat down. In a minute she had the fire roaring, and the heat of it warmed his face. She stood once again in front of him, her hands pressed to her face, the words muffled. "I'm not sure this is going to make any sense to you, and you're right that it probably doesn't make any difference, but I'm going to tell you what happened anyway." She walked to the window and stared out.

"I guess you think I abandoned you for your brother, and maybe that's right, but you don't really know the half of it, Wes. I was fifteen years old." She turned back toward him. "Fifteen years old, and your brother was the most popular guy in school then. That he was interested in me was too much for me to imagine." She turned, squatted down and took his hands in hers; hers

A Sense of Place

warm, his cold. "Do you remember what it was like to be fifteen? Do you remember what it was like to want to be popular? No, come to think of it, you don't, because as I remember it, you really didn't seem to care about that, but everybody else did, and I was as much a victim of that as all the other girls, and guys too for that matter, in our class. The whole thing was like some play where I was the little poor girl who got selected by the prince. I always felt that when he discovered who I was, that I really was the little poor girl, the play would be over, and you and I would get back together. But before that could happen, your Grandpa was killed, and the next thing I knew, you were gone." She paused and squeezed his hands.

"Wes, don't you see how it was? When you left, I didn't have that many options. My daddy died during the winter of my senior year. There was no way I could run the mint farm by myself, and we were so far in debt, the creditors just took the farm. They let me stay on in the house until after I graduated, but then I had to make a choice. I'd put Pat off during all of senior year, but you didn't come back. I wanted to leave town, to go see those places we always talked about, but how could I do that? No money. No possibility of any kind of job to save any, and your brother still hanging in there, waiting with more patience than I had ever believed he was capable of." She gripped his hands even tighter. "Does any of this make any sense to you at all?"

She looked searchingly at his face, and he closed

his eyes because he couldn't bear to see her this close. She waited for him to answer, but he couldn't say anything. Finally, she stood up, let his hands slide slowly out of hers and turned toward the door. "We better get back up to the house and get you some breakfast if you're going to work on that barn today. Can't do that on an empty stomach."

Her tone was flat. He stood up, the blanket dropped from his shoulders. "Nora." She looked back over her shoulder, her hand on the door knob. "I do understand, and I guess on some level, I always have. I don't blame you for anything."

She smiled a sad little smile back at him. "I know, Wes, and I don't blame you." And she was gone.

A week of intense cold with temperatures hovering in the teens followed their exchange, Nora and Wes went their separate ways, the carpentry consuming his every waking moment while the winter chores of barn cleaning, machine repair, planning and ordering consumed hers and Pat's. Wes threw himself into the work, pushing down the confusion of feelings he had about what had happened. All he wanted now was to complete the project because he had determined now that he would head south as soon as he finished the lean to. By the end of the third week in November the new rafters were ready for the roof boards, and he was more than ready to be done with the job.

At supper on Friday everybody seemed unnaturally quiet, and more than ever he wanted to be on

A Sense of Place

his way. He pushed his plate back and looked across the table to where Pat was lighting up a cigarette. "Can I get a little help from you tomorrow? I need to bring up those elm boards you have stacked out behind the barn. I guess you wouldn't mind using them for the roof boards, would you? Seems like they would work out all right."

Pat took a long draw on the cigarette and as usual broke into a fit of coughing. When he finally got it under control, he stared back at Wes through the smoke. "You mean you're already to put the top on her? You moved right along, didn't you. Sure, I can take a day to do that. All I have right now is rebuilding the engine on the Massey Ferguson and I got most of the winter to take care of that."

"We'll bring them up in the pickup, and you can hand them up to me as I need them. It'll save me some time. I'd like to get this wrapped up this week."

Nora looked up at him for an instant and then stood, picked up her half-finished plate and walked to the sink. She paused for a few seconds and then bent and scraped the food into the garbage and left the room without saying anything.

Pat studied him through the haze of cigarette smoke. "You ain't plannin' to move on when you're done are you? I got plenty more projects that need doin' around here. Farm report this morning said corn prices were headin' up, so I'll have some cash for you by the end of the month."

"No need for that. You keep the money," he said.

Dennis Hurley

"I've pretty much made up my mind though. I don't figure to spend a winter up here in the cold when I can be working down in the warm and sunny south." He tried to make it come out light and funny, but the words just kind of hung there between them like some old bitterness.

"You sure as hell will take the money. I ain't takin' your work for free. I hope you know what you're doin'," he said and stood up and followed Nora out of the room.

Saturday broke cold with a few light snow flurries. During the night the wind had swung from the west to the north and bore with it the promise of worse to come. By the time they finished the milking and breakfast it was howling around the eaves, sucking the warmth from the house. After breakfast Wes went back to the cabin and added a pair of bib overalls on top of his jeans and slipped on an extra pair of socks. Still the wind cut through each layer as he and Pat loaded the boards into the back of the pickup.

"Blowin' like stink, ain't it," Pat said rhetorically. "Been aimin' to do this for quite a while now. I'm damned sure surprised it held off this long. Normally we'd have had a sure enough snow by now." He flipped another board into the pickup bed.

"I think we're going to get it by the end of the day," Wes said as he flipped the last of the boards into the truck. "Let's haul this up to the barn before we blow away."

The wind grew even more intense as he started up

the ladder. He thought seriously about forgetting about it for the day, but the need to get the job done and get out drove him despite his fears. He clutched the rungs and carefully climbed to the top. He stepped off the ladder and swayed precariously on the top wall girt. Nausea swept over him, and he squatted down and gripped one of the rafters with his right hand until the feeling passed. Pat pulled one of the twelve-foot pieces of elm 1 x12 out of the pickup and held it up for him to grab. With no place to stand but the narrow wall plate he struggled to pull the board into place along the edge of the eave. The wind and the weight of the board fought against him, but he finally managed to drop it into place and drove home a sixteen-penny spike. By the time he had nailed it in place he was shaking.

"You all right, bud? You look a little peaked."

"Yeah, I'm OK. Just keep those boards coming."

He willed himself to get into position for the next board, took it and nailed it down. By the time he had nailed in the third board he had a place to stand and felt slightly more comfortable. He still strained against the wind which came in powerful gusts and then eased off so that his swaying appeared like some crazy dance. At least the roof had a low pitch so, as the platform widened, it became easier to stand. He built a platform to hold the rest of the boards and Pat handed them up for him to stack. When Pat finished that, he headed back to his work on the tractor. By noon Wes had nailed off half the roof.

During lunch the snow flurries increased to a

genuine snowfall. Pat laid down his baloney sandwich and looked out the window. "I think you're done for the day, little brother. That roof can wait."

"No, I'm set now to at least get the rest of the roof boards on. I'll quit if it gets too slick."

"You suit yourself, but it ain't so important you got to get your neck broke doin' it."

Nora watched Wes intently from the other side of the table. Finally, she stood up. " I'll get my clothes changed and give you a hand." She disappeared into the other room before he could protest.

"Pat. You keep her here. Don't let her come out there. It's too cold and too dangerous. I can break my own damn neck, but I don't want her risking hers."

"I'll tell her," he said, "but I wouldn't count on her listenin'. You ought to know that by now."

Wes rinsed his plate and walked to the door. "I've got everything I need up there now. It won't take me any time to finish up this part of it." Pat nodded and took another puff on his cigarette.

The wind had settled down a bit by the time he got back out to the ladder, but the snow came down heavily,   muffling the sounds of the cattle in the barnyard, all enveloping, all isolating. He went into the barn, grabbed a push broom and returned to the ladder. The whirling snow made him dizzy as he looked up to the roof edge, and once again he had to steel himself to climb up there. He took his gloves off and blew on his hands to warm them. Finally, he slipped them back on, ascended

A Sense of Place

the ladder and stood on the edge of the roof. The house appeared as a ghostlike outline through the veil of snow, and from Nora's window a light appeared and then, just as quickly shut off. He turned back to the roof and began sweeping the area that he had to work on. Maybe it was the connection to his work on the barn, but somehow, he got to thinking about Cassie again.

•••

On the last Saturday of November, 1942, Wes rolled out of bed at 4:30 and dressed quickly in the darkness. Since September he had followed the same routine every day, rising early, grabbing a glass of water and a couple of whatever kind of cookies that were in the jar over the stove, then out into the barnyard to dig traps out of the manure pile where he kept them to take away the man smell. Steel Victor traps, rusted now from exposure, but new and shiny when they arrived in their package from Sears in the late summer of his freshman year of high school. During the summer he had pestered his grandfather until he had let Wes try his hand at trapping under Cassie's guidance.

He loaded the pack basket with traps, and the bait scent he kept on a shelf in the barn. Pungent and acrid, it had a fatal attraction for the muskrats in the pond. Finally, he added the short-handled ax, swung the lot of it onto his shoulders and walked through the fog of his own breath until he reached the pond. He stood and looked out into its perfect darkness as he waited for Cassie. The cold smell of approaching snow came down with a north wind, and a rime of lacy ice had begun to form along the edges of the pond. He heard the creak of Cassie's pack basket before he saw him. Cassie seemed to rise out of the darkness, appeared to float toward him across the sea of dead marsh grass that rimmed the pond. His thick hands were jammed deep into the pockets of his old mackinaw and he merely nodded to Wes as he drew up alongside. Together they made their way along the shore until Cassie paused and stooped to look closely at the bank in the darkness. "Here," he signed. "Give this spot a try."

Wes bent to see what Cassie saw, but hard as he tried, he still couldn't figure out what he found that told him where to set the traps. He moved off into the darkness and Wes waded slowly into the icy water, feeling it through his rubber boots and thick socks, wanting to step out, to escape its grip. He took out a stake and drove it at least a foot into the soft muck. He slipped the ring of the trap chain around the peeled cedar and then carefully pressed the jaws open and set the trap down into the water next to a log. Finally, he sprinkled a little of the bait scent along the log just over the trap, closed the bottle and stepped out of the water onto the bank. He shivered as he loaded up his basket again and then swung it onto his shoulders and moved further down the pond edge to where Cassie worked at setting two traps in the water under an overhanging bank.

"Cold?" he signed.

Wes nodded his head, and an involuntary shiver

shook his frame. He smiled. "I'll survive," he answered.

They continued along the shore and each made two more new sets before they started to check their lines from the day before. Where a spring fed into the pond, a small dark shape lay quietly on the bank. Cassie pointed at the muskrat. "A big one," he signed. "At least a dollar for that one." He moved carefully, almost reverently, toward the muskrat, which raised its head in a resigned way. Now came the part that Wes always found hard, but Cassie seemed to do with little thought. He raised the flat of the short ax he carried and brought it down quickly on the muskrat's skull. The animal never moved to avoid the blow.

Cassie stooped and gripped the spring, releasing the rat's foot from the jaws of the trap. He held the limp carcass in his hands, studying it, slid his hand along the back over the smooth thickness of the fur, and then reached over his shoulder and dropped the carcass into his pack basket. Next, he stooped, reset the trap and sprinkled new scent around it. He worked quickly and with a practiced efficiency that came of years of experience. When he finished, he turned toward Wes, and only then did Wes realize that he had been staring intently at everything Cassie did. "What's the matter," he signed.

Wes looked away, embarrassed at first to say what he had been thinking. Finally, he signed, "I just wondered how you kill the muskrat so easily. Doesn't it bother you?"

Dennis Hurley

"You mean do I feel sorry for the muskrat?"

Wes nodded, "Yes I guess so. I mean doesn't it ever make you feel sad?"

"No. The muskrat gives himself up to me. You watch carefully. When the hunter corners the game, whether the hunter is a man or another animal, you don't see a struggle in the end, only an acceptance of things. That's the way it's meant to be."

...

Wes thought about that now. Had his grandfather given himself to Cassie? Had he offered himself up to the club, eyes bright, alert, waiting? He tried to picture it, the two of them standing there in the barn loft, some old anger between them, a hatred hidden from the rest of the world until that moment when it found itself focused in the club. It didn't seem possible, never had from the day it happened. There was no anger in Cassie's killing. He saw it as a necessity, a part of the process of trapping, farming. It didn't fit that he would kill his grandfather out of anger. The images in the loft that day were only in Wes' imagination, but maybe because of that, they were colored in deeper hues than what reality probably offered. He shook his head to clear the image.

"What's the matter? Are you OK?"

He turned and looked behind him at Nora standing at the top of the ladder.

"Yeah, I'm fine. I just love working on a roof in the middle of a snowstorm."

A Sense of Place

"Pat said you didn't want me out here, but it sure looks like you could use some help."

"I'm fine, really," he said. "I have a couple dozen boards left to put down and I'm not going to nail them off until it clears. A half hour at most."

She watched him for a minute and then stepped off the ladder onto the roof. "You grab the other end of the board. We'll swing them into place together," she said. It'll go a lot faster that way." She bent and picked up one end of a wide elm board and swung it toward the next open spot.

"Not going to take no for an answer, are you? OK then. Let's get the rest of this roof deck laid and get out of this weather."

For the next half hour, they dropped one board after another into place, nailed it enough to hold it temporarily, and moved on to the next. By the time they had reached the last slot the snow had covered the roof to a depth of three or four inches and the footing had become really treacherous. As they dropped the last board down, Nora's feet went out from under her and with a muffled little scream, she started sliding toward the edge of the roof. Without thinking, Wes dove for her outstretched hand before she reached the edge, dug his toes into the wood, and they slid in a kind of slow motion toward the drop, Nora on her back, Wes on his stomach. With agonizing slowness, the friction of his boots worked against the wood, and they came to a stop, Nora's feet dangling over the eave.

Dennis Hurley

"I can't get up. I don't have any leverage this way," she gasped.

"Hang on. I'll try to help you roll over and then I can help you get up. Reach your other hand up here, and let me grab it."

She stretched out her hand and he took hold of it and pulled with a twisting motion as if spinning her in some weird dance move. She struggled to help him, arching her back and pushing with her head against the rough boards. Finally, she rolled over, their arms crossed facing each other, lying on the cold roof deck. Tears streamed down her face.
"Are you OK?"

She nodded her head. "I suppose you mean, am I injured? No, I'm not." Her voice angry, quivering.

"What is it then?" he asked, but he didn't really want to know.

"You know what it is. Why do I have to say it? Why do I always feel like I'm exposing some open wound to you?"

He dropped his forehead to the snow for a moment and then raised his head up and looked intently at her, at her tear stained face, a loose lock of hair trailing across her cheek. "What do you want from me, Nora? I can't promise that I can give it, but tell me clearly what you want from me."

She seemed to hesitate a moment, and then, "Stay. I know I've asked this before, but before I mostly asked you to stay for him. Stay, but stay for me. Stay because I need you. Stay, Wes, because there was something true and special between us once." She stopped and stared at him, and he felt like squirming, like some schoolboy caught in a lie.

"I don't know, Nora. I don't know if I can stand it, you there every day with Pat. Can't you see how it would be salt in a wound."

"Wes, I'm begging you now. It's not like that between Pat and me, hasn't been for a long time. There is really nothing left for you to be jealous of, nothing left to envy." Tears rolled freely down her cheeks now, and feelings from a time he thought long passed washed over him.

"You need some help up there?" Pat's voice.

Nora froze. Wes locked eyes with her for an instant and then, "Yeah. We had a little fall." He hoped his voice wasn't shaking. Could you push Nora's feet up, give her a little leverage so she can stand? I'm holding her now, but we can't really move."

"Sure. I've got it. Let me move the ladder over there. Hang on."

He could hear the soft sounds of the ladder dragging through the snow, and then a bump as Pat placed it against the fascia board.

"Hold on there, babe. I'm right under you. Just slide on down and I'll put your feet on the ladder and you can come down."

Nora gripped Wes' hand tight, mouthed the word, please, and then let go and slid down over the roof edge and out of sight. Suddenly, Wes felt his body shaking uncontrollably. In all the time we had clung there, he hadn't felt the fear of falling until then, and now it was all he could do to get to his knees and move toward the edge.

"You all right up there, kid?"

On all fours now, he still felt the spasms roll through him, but he didn't want Pat to know. "I've got a couple of things to tie up. I'll be down in a minute. You take Nora and get in out of the cold." He hoped that his voice hadn't shaken too much.

"OK, but you be careful now. We'll see you inside."

He stayed on all fours until the spasms slowed, maybe five minutes, before he could stand and make his way to the edge of the roof. As he got there a wave of dizziness swept over him, and he had to squat and then lower himself carefully onto the ladder. Finally, he stood at the bottom and felt the snow wrap around him like a shroud.

A Sense of Place

Chapter 11

They had filled the summer before their sophomore year with experiences, with learning about who they were under the superficial layers that they showed to the rest of the world. Nora had little to do prior to the mint harvest so she came early and helped with the milking and stayed for breakfast. Afterwards would depend on the day. Sometimes it would be working a field with the Massey Ferguson and a cultivator. Nora would ride on the fender and they would talk the entire time about whatever came into their minds at the time. Sometimes it was just school gossip. Sometimes it became more personal. Whatever the topic, they gained more insight into what the other one deemed important and how they fitted into that picture.

After whatever work they had done, they would disappear together, sometimes to just walk the fields, find a shady spot and lie in the sweet grass of summer. On rainy days, they climbed up into the loft and lay in the hay. No matter the location, they always found a way to hug and kiss and touch one another. One rainy day they climbed up the dusty, chute ladder and stepped across the shaft into the loft only to find Cassie sitting in a corner behind a pile of alfalfa, a bottle in his hand and clearly on his way to being drunk.

"What are you doing, "Wes signed.

"Just taking rest," he answered.

"Nothing to do in the rain?"

"Just taking rest." The sign came fast and clipped like Cassie was irritated to be questioned.

Wes looked at Nora. "What do you say we swing on the mow rope" She nodded, eyeing Cassie. She didn't know him the way, Wes did, and was always a little frightened by him.

He turned away from Cassie and whispered to her, "It's alright. He isn't going to hurt you. Let's just have some fun." He grabbed the mow rope where it hung down from the pulley and climbed up onto a pile of loose hay, reached higher until he had taken up all the slack and swung out across the piled, loose hay. Nora grabbed the rope next and climbed to an even higher spot, swung out and at the apex of the swing, let go and dropped fifteen feet into the hay. She lay there laughing hysterically.

Cassie shook his head, slipped the bottle into a niche in the wall beams, crossed the loft and quickly, if a little unsteadily, climbed down the ladder.

A Sense of Place

"Let's have a look at what he was drinking." Nora ran across the loose hay, slipping and laughing. She reached into the niche and took out a pint bottle of whiskey, more than half empty. She unscrewed the cap and took a sniff. "Whew! That is nasty stuff." She touched the bottle to her lips and let a little of the liquid wash into her mouth. She swallowed and then made a face. "Here, you give it a try." She handed him the bottle and he held it gingerly.

"Come on. Give it a try. Not going to kill you. Don't be a chicken."

He held the bottle up to the dim light, eyed it dubiously and quickly took a small sip. He squinched his face into a pained grimace and recapped the bottle. He felt the tiny amount burning all the way down and couldn't imagine what it would be like to have taken in more.

"Not for me. I don't see how anybody could get to like that."

"I hear you have to drink more of it until you start feeling good. That's what they drink it for."

"I always feel good." He yelled it, jumped up on a pile of hay and then slid down on his belly like he was riding a sled.

Nora laughed and grabbed the rope again, climbed up a mound of hay and swung out over, Wes' head. This time she just hung on and swung back and forth until the rope slowed. Wes grabbed the bottom of the rope and began to twirl it so that Nora began to spin. She laughed her clear, bright laugh again and then started to slide down. Suddenly, she lost her grip and dropped backwards onto Wes. They both fell in a tangle on the floor of the loft. Wes rolled over and touched her hair. "You ok?" His face registered the worry he felt. She lay face down and then her shoulders began to heave in silent spasms at first and then faster until she couldn't hold it in any longer and she burst into another fit of laughter. He smiled and rolled her over.

"Don't do that again! You scared the heck out of me!"

She smiled again and reached up and touched his face and he leaned down and kissed her tenderly first on her forehead and then on the lips. They lay there next to each other, each letting their fingers exploring the contours of the other's face until they felt they would know the other by touch. Wes sat up, brushed hay from his hair and then stood up and offered her his hand. Nora reached up, took it and with her dark eyes locked on his, she stood in front of him and put her arms around his neck. He touched her cheek and then turned away. She kept her hold on him and pressed against his back.

"We can't keep doing this'" he said. "I can't stand it anymore and I am going to explode if we keep making out like this."

A Sense of Place

She leaned her head into him. "I just can't get enough of you, Wes. I understand though if you are worried about going farther."

Wes turned and took her face in his hands. "You know how I feel about you. I just don't want to do anything that wrecks your reputation at school. Those things have a way of getting found out no matter how much we try to hide it." He hugged her and kissed her on the forehead.

"Let's get out of here and go take a walk in the rain. We can get some crawlers on that wet grass and go do a little fishing off the high bank." He smiled and she smiled back.

"Only you would think of going for a walk in the rain. I think you've been hanging around with Cassie too much. You think you're some kind of mountain man or something."

Wes laughed. "Cassie's a good guy. I know it's hard for people to see that because they don't have a way to talk with him, but he's really smart and he has taught me a lot about carpentry and trapping and lumbering and …" he hesitated. "He's taught me a lot about life in general. I mean a lot of what we see about people is just surface judgement. It takes a lot more work to get inside their mind, see things from their perspective. It's opened my eyes to a lot of things. Take you for example. BC-before Cassie, I probably would have just seen a pretty face and a beautiful figure and never come to know the funny, smart, perceptive woman under that fancy exterior." He laughed and dodged away as she swung a playful punch at him.

They climbed down the chute to the barn floor, wound around stacks of feed sacks and opened the barn door. The rain was light now, coming in quick, bright waves from a windless sky. They waded through the puddles near the barn and stopped behind the milk house to get two cane poles and an empty can for the worms and then headed back along the lane and into the open pastures that stretched over gentle hills to the edge of the millpond. The southern part of the farm backed up to Partridge Creek where the water ran through a swampy stretch, and then broadened out as it entered the millpond.

They stopped in a loamy section of ground that had been grazed nearly bare and, on the dirt, lay a dozen or more night crawlers that had risen to the surface and lay resting in the cool dirt. Wes quickly grabbed a half dozen and plopped them into the can and they made their way from there along the edge of the pond until the low shore started to rise up and form a drop off overlooking the water. Here, the rain hadn't penetrated as much since the ground was protected by the leafy canopy of ancient oaks and maples. They found a flat spot to sit, their legs angled down the steep bank, baited their hooks and dropped them into the dark, still water beneath them.

Fish circles appeared all around their lines, rippling, concentric circles where fish rose to feed on surface insects. Suddenly, Nora's line went taut and she pulled up sharply to set the hook. In less than a minute she pulled a large, scrappy sunfish up onto the bank beside her.

"Dinner," she laughed.

"I don't think that dinky thing is going to go far." Wes grabbed the line and held it up. Maybe we should just let this little baby grow up a bit."

"Oh, no! You are just jealous because I caught the first fish. I'm going to clean this beauty, filet it and have it for supper. You are going to be sorry you didn't catch one half as nice!"

Wes stood up, laid down his pole, and in one swift move picked Nora up and pretended he was going to throw her into the pond. Laughing, she struggled and he lost his balance and together they slid down the muddy bank and ended up head first in the shallow edge of the pond. They struggled up, hair muddy and hanging in dripping windrows around their faces and then they both erupted in laughter once again. They stood holding one another, knee deep in muddy water until Nora broke free. She started to strip off her shirt.

"I am going to wash up." She threw the shirt on the bank and then reached down, and slipped out of her jeans.

Wes stood still for a minute, and then followed her lead. He was down to his underwear almost as fast as she was and they both dove under together, rose back to the surface and swam with a steady rhythm until they floated in deep water. He dove under, grabbed her ankles and pulled her down with him. He tried to kiss her but they both started laughing and then choking and had to thrash their way back to the surface to catch their breath. They floated and drifted, swam and played for the better part of an hour and finally swam ashore and dressed. When they had finished, Nora wrapped her arms around his neck and stood gazing up at him.

"You have the bluest eyes." She stood on her tiptoes and reached up to kiss him. I better go. Mint pressing starts tomorrow and I am sure my dad has things for me to do now that the weather has cleared." She picked up her fish, handed the poles to Wes and turned to walk away.

"Better luck next time! If you want some pointers on fishing, let me know." She laughed again and he picked up an old acorn and flipped it at her. She laughed again and then she was gone.

That summer Wes got his driver's license. Pat had gotten his at fourteen, two years before, but Wes had waited until he turned fifteen to take the road test. He had been driving the small Massey Ferguson tractor since he got to the farm, at first mostly for non-technical work like moving through a hay field while others loaded the wagons. The Ford pickup was another matter though and in May when his grandfather gave him a brief lesson, he

A Sense of Place

kept popping the clutch and stalling it. In his nervousness he started laughing and couldn't stop himself and after a few failed attempts, his grandpa started yelling at him and finally told him to just get out of the truck and go in the house. From that point he took every opportunity he could get to take the truck when no one was around and practice until he could clutch and shift smoothly. By the end of June, he felt he was ready and told his grandpa so.

"So, you think you're ready now, eh. From what I saw the last time I would be real surprised."

"I've been practicing a lot and I think you will be surprised." Wes smiled nervously.

"Well, let's see what you can to do."

After a short ride to assure him that he had indeed learned to drive, his grandpa had Wes drive into Lapeer. They stopped at the Department of Motor Vehicles office to sign up for the testing. An hour later he was back on the road with a date for testing. He hadn't cared much about the license until then. He hardly left the farm most of the time, but as his relationship with Nora grew, he wanted to be able to take her places, do things that the farm alone didn't provide, so the license became a priority.

Nora was changing too. She still seemed content to spend time with him but her beauty hadn't gone unnoticed at school in her first year and other guys started hanging around her, asking her out. By the end of the year she had started to hang out with some of the more popular girls in the school. She wanted to go places and do things and Wes occasionally felt like he didn't fit in anywhere in her life anymore. Many of the things she wanted to do took money and though he worked nearly full time on the farm, all his grandfather could give him was a small allowance. He had saved what he could and seldom bought anything for himself, but even little trips they took together took money, and he quickly ate up what he had saved. One hot morning as he started the mowing for the second cutting alfalfa, Nora came striding across the field in jeans and a red checked shirt, tails tied up her waist.

"Hey, you," she called, barely audible above the sound of the tractor and sickle bar mower. He turned in his seat to watch her, put the tractor in neutral and disengaged the PTO.

"Can I ride along? I promise I won't talk your ear off." She smiled and as usual he melted to see it.

"Sure. Climb on up here onto this comfy fender and I'll take you on a tour of the field. You're always wanting to see the country. Well, here's your chance." He laughed at his own joke and she hit him on the shoulder as she climbed up behind him.

"Not exactly what I had in mind, but it will do for today." She leaned forward and kissed him on the cheek.

Wes engaged the PTO and the sickle bar slid noisily back and forth in its track. He put in the clutch, put the tractor in second gear and began to move slowly ahead as the cutting knives laid the alfalfa down in a five-foot swath. Nora leaned forward, her lips close to his ear so he could hear her over the noise.

"What would you think about going to the show in Armada? I know it's a long drive but they are playing "For Whom the Bell Tolls" Saturday night and we both read the book. I'd really like to see the movie." She blew warm breath into his ear.

"Pretty please."

Wes turned to look at her. "Blow in my ear and I'll follow you anywhere, I guess. Not sure though where I am going to get the money. I am about tapped out on my allowance."

"Borrow some from your brother. He always seems to have money to spend."

"No way I am doing that. First off, he would never loan it to me, and if by some miracle he did, he would never let me forget it. Ok. Let me think on it. I might be able to pick up some money for a job over in Partridge Creek for Mrs. Randolph. She needs a little carpentry done and with it not getting dark until nearly ten, I might be able to go over after we milk and get it done in the next couple of days. I'll let you know when I find out if that will work or not."

She leaned forward and kissed him again and smiled that smile that he couldn't resist. "I need to get back home. We are pressing mint today and they are cutting this morning, then I have to work the press until that is all processed. I'll see you at milking."

He stopped the mower so she could get off. Before she did, she hugged him around his neck and then lightly stepped back off the tractor and started walking back toward home. He shook his head as he looked after her. She turned, walked backward for a few steps and waved to him, and then turned and started to jog off across the cut portion of the field. He watched her until she disappeared into the tree line.

Wes finished the mowing by noon and took the tractor back to the machine shed. His brother was there ahead of him and was greasing the hay rake fittings.

"Hey little brother! You got that look like you ate the canary. What are you plannin'?"

"Nothing. What's it to you anyway?" Wes paused and took the other grease gun and started to work on the mower fittings, carefully wiping the grease zerks and then filling them with grease. Finally, he asked, "What are you doing this weekend?"

Pat looked up. "Why? You got some plan?"

"I was thinking I might like to use the truck."

"Yeah. I'm sure you would. I got plans. We got summer practice and then afterwards a bunch of us is going to do a little drinkin' down at Sam Morris' barn. "You want to join us, little brother?"

Wes, took a bandana from his hip pocket and wiped the sweat that had beaded on his forehead. "You know I don't. Why don't you just ride with John?"

"What'd you have to trade me for the truck? How about a date with your little girly, Nora? Nah., I don't need you to give me that. I could get her anytime I wanted her. What else you got?"

"You're an asshole; you know that? I am out of allowance money, but if you can wait, I'll give you the next two weeks allowance when I get it."

He greased the last of the fittings and straightened up to look over at Pat. Pat was finishing up the rake and he had a big smile on his face.

"Sure. Why not. I wasn't plannin' to use the truck anyway. Thanks for the gift though. A deal's a deal so I expect to see that money in my hands the next two weeks." He flipped the greasy rag at Wes, turned and walked out of the shed and headed for the house.

Wes spent the afternoon working with Cassie on the new barn. They were placing rafters and it was a two-man job with Wes on the bottom end setting them in place and Cassie working along the ridge beam to fit them at that end. With half the rafters set, they took a break and sat in the shade of a Sugar Maple tree, a slight breeze cooling them as they drank some water and stretched out their legs.

"Cassie, you think I learned enough carpentry to do my own work?"

"You are pretty good carpenter now. Best teacher." Cassie smiled at his own joke.

"I need to earn some money."

"I know. Got girlfriend." He smiled again and poked Wes in the ribs.

"I been thinking maybe I take a carpentry job in town. You think I can do that?"

"Sure. You getting to be fine carpenter. You just take your time and work careful like I teach you. You do fine."

Wes leaned back against the tree and closed his eyes an odd feeling of accomplishment welling up in him.

After the milking, Wes asked to borrow the truck to go see Mrs. Randolph. An hour later he was hanging shelves and tightening doorknobs throughout the house. By ten o'clock he had finished and Mr. Randolph gave him $2.50. He said goodbye to Mrs. Randolph and headed back.

It was a full moon night and the road home seemed almost as clearly lit as daylight. A deer crossed in front of him as he turned into the drive, and he braked

A Sense of Place

hard to avoid hitting it. He sat for a minute breathing hard from the close call and then parked the truck and went into the house. The rest of the house was dark, but his grandmother had left a light on and a plate of food for him in the kitchen. As he sat eating, he thought about the money he had made. Two dollars and fifty cents. A fortune for him. Sixty cents for the two of them to go to the show. Fifty cents for gas. He could hardly believe his luck. The loss of the allowance was well worth it now that he knew what he could get doing carpentry. He cleaned his plate, put it in the sink and headed up to bed.

Saturday came and with it a warm rain. All day his grandfather gave him all the cautionary advice he could about driving in the rain. After milking, Wes took an early bath and dressed in clean jeans and a blue denim shirt. He carried a light jacket with him. At 8:00 he drove the truck to Nora's house, parked, threw the jacket over his head and went up to the door and knocked. Nora's father answered and let him in. Wes stood dripping in the entryway while her father went to call her down from her room. When she came down the stairs, Wes was stunned. Nora wore a light blue dress, her short, dark hair shining and curly and framing her face in a way that brought out the blue in her eyes. He had never seen her so beautiful and he felt at a loss for words, could hardly get out a hello when she greeted him.

"Hi, Wes. Are we all set?"

He nodded his head. He couldn't take his eyes off her, stumbled as he tried to hold the door for her, managed a goodbye for her dad and they stepped out onto the covered porch. He recovered enough to throw his jacket over her head and shoulders and they made a run for the truck. She laughed as he opened the door for her and then again as he got into the driver's seat.

"We're going on a date, Wes! She glanced at the house to see if her dad was standing in the window, then slid over and kissed Wes on the cheek.

He wanted to say something but felt tongue tied. Finally, he blurted out, "You're beautiful!"

She laughed again and then turned his face to hers, looked into his eyes and then kissed him long and hard on the mouth. All through the drive to Armada, Wes tried to concentrate on the road and on his driving, but he could hardly resist looking at Nora and at one point nearly went off the road at a curve. As the wheels caught in the drop off at the edge of the road, he fought to get back on the pavement.

"Well that was exciting." Nora slid over and threaded her arm though his, leaned her head into his shoulder. He turned his head and lightly kissed her hair.

At the show he splurged and bought popcorn for them both and they sat in the back row with the flickering light of the projector directly over their heads. He couldn't concentrate on the movie at all and by the end couldn't have told anyone what the story was about, but he could tell you how she smelled and how warm she was against his arm and what her mouth tasted like when she kissed him.

When the show ended, they waited in their seats until the theater emptied and then made their way into the lobby, now semi-dark, and out into the night. The rain had stopped and a full moon lit the street, and when they got to the truck, he spun her toward him and kissed her long and passionately. Afterwards she leaned her face against his chest and then turned her face up to him.

"Maybe tonight we should stop up on Turner's Ridge Road and watch the moon for a while." A shiver coursed through him at her words. He looked into her eyes and knew that whatever she wanted, he could never say no.

That night they lay on a blanket in the back of the pickup and made awkward love for the first time. Afterwards, they lay side by side and watched the moon as it made its way across the sky.

Chapter 12

The weather broke the next day and the short days of November turned an unusual bright blue. The shingling went quickly in the mild forty-degree temperatures, and the day before Thanksgiving Wes took down his ladders for the last time. There were still two hours left before sunset, and so he set out across the hay stubble field toward the old homestead with his tool belt slung over his shoulder. He wasn't sure in what way or why he had decided to stay, had hardly admitted it to himself, but somehow, he had reluctantly come to the decision that he couldn't leave just yet. More than Nora asking him, he felt that his homecoming had raised more questions that as yet had gone unanswered, and if he left now, he knew that there was no way that he would ever come to any peace about his grandfather's death and Cassie's part in it, maybe even his own culpability.

The only thing he knew for sure was that he couldn't go on staying in the yard outside Nora's and Pat's room. He'd thought about renting a place in town, but

A Sense of Place

somehow that didn't seem right either. Now, as he crossed the fields in the low angled light, he wondered at his decision. He almost felt like he was being controlled by some outside force and yet, he knew that deep down it was his own decision to stay. Was it weakness on his part or strength? He couldn't tell. He did know that sometimes you are so close to a decision that you have no perspective on it. Right now, he wanted to believe it was strength.

The house presented itself like a shabby bit of flotsam against the flow of fading green buckthorn that seemed to be trying to sweep it up and send it on its way.He hesitated a minute, a breeze stirring the gnarled branches of the lilac that overgrew the east end of the porch, and watched a bit of lacy dried weed as it slid back and forth across the weathered boards in a crazy dance. Finally, it broke free and rolled across the yard until it came to rest against the spring house, and with that he stepped onto the porch and removed his hammer from its loop on the side of his tool belt.

The boards came away easily from the door frame as if someone had been here before and worked the nails loose more than once. When they were all down, and laid carefully aside with the nails pounded back so that no points stayed exposed, he swung the door open and stepped across the threshold into the past. If he had felt the history in Pat's new place, he realized that he was a major part of the history of this place.

Right now, it appeared as it had the day he'd left.

Dennis Hurley

The front door opened onto a hall that ran through the center of the house, the wood floors, dusty now but solid and virtually unmarked. His grandmother had cared for them well, but that had been easy, since they rarely used the front door, and when they came in the back, it was a rule that the boots came off. He walked now through the dust, his boots leaving their tread marks to testify to his passing. Each door he swung open revealed the same picture frozen in time- the same furniture that had been there when he left thirty years before, covered now with old sheets, but each form familiar, waiting.

Up the stairs and under the eaves where he and Pat had spent their first night so long ago, he found the only signs of deterioration, the beginning of the end for the old house if not checked now. Chunks of plaster covered the floor boards where the rains had finally worked their way through the rotting shingles and soaked the ceiling until it collapsed. Ropy strands of horse hair plaster hung down like cobwebs from the stained and exposed rafters. He poked at the wood- nothing rotted, the wound too recent, just starting to fester. A half dozen shingles and a half day's labor to repair.

He walked over to the little dormer window and squatted to stare out at the darkening fields. Pat farmed most of the land on the old farm, but the area behind the barns back to the pond, he had left fallow until the wild had taken over and made the fields virtually unrecoverable.

As the light dimmed around him, he could

A Sense of Place

visualize his grandfather loading manure on the spreader out behind the barn, the team of black Percheron's, Carl and Jake standing steady and quiet, steam rising from their backs.

...

"Hard work, boy. That's what this is all about." His grandfather paused and waved one square, freckled hand vaguely at the fields behind him.

"Your brother don't seem to get it. All he's interested in doing is hanging out with them friends of his. Looking for trouble is all." He drove the long-handled manure fork deep into the pile as if for emphasis.

Wes redoubled his own efforts so as not to be lumped in with Pat and his friends. He had guessed long ago that in general Gramps favored him, probably because he didn't cause him any real trouble. None-the-less, he was afraid of him. Overall, he didn't guess you'd have called Gramps a big man, but he left the impression of bigness. His square body and thick neck gave the feeling of great strength, and even though he had entered his sixties, he seemed to have an intense energy about him. Most of the time Wes remembered him as funny and easy going, but every now and again he was prone to fits of anger that were frightening to behold, especially if he'd been drinking.

"You keep your nose clean, boy, and you'll be working this place for yourself someday. Unless Pat starts walking a new road, it ain't likely I'm going to let him have a piece of it."

Dennis Hurley

...

Wes stood up and with one last glance out the window, headed back down the stairs. It seemed strange to be here now, to go from boy to man in a single step and still feel comfortable in the same place, but here it was. The house itself held nothing bad for him. Oh, those days of the trial had been a bad time for sure, but in the house, there had only been a silence about what happened. Nobody talked; not Pat, not Grandma. After the funeral, that silence draped everything and stayed there until Wes left. The thing was, over the years he learned to live with the silence, even to welcome it, so coming back to it was like a homecoming.

As darkness settled fully onto the landscape, he headed back across the fields toward Pat's barn. The barn lights showed dimly through the dirty window panes and the light cast itself in pale squares on the ground along the walls. When he opened the door, he saw Pat, back bent over the feed cart. Pat turned from the feed cart and eyed Wes as he shut the door behind him.

"What you been up to li'l brother? I see your ladders down and no sign of you. Thought maybe you'd taken off on us. Found your truck though and figured you wouldn't a hoofed it out of here no matter how anxious you was to hit the road." He grinned at his own joke. Wes picked up a fork and started to clean the aisle of hay thrown out by the cows as they ate.

"I guess you've got me for a while longer, Pat. I'll stay for the winter anyhow. After that we'll have to see."

A Sense of Place

"That's great, buddy. You know I can use the
help, and at the same time winter time is easy enough so's
you'd kind of be on vacation." His voice registered a
relief that surprised Wes. He knew Pat wanted him to
stay, but that he would be so open about it left Wes
feeling uncomfortable and a little unsure about his
decision.

"There's all kinds of equipment that needs repair;
that'll be the bulk of it. And there's always manure to
clean up and spread. That never stops. The machines
aren't the same as when you was here before though. No
sirree Bob. No simple horse drawn stuff now, but the
principles is the same. You'll catch on quick. With two of
us though, it'll go fast and you'll be able to pick up some
cash work in town if you want."

"Yeah, I've been thinking about that. Might put up
a little sign down at the store, see what pops up."

"Good ideee." He let the word roll off his tongue
and hang out there. Maybe we can get you a few more
home comforts for that cabin too, maybe a better bed.
They have that auction over in Lapeer every weekend.
Oughta be somethin' would crop up there soon. Maybe
even get you a little double case you find somebody'd
share it with you sometime, you know what I mean." He
winked up at Wes as he squatted and stripped the last of
the milk from the teats of a huge, mostly black Holstein.

"I've pretty well decided to move on over to the
old home place." It came out before he had a chance to
think about it, to know if that's what he really wanted to

do.

"You don't say. That place still standin'?" Pat's head buried in the cow's flank.

"Yeah. Been over there to look it over. In pretty good shape really. A few repairs and some oil for the old furnace and she'll be good as new." He needed a reason for moving. "Give me a little more room and all. Besides, it'll get me out of your hair for a while, give Nora a break from feeding an extra mouth."

Pat stood up, the half full bucket swinging from his left hand. "Don't hear her complainin' none about it. If I didn't know better, I'd say she likes cookin' for you over me." He looked hard at Wes, moved off down the aisle to dump the bucket and then turned back toward him. "You move if you want, though I can't say as that place don't make me as uncomfortable as hell, but keep comin' for dinner. No use to you down there eatin' by yourself."

He nodded. "If it's OK with Nora."

"There ain't no doubt in my mind about that."

Wes had reached the end of the aisle where the silo access door stood in deep shadow. "You never did tell me why you ended up here at John's family's place. And why did you move out of the home place? Seems like it is in as good a shape as this."

"Long story, but I guess it starts way back in high school. You remember me and John were buddies, did everything together. We were both plannin' to enlist as soon as we was done with school but my football injury shot that plan. It didn't stop John though. He up and went direct into the Marines as soon as he graduated. Actually, left the day of graduation. Right after boot camp he got assigned to a company that went to Germany for some of the cleanup operation. John hadn't changed all that much, big kid at heart still, and so he was screwin' around with another guy, pushin' match you know, and stepped on an old land mine. Hardly enough of either of them left to bury.

His dad took it real hard. Tried to bury it by workin' extra hard but everybody thinks the stress killed him. Died in the field one day. John's ma called me and asked me to go out and look for him when he didn't come home. I found him right off. He was layin' beside his tractor like he had just decided to take a nap. Broke my heart to have to tell her after John dyin' and all. Anyways, she couldn't work the farm by herself, so she asked me to start doin' it on shares. That was about the time where everybody was getting' bigger and so I jumped at the chance. I took my share and banked everything left after expenses. After a few years of that, I made her an offer and she took it. I paid off the loan seven years ago. Both farms belong to me now, 100%." He turned to look at Wes leaning against the barn wall.

"I know you think I'm crazy usin' all this old crap equipment. The thing is even though Gramps didn't think so, I was payin' attention all those years ago and I saw how he didn't buy anything new if he could fix the old. Now most of these farms around here are deep in debt cause they bought all that shit from the ag schools about needin' the latest, expensive equipment ever' couple years. They miss the point that the value is in the land and if you lose that because you got too much debt, you got nothin'."

"Phew! Longest damned speech I ever heard you make! I got to hand it to you brother. You got it figured out. Still, why'd you move up here and leave the home place?"

"You know I never felt comfortable there after Gramp died. And then when Grandma passed, well I just felt a change of scenery would be good for both me and Nora. So here we are. If you want to fix up that place, you be my guest. You are welcome to it. Let me know if you need any help." He turned and walked into the milking parlor.

Wes busied himself with the manure clean up, shoveling the fresh piles to the end of the gutter to be loaded into the spreader in the morning. As he did, he thought what Pat had said and especially what he had said about his grandma and a feeling of guilt began to creep over him. She always had seemed so distant to Wes, kind of sad and alone most of the time. He had rarely seen her laugh and after Gramp's death, she had become more distant and sadder. Wes had heard her quietly crying in her bedroom at night and had covered his ears with his pillow. Now he felt like he had let her down by leaving. Maybe he could have done something to help her if he had stayed. At the very least he wouldn't have been another burden for her to bear. He had been so lost back then and had only thought about himself, but he couldn't excuse himself that way now. There were so many things he would have liked to change now as he thought back on it. So many things to examine now that he had buried for so long.

Chapter 13

Thanksgiving morning Wes woke in the predawn darkness. He was sleeping better now than he had in years. Rolling over to look at his alarm clock, he saw that it was 4:30. Another hour before he had to be up at the barn. He rolled onto his back, hands behind his head and stared up at the incongruous decorative plaster medallion on the ceiling. Staying here for the winter had seemed the right thing to do when Nora had asked him. The problem for him was that he couldn't be sure of his motivation. He thought he had managed to put his feelings for her behind him after all these years, but seeing her now here with Pat had brought everything back in a confusing way. He could see that they needed the help, but he couldn't be sure he would be able to keep his feelings contained with her so close.

When the alarm went off at 5:30, he realized he had fallen back to sleep. Groggier now than when he had first awakened, he threw the covers back and swung his bare legs out and sat up on the edge of the bed, rubbed his eyes and reached for his jeans. They were cold and clammy as he slipped them on and he shivered as he pulled

A Sense of Place

on a wool shirt, stood and walked over to the small chest of drawers in the corner. He took out a pair of thick, wool socks, sat on a kitchen chair to slip them on and then walked to the back door where he pulled on his boots and then his chore coat and a dark blue wool cap.

His breath circled his face like a mini climate as he headed up to the house. He could feel the hairs in his nose crinkle as he breathed in and knew that meant that the temperature was in the single digits. He felt his hands numbing through the leather gloves he wore and made a mental note to get something warmer the next time he was in town.

He hurried across the yard and entered the kitchen, where Nora bent over the oven taking out the first of two pumpkin pies. On the counter were the makings of a mincemeat pie waiting it's turn.

"Smells mighty good. I can't even tell you when the last time was that I had a piece of homemade pumpkin pie."

She turned, the pie in her hands, a lock of hair hanging loosely over her right eye. She pursed her lips and blew it out of the way, and her face, glowing with the heat of the oven, broke into a sudden smile.

"Only the best for the hired man. Wait until you see the whole spread I have planned for you. You won't ever want to leave again." She set the pie down quickly and turned away. She took the mincemeat pie and set it in the oven, closed it and then turned back to him. "Pat told me that you are planning to stay the winter."

Dennis Hurley

He nodded his head, "Yeah, I guess."

She pushed the offending lock of hair back into place, and then moved to get a coffee cup from the cupboard. She poured it full and set it down on the table along with a couple of oatmeal cookies. Wes pulled out a chair and sat down.

"You better eat up. You're running a little late today. So was Pat though. It's not like him to not get out of bed on time for morning milking."

"The bed felt a little too good this morning. Probably felt the same for him." He looked up at her and he could feel a flush of embarrassment rushing to his cheeks. "Getting up in the dark never was my favorite part of farm life." He held the cup in two hands to warm them and sipped a mouthful, ate one of the cookies and drank deeply from the rapidly cooling liquid.

"I'd better get out there. It seems like I'm always running late here." He set the cup down and picked up the second cookie. Nora wiped her hands on her apron and walked over to him. She took his free hand.

"Wes. Thank you." And she leaned close and kissed him lightly on the cheek, her breath warm and soft. She looked at him for a long moment, squeezed his hand and turned back to the stove.

"I'll have a small breakfast for you two when you come in. Don't want to spoil your appetites for our big Thanksgiving meal." As if nothing had happened.

The smell and feel of her stayed with him as he walked out to the barn. A kiss on the cheek, that's all. An expression of warmth between old friends, but the feeling for him held something more like the experience of a teenager's first kiss. He tried to fight it down, to put it into perspective, but he couldn't. He wanted to turn around and go back into the kitchen, take her in his arms, the dream he'd had a thousand times since he'd left, but he didn't. He hesitated for a moment and then swung the barn door open, entered the hazily lit warmth of forty cow bodies and went about the chores like any other day.

After breakfast he spent most of the morning packing his gear and tidying up the cabin. He figured to spend one more night there to give him time to get things cleaned up a bit over at the homestead, get the well going and get some firewood in to get the place heated up. He knew that it would be a couple of weeks before He got things really under control, but he was anxious to get started.

Dinner consisted of roasted turkey, mashed potatoes, sweet potatoes, canned corn, cranberry sauce, mountains of rolls and all the gravy you could want to put over everything. They said no grace, and pretty much ate in silence but not really an uncomfortable silence. Wes guessed it came as close to feeling like a family meal as they had had together, and yet every time he glanced across at Nora, she looked away, and he couldn't read her thoughts. Finally, they had eaten their fill, and Pat pushed himself back from the table and lit a cigarette.

"Lions game'll be on in a few minutes. What say we go out in the living room and make ourselves comfy?"

Dennis Hurley

He stood up and stretched and shuffled across the kitchen
and out to the tiny arena of seats he had set up around the
TV. Wes picked up his plate and Pat's and took them to
the sink, and then followed him out. In general, he would
have been just as glad to have headed out to the cabin and
read until dark, but somehow, he got caught up in the day
and the mood. He sat down in an over-stuffed chair and
leaned back and waited for the Lions to take the field so
they could see what way they would manage to lose it. As
the crowd roared to signal the kick off, Nora came into
the room with cups of coffee and set them down next to
each of them.

"So, when's the big move goin' to take place?"

Nora looked up. "What big move? I thought you
were staying."

"I thought I told you. Wes here's goin' to move
over to the old place, Grandma's place. Says he's had
about enough of bein' this close."

Wes pushed back in his chair and clasped his
hands behind his head. "Now that's not exactly right. I
said I could use a little more space and since the home
place is just sitting there, I might as well do a little repair
and take advantage of it, that's all. Besides, you don't
really need me underfoot so much. I can be close enough
to be able to come over and do the work, but far enough
away so that you can still have your privacy."

Nora sat down on the edge of a stiff-backed
Windsor chair.

"I told him we still expected him to eat here, ain't

that right, Nora? Can't have a man workin' for us and livin' on his own damn cookin'." Pat started to laugh and then broke into a coughing fit that finally left him teary eyed and gasping for breath.

"I guess you do what you need to do. You're welcome to eat here, but it's not required," Nora said, her voice a little strained.

"I love eating with you folks, but I feel like a fifth wheel here. You've been living together for a long time and always had your time alone, and I've come along and disrupted that by being around at every meal. I just thought you might like to get back to your normal routine." He felt like getting up right then, making an excuse and getting out, but he sat frozen in place.

The Lions fumbled on the second play from scrimmage and Pat had now totally turned his attention to the game. Wes looked at Nora, and for a change she looked back. "No need for that, Wes." She glanced at Pat, but he appeared not to be listening.

"No need for what?"

"She wiped at her forehead with the back of her hand, glanced at Pat." I mean, we still have enough time to ourselves." She didn't say 'together.'

He stayed through the game and the pie course and by then it was time for the milking to start again, the inevitable rhythms of the farm, but by the time Pat finished his pie and his cigarette, he couldn't stop coughing. Between coughs he complained of being chilled and asked Nora to turn the heat up. Finally, Wes stood up.

"You head on up to bed, old man. I'll do the milking tonight." After he said it, it sounded too dramatic somehow, like some heroic gesture. He regretted it as soon as it came out.

"I can't let you do that," Pat managed to get out between coughs. How am I goin' to trust you with that expensive parlor set up?"

"You just sit tight and get healthy. I've watched you enough to know your part of our little song and dance routine out there. I'm serious now. You take care of yourself. I don't plan to be milking alone all winter."

Pat broke into another fit of coughing and finally nodded his head and waved him out as Nora helped him off to bed. Wes stood in the kitchen's fading warmth and drew on his old canvas coat, a knit cap and the knee-high rubber boots he used in the barn. He stood for a moment and listened to the sounds from upstairs, the coughing, muted conversation. He opened the door and stepped out into the deepening cold.

The cattle had been in their stalls since morning, and the heavy manure smell filled the air. They lay or stood quietly, waiting with a stolid bovine patience for the routine they knew so well.

...

"Cows aren't like wild things," Cassie used to say.

"What do you mean?" Wes signed.

"Well now cows are pretty predictable. You take a cow, and even when it is in a panic, it will act a certain

A Sense of Place

way just about every time, but a wild thing, you never know. Sometimes they'll turn and run, others they'll cower and wait for what they think is going to happen and another time they'll attack with almost no warning."

"I always thought that's the way cows acted."

"No. You watch them real close for as long as I have and you get to know what's coming before they even think about it." He paused, his hands resting on the worn oak edge of a manger, and then his hands started up again. "Some people are like that too, but others are like wild things. No matter how much you think you know them, they're going to surprise you sometimes."

...

Now as Wes went about getting things set up for milking, he tried to think which people he had known in his life who fell into the wild and which fell into the bovine category. For sure some of the men he had worked with over the years had been wild things, peaceful and easy going one day and suddenly throwing a hammer at your head another, always hard to read. Pat, he had been a wild thing when they were kids, but now, Wes wasn't so sure. He turned on the compressor and listened to the vacuum suck through the lines. He climbed up into the loft, more easily now after weeks of practice, and threw down enough hay to hold them while he got going on the milking. Nora-- now when they were kids, he had thought Nora to be predictable until she went off with Pat. Now, he couldn't be sure whether she possessed more wild thing or predictability (He couldn't think of her as bovine).

He had started to wash the udders of the first cows into the parlor when he felt the cold draft of an open door cut through the barn. He looked up and Nora stepped into the light, dressed almost identically to him except for her denim barn coat.

"You get the silage going, I'll wash and milk," she said matter of factly.

"How's Pat doing?"

"He's for sure sick. I can't remember him not coming out to milk no matter how bad he felt, so I'd say he's pretty low right now."

Wes stood up and handed her the bucket of disinfectant, took off the heavy rubber gloves and hung them over the edge of the bucket. "I'll take care of the milking until he gets back on his feet. Maybe you should take him in to the doctor tomorrow. I know he'll fight it, but he needs to get checked up, that's obvious."

"We'll have to knock him out to do it. He won't go willingly, I'm sure of that."
She picked up the gloves and slipped them on. "Maybe he'll listen to you. After breakfast in the morning let's see if we can get him to act like a real human being instead of some superman."

Wes rolled the silage cart down the aisle to the silo, opened the small door at the base. The rich scent of fermenting fodder settled like a living presence in the aisle. He picked up a fork and dug away at the packed green layers until he had filled the cart to overflowing.

A Sense of Place

From the parlor he could hear the sound of a radio, Carol King's voice floating through the barn, "Both Sides Now" filling the air. He turned and wheeled the cart toward the mangers, and then dropped a pile in front of each cow as he moved along the line.

When he had emptied the cart, he turned it up against the wall and entered the parlor. Nora crouched beneath a giant Holstein, its size dwarfing her as she washed its udder with disinfectant and slipped on the suction cups. She stood, wiped the hair from her eyes with the back of her wrist, and then noticed him for the first time.

"Like old times, eh Wes? You and me working at the milking routine. Feels a little odd though."

...

When they were kids, Nora would be at their place so much that it always seemed natural that she shared in the chores. Her dad's farm had no livestock with the exception of a few chickens and a foul smelling billy goat that he would lease out for breeding to the few farms that had milk goats. It seemed to him though that she always seemed to enjoy the work somehow, made a game of it often so that they both enjoyed it really. He remembered one day in particular in early June just after school let out in their freshman year. The evening sun slanted through the dirty windows on the west side of the barn, sliced through the suspended dust particles in the air and came to rest on the side of her sun-browned face. He had finished hand milking the one old Jersey they kept and squatted next to the manure gutter watching her finish stripping out the last of the milk from a Guernsey. She pressed her head into its soft flank and pinched its tail behind her knee to keep from being swatted as the cow tried to keep the ever-present flies off.

"What do you want to be, Wes? I mean what do you want to do with your life when you grow up?"

The question took him aback for a minute. No one had ever asked him that before. When he finally answered, it came out as the foregone conclusion that he thought it was.
"I'm taking over the farm when I get old enough."

She slid her finger and thumb slowly down the teat stripping the last of the milk in a thin stream into the bucket and then stood up.

"No, I mean what do you want to do? I know what you think you have to do. What would you really like to do?" She drew out the 'really' for emphasis.

"I don't know. I guess I never thought about it."

"Well, I know what you should be, and I know what you should do. You should be a writer and you and I should travel all over and live in different countries and see the whole world."

"I don't know, Nora. I can't picture myself ever leaving the farm. I feel..." he hesitated. "I feel safe here." It felt stupid as soon as he'd said it.

"Safe? What do you mean?" She stood close to him now, the bucket dangling from her fingers, her eyes locked on his.

A Sense of Place

"I don't know exactly. Maybe safe isn't the word. Maybe comfortable, maybe happy. I just don't know. Anyway, I can't picture myself traveling all over the world. Doesn't seem natural."

She turned away and started toward the milk house. "I think it sounds great," she said. "I can hardly wait to get out of here, to see some of those places like in the National Geographic. I just want to leave this place behind." She stopped so suddenly that he almost bumped into her. She turned and faced him. "I'd hoped you'd want to come with me." She spun back around and disappeared out the door of the barn. He caught up with her as she went into the milk house, a ten foot by twenty foot shed with an artesian well running into long cement troughs along the north wall. The cold water circulated around the ten-gallon metal cans and then slid over a low lip at the end and out the side of the shed and into a wooden trough that carried the water to the barnyard to water the stock. Cold air rose from the tanks even in the heat of the summer. He caught her hand as she stepped through the door and spun her toward him. He took her face in both his hands, felt the warmth of her cheeks in the chill room, and kissed her softly.

"I'd go with you wherever you wanted to go," he said.

···

Now he took the bucket from her hand and carried it over to the ten-gallon container in the corner. Pig food now. You couldn't sell the hand milked stuff, not sanitary enough for the processors. It had put a lot of the small producers out of business when the rules took effect. The cash outlay for the new equipment had been too much for them, so they had simply gone under, taken jobs in the auto plants in Pontiac and Warren, made the long commutes until they couldn't stand it anymore and then sold out to move to the suburbs where they worked. Now they farmed lawns sixty-five by one hundred-twenty, and watched the sunsets over the neighbor's roof...

He'd meant it then. Somehow, she always gave him courage he didn't have on his own. As he watched her milking again just as he had then, he wondered what she wanted from life now or if she had already gotten it.

The next morning after the milking, they ate a quick breakfast and loaded Pat into the car. He protested loudly, but his weakness and constant coughing combined to give them an easier time than they'd thought. He was just too weak to fight it. He sat next to Nora, his head flopping back and forth in half sleep as they headed out to the highway and then south into Lapeer.

The doctor's office was up a flight of stairs in an old brick storefront- a now empty pharmacy whose dusty windows still contained cardboard displays for cold medicine and aspirin. Pat had labored up the stairs, stopping frequently to catch his breath. Nora had called ahead so when they arrived, the receptionist went back into the examination rooms to let the doctor know they were there. They sat in the dim waiting room, Pat alternately shaking and sweating, coughing and smoking. Finally, the nurse called him in.

Nora and Wes thumbed through the greasy pages of old Field and Stream magazines while they waited. When Pat came out, he headed directly to the door without saying anything. Nora and Wes stood up and followed.

Pat was already in the car when they got there, his head slumped back against the seat. They climbed in and Nora started the engine before she turned to him. "What did the doctor have to say?"

"Nothin'. Just the flu or somethin'. Stop up at the Rexall and I'll get this filled."

He held up a prescription slip and then let his hand sink back to his lap.

"I'll run it in for you," Wes said.

"You damned well won't. I can handle my own shit."

He said it with such intensity, it took both Nora and Wes off guard. Pat just turned and stared intently out the window at the storefronts as they passed by.

After they got back to the farm, Wes helped Nora get Pat settled in and then went out to the cabin to load his stuff into the pickup. He planned to get the furnace going at the old homestead, settle some of his things in place and then head up to do the evening milking. As he climbed in and started the engine, Nora came out of the kitchen door. She motioned for him to stop, and came over to hand him a waxed paper packet filled with warm oatmeal raisin cookies.

"Thanks for going with me today. I know you had other plans." She nodded toward the back of the pickup. Then she leaned in and kissed him on the cheek.

"I'll see you tonight at milking time," and she turned back toward the house. Wes sat and watched her, and as she opened the door, she turned and waved. He waved back, watched her disappear inside and then put the truck in gear and drove down the hill to the only place he had ever really called home.

A Sense of Place

Chapter 14

While Pat recuperated, Wes put everything on hold. The house repairs could wait. He had finished the essential repairs on the roof and had the house functioning again. He had the furnace running and had an oil delivery set up. Now he spent his time repairing machinery and getting everything ready for the spring planting.

The routines had changed somewhat now. He still ate supper at the main house, but for the first week, Pat didn't appear at the table. Nora made up a plate and took it up to their room for him. Wes could hear the wracking cough coming from there as he and Nora ate each night and Wes thought Pat sounded no better.

On the fourth night of the first week, Wes couldn't hold back anymore. "How's he doing? He doesn't sound good to me. Should we get him back to the doctor or maybe the hospital to have somebody take another look at him?"

Dennis Hurley

"You know how he is, Wes. There's no getting him to do something if he doesn't want to do it. I have tried everything I know to get him to go. He says he is fine, just needs some rest. I've moved out of the room and sleep down the hall. I can't stand the coughing. I am exhausted all the time because he is either coughing or snoring. I guess we will just have to let him come to his own decision on this." She stood up and started to clear the plates. Wes stood up and carried his over to the sink.

"I don't know, Nora. If he doesn't show some improvement, I think we are going to have to force the issue. If he isn't showing improvement by next week, we'll hog tie him and at least get him back to the doctor."

Nora rinsed the dishes while Wes stood leaning against the counter sipping a cup of coffee. Finally, she picked up a dishtowel and dried her hands and turned, slipped her arms around his waist and hugged him tightly, pressing her face to his chest.

"Wes, what would I do without you here?" She raised her head, and then took one hand and ran it along his cheek, hesitated for a moment and then put her hand on his chest and pushed herself back and away from him.

"You better go back on down to the home place now, I think I need to stay away from you for a while." She turned and shook her head and walked out of the kitchen.

A Sense of Place

Wes sat down at the table, his coffee cup cupped in his hands, and stared off into the darkness of the living room where she had disappeared. A last fly caught on the flypaper strip, buzzed and struggled and then nothing. Silence engulfed him, and he stood, took his cup to the sink, slipped on his jacket and stepped into the cold.

...

The summer of the driver's license, also marked the beginning of Wes' carpentry career. Word got out that he was a good carpenter and so he spent many nights after milking working for people in and around Partridge Creek. Even with the dates he and Nora had more often now, he put away a good amount in savings. Their summer took on a routine. Nora still came over to do the chores with him and then they swam, and fished and went to the movies and spent hours just lying on an old quilt in the sun. One evening they were sitting on the swing together and off in the distance they could see the light from Cassie's cabin.

"Let's go visit him." Wes said. "I mean he always sits by himself in that cabin with nobody to talk with. He has to be lonely sometimes." He turned to her and saw that she seemed uncomfortable. "It's ok. I'll interpret for you. He likes to talk about books and ideas. He is a really interesting guy. If he has been drinking, we won't go in." He smiled at her and touched her cheek lightly. She smiled back but still looked unsure. He stood and took her hand. "Come on. I won't let him bite you."

Dennis Hurley

The tamaracks brought darkness earlier to the little clearing and the hand-hewn door lay in deep shadow as they approached. Wes knocked firmly so the door moved a little with each knock. Inside a chair slid across the wood floor and then the door swung open and Cassie's figure formed a dark silhouette against the lamplight. He stepped aside and waved for them to enter, the light now striking his face revealing a large smile and its stained and missing teeth. The cabin was as meticulously clean as it had always been when Wes had visited before. He turned and caught the brief look of surprise on Norah's face. He put his arm around her shoulders and gave her a reassuring smile. She smiled back and Cassie arranged the chair alongside the bunk so that they could sit there while he sat on the chair. They started tentatively with Wes asking about what Cassie was reading and then interpreting his answer for Norah. Before long though they were in the middle of a three-way discussion of Shakespeare's Macbeth with Wes signing for both he and Norah and interpreting the responses. Wes could see Norah getting more and more involved and more and more comfortable. Finally, darkness had fully engulfed the cabin and Wes rose to go. Norah, stood up with him and then she stepped forward and hugged Cassie briefly.

"I had a great time. Thanks for letting us visit with you," she said and Wes signed it and then shook Cassie's hand.

A Sense of Place

Wes walked her slowly back to her farm, the stars and a crescent moon lighting the way.

Early in that summer Pat had found an old Ford coupe that someone had given up on and he got it for a bit of work exchanged. He spent most of June tinkering with it until he had it running well. It freed Wes because now, he didn't have to share the truck and so he and Pat seldom talked anymore. Pat would be a senior and his football prowess had made him a big deal at the high school. He and John had their pick of the girls and so their nights were often spent partying and dating. The late nights caused constant friction in the house with Pat and his grandfather in a heated battle for dominance. Finally, their grandfather tended to give up and from that point on Pat did pretty much as he pleased for the rest of the summer, doing only what interested him or absolutely had to be done around the farm.

By August football had started in earnest and because Pat had to be at practice every day, much of the farm burden fell on Wes. He never complained. The rhythm of the farm felt familiar and comforting to him now and so he worked by himself or beside his grandfather or with Norah and felt a joy in the season, in the smell of fresh cut hay, in the dust and sweat that he washed off at the outside hand pump each day after work. He grew taller that summer by almost four inches and filled out with long, stringy muscle, its definition running along his shoulders and down his arms.

Dennis Hurley

They put up more than four tons of loose hay in the loft and as they headed into the last week of August, the rains came and boosted the alfalfa crop. His grandfather had decided to make silage with the alfalfa so it didn't matter that it was a little wet when they cut it. They needed to install the blower tube to carry the chopped alfalfa from the hammer mill up to the top of the silo and Pat volunteered to climb up and pull it into place. He climbed the inside ladder to the top of the silo, a long rope slung across his shoulders, and inched around the rim until he was over the hammer mill below. He peeled the rope off his shoulders and lowered the end to his grandfather waiting on the ground. Wes couldn't watch. It made him dizzy to see Pat like some large bird of prey balanced on the tiny rim of concrete forty feet above him. He busied himself with tying the rope to the curved top end of the steel tube that would shoot the chopped alfalfa up and into the silo. When he was sure it was secure, he tugged lightly on the rope and let Wes know that the tube was ready to be pulled up.

"Take it away, Pat." The tube started to move and then the top end came off the ground and began to snake its way up the side of the silo. Wes looked up for a moment and saw Pat leaning out to tug at the tube whose hooked end was caught on one of the steel rings that supported the silo walls. Suddenly, it broke loose and the suddenness of it caused Pat to slip and cling precariously to the lip of the silo, one leg hooked over the back side;

the right foot barely balancing on one of the outside steel bands.

"Shit. Pull the bottom of that thing away from the wall, Wes. Stop standin' around with your thumb up your ass!"

Wes grabbed the tube and tried to walk it out away from the silo wall. He couldn't look up but then he heard the banging of the blower tube as Pat hauled it the rest of the way to the top and then maneuvered it into place and hooked the curved blower end over the lip of the silo. Wes could hear his brother breathing hard and looked up. Pat sat straddling the rim, both hands in front of him supporting himself on the silo lip as he tried to catch his breath. Finally, he began to slide carefully back along the rim until he reached the interior ladder and then swung both legs over the side and disappeared

When Pat came around the base of the silo, he was laughing. "Now that was exciting, eh?" He poked Wes in the stomach. "I love a good challenge like that. You need to pay more attention, li'l brother. You'll be doing that next year when John and me sign up for the Marines."

Wes gave him a dirty look and set about getting the tube attached to the blower. He didn't want to admit how scared he had been for his brother. As mean as Pat was, they were still tied by blood.

Dennis Hurley

By late August, Wes had established a fairly large carpentry business and so had less time to spend with Nora and with Cassie. He had a hard time turning away the work since when he and Nora did get together, their dates had become more and more expensive. For the first time in their friendship, they argued. What they argued about most was his lack of time for her. By the time school started in September, they were no longer doing the milking together.

Nora at first made up excuses that she had to help her dad and finally, she just stopped coming. They no longer did their homework together and drifted further and further apart. Through it all, Wes missed her intensely. He missed their easy relationship, their quiet conversations, the smell and touch and feel of her in his arms. Somehow, he couldn't bring himself to talk with her, to see what had gone wrong.

He went through the first days of school alone and distant. He had never been one to have many friends and now the few that he had didn't interest him. He mainly just wanted to be left alone and so for the most part, that is what people did. Instead he spent his limited free time reading or sitting in the woods and just observing the nature around him. He loved the changing season with its riot of color. He loved watching the woods go from their green obscurity to golden, to open, as the vines and low brush dropped their leaves, clearing views of trunks and limbs. He felt like it was as if he could now see the skeleton of the forest, its symmetry stripped bare.

By mid-October the football season was well under way and with Pat and John, the team was undefeated going into their sixth game. Wes rarely went to the games, but at school talk had started about the possibility of an undefeated season and the excitement of it even infected him. Around the dinner table, Pat could hardly contain himself.

"Undefeated! Yessir. That's a real possibility now! The schedule is real easy from here on out. Me and John dominate the line! You comin', little brother?" He punched Wes in the shoulder.

Wes, gave Pat a dirty look and then surprised even himself when he said, "Maybe. I'll have to get back in time to do the milking, so if it's not over, I won't get to see the ending, but I am sure you'll fill me in, won't you Pat."

"Well I'll be! What? You turn over a new leaf? You got some school spirit hidden deep down in that scrawny body of yours?" He dug at Wes' ribs with his fingertips. Wes slid way and picked up his plate from the table.

"May I be excused, Grandma? I have homework to get done." She nodded and Wes took his plate to the sink, rinsed it and set it on the drainboard.

Dennis Hurley

He climbed the stairs to his room and shut the door behind him. He had been thinking about Nora all day and now he sat at the table where he did his homework and took a piece of notebook paper and started to write everything he had been thinking, everything she had meant to him, still meant to him. In the end it became a love letter and he was determined to give it to her on Friday if he got the chance, maybe be able to have a date with her on the weekend. He tucked it into the back of his class notebook and put the notebook into the neat pile of his schoolwork.

On Friday the school quivered with anticipation for the afternoon game. Wes walked past Nora's locker several times during the day, but never caught her there. The day passed and he decided he would have to give her the note at another time. The game would start at 4:00 and so Wes stayed in his last classroom and finished all his homework so he wouldn't have to take any home. By 3:45, he had packed up all his things and put them in his locker. He walked down a flight of stairs and out into the late afternoon October sunshine. Most of the school already had filled the bleachers with a small contingent from Imlay City sitting on the opposite side of the field.

Wes stood along the fence and half watched the field and half watched the crowd. Finally, he spotted Nora sitting four rows up near midfield next to one of the most popular girls in the school, Nancy McIntosh. Wes hadn't even known they were friends but then he knew little about her now after their quiet breakup.

The Imlay City team was already warming up on the field when the band played a little bit of the school song and the Lapeer team ran out onto the field. His brother, as captain, led the way and they swung into a double line and began their warmup routine. At four o'clock the teams went to their benches; the captains came to the center of the field for the coin toss and the Lapeer offense took the field for the kick off.

The game seemed mostly one side as it progressed with Imlay City taking a beating on both sides of the ball. Pat and John opened up huge holes for the running backs on the right side of the ball and by midway into the second quarter, Lapeer led 21-0.

Imlay City received the kick off and because of a missed tackle, were able to run the ball back to their forty-yard line. Suddenly, Imlay began to move the ball, gaining large chunks of the field on every run. Lapeer called time out and the coach called Pat over to him. At the end of the time out, Pat was in at defensive tackle.

The Imlay City team came directly at him on their next play. The quarterback handed off to a big farm boy who, if not fast, was definitely strong and he slammed his shoulder into Pat as he drove through the line. Pat's body spun, but not his cleats and Pat went down in pain. The whistle blew and Pat lay on the field, his knee at an odd angle. As they brought him off the field, Wes, met him. He looked at Pat and turned to the coach. The coach took Wes aside.

"It doesn't look good. He needs to go to the hospital. Is your grandpa here?" Wes shook his head.

"Do you have a car? Can you take him?"

Wes nodded his head yes and suddenly realized that Nora was standing beside him. Wes went to get the pickup and with some help from the crowd they made a bed of blankets in the back and Nora climbed up and helped them place Pat on it. She sat beside him and waved for Wes to get going. He could see her stroking Pat's face and wiping away tears from his cheeks as Wes drove as quickly as he dared to the hospital.

...

The house was cold when Wes got back from supper. Still in his coat, he checked the furnace and found that the thermostat wire had worked loose at the furnace connection and reattached it. The furnace came on immediately and Wes, climbed the stairs up into the kitchen. He turned on the stove to warm up and decided to make himself some hot chocolate. He found the cocoa, took a cup from the counter and spooned chocolate into it and then added some milk from the refrigerator. While he stirred it as it heated, all he could think of was Norah and her touch and whether he had made the right decision to stay or not. He wasn't sure that next time he could stand not to cross a line that he had set for himself.

Chapter 15

Pat seemed to recover somewhat after a week of rest and tentatively joined Wes and Nora in the milking routine once again but it was obvious that he had not fully recovered his strength. Nora still helped in the barn, but now returned to the house and let Pat and Wes finish the milking and clean up. Things seemed to return to what they had been before. Somehow though, Wes didn't really fully settle back into the routine.

Having Nora to himself each night for the past week as they milked, time to just talk casually, normally like they had as kids, had changed things in a way that made going back all but impossible. Instead, he found himself thinking about her all the time, mooning over her in a way that he hadn't even as a teenager. He wasn't clear yet about what he felt, but the intimacy that he had missed out on for over thirty years, the longing to spend time with another human being that you really cared about had created a powerful desire to fill the emptiness

A Sense of Place

that he hadn't allowed himself to recognize until now. That emptiness had settled into every crevice of his being and dragged him down. Now he felt released, given permission, and he couldn't get enough of it.

On the surface they moved in the same circumspect ways, a quiet distant dance with each other that allowed them to maintain a normal façade. Actually, it allowed him to maintain a normal façade. He didn't know what Nora felt or thought. It seemed like moments passed when they might have talked, but something always got in the way- a small disaster, Pat entering the room, his own self-consciousness. All in all, two weeks passed before they had another chance to be alone.

Pat's next doctor appointment found him well enough to drive in on his own. After the morning milking, he cleaned up, climbed into the pickup and drove off without a word to either of them. Wes had just walked back up to the house with a load of eggs from the hen house as Pat pulled out onto the road.

Wes stood at the foot of the porch steps and watched until the truck disappeared over the hill. He felt a little odd going up to the house with Pat gone and for a moment contemplated leaving the basket on the porch, but finally convinced himself that if he did, the neighbor's dogs would get the basketful. He knocked tentatively and waited. Nothing. he tried again and when he didn't get a response, quietly opened the door and walked across to the kitchen. He left the eggs on the counter and turned to head back out when Nora walked into the room, her thick hair falling down across her face as she dried it with an old green towel. She wore only a thin robe drawn loosely about her waist. He stopped, unsure what to do. She threw her hair back and as she looked up, a startled expression rushed across her face and then just as quickly vanished. She laid the towel across her shoulder.

"Well, welcome to my kitchen said the spider to the fly. What are you up to, Wes?"

"I just brought up some eggs and didn't want to leave them on the porch." He tried not to stare but he couldn't stop looking at her. "I hope you don't mind, I mean I'm sorry for just walking in on you." He tore his eyes away and started for the door.

"No, wait. Sit down and have a cup of coffee with me. I won't bite. I promise. "She moved to him in a step and laid her hand softly on his arm.

He looked down at her, so close, and started to move away. "I really should get back to the house. I have some things I need to get done and since Pat's not here…" The words just hung there for an instant. She slid her hand down his arm and took his hand in hers.

"No, please, Wes. Come sit down."
He couldn't really help himself. He let himself be led across to the table and sat down. Nora sat across from him and reached out and took both his hands in hers.

"Wes, there is so much I want to tell you, to ask you. I've held it all inside for too long."

A Sense of Place

"Nora, I don't think we should be doing this. It's not right. You've made your choices and I've made mine and there's no going back now. What's done is done."

"No, Wes. We didn't make our choices. That's just the point. They were made for us. We didn't really participate at all. We were kids caught up in something that we didn't understand and it swept us along like a wave."

"Either way, there's nothing we can do about it now?"

"That's just the point, Wes. We can do something about it now. We can go back and undo at least the one mistake- the one that split us apart thirty years ago."

"What are you talking about, Nora? You and Pat have a good relationship. You've spent thirty years developing a partnership."

"We've spent thirty years together. That much is right, but it is no partnership, never has been." She hesitated, let his hands go and covered her face. When finally, she dropped them back to the table she stared at him intently.

"I want more than that, Wes. I want someone who cares for me beyond what I can do in the barns and the fields. What I can do to support him when he is down with never a thought for what he can do for me. Do you understand that? Wes, I always thought you were that person. I still think it."

He stood up, walked to the window and leaned on the sill. His legs felt weak and he stood staring out at the

bleak winter landscape trying to steady himself.
Suddenly, he felt her arms around his waist, her warm
breasts pressed against his back. He turned and drew her
closer to him.

"In a hundred lonely places I've pictured this
happening with no hope of it actually coming true. Even
now it doesn't seem real. Have I heard you right? Are
you really here or am I going to wake up under yet
another unfamiliar roof in some distant place and roll
over with the emptiness still inside me?" He drew her
tighter to him and kissed her hair, drew in the smell of it,
the feel that he had imagined a thousand times over the
years. She tilted her head back, and he kissed her.

She leaned back and took his face in her hands,
staring so long into his eyes that he felt she could see
right into his soul.

"Why did you come back, Wes? What did you
expect to find here?"

He pulled her head into his shoulder, buried his
face in her hair, in the silky, damp softness of it. "I don't
know, Nora. I tell myself that I came back for Cassie, but
most of the time I don't know."

"Did you ever…" She hesitated. "Oh, it doesn't
really matter." She kissed him again, slid her arm around
his waist and guided him toward the hall.

They made love in the bedroom Wes had slept in
the first night he had come back, long and tender and
filled with all the longing of thirty years of separation.
Afterward, Wes rose, stood beside the bed and reached

down and ran the back of his hand along her jawline, tracing the curve of it.

"Nora, I…" He hesitated and then, "I don't want this to end."

"It doesn't have to, Wes. Pat and I don't do this anymore, hardly ever did. He doesn't love me. I am not even sure he has that capability."

"Then why didn't you leave him?"

"And do what? Go to work in a dime store? I had no training, nothing to fall back on. Besides, he just seemed to need me. I wanted to leave. I really did. I just couldn't do that to him. I felt trapped." She hesitated a moment, looked away and then turned back to him, stared at his face, reached up and touched his cheek. "If I had gone someplace else, how would you have found me? I know now that deep inside I waited for you to come back."

Wes sat down next to her. "So where do we go from here?"

Nora sat up, leaned against him, laid her head on his shoulder. "I don't know Wes. I just know that I have waited for you to come back to me for thirty years and I don't want to let you go now."

Wes stood up again and started to dress. "We sure can't do this again here with Pat around. He already sees more than he is happy about. He said something the other day about me already having you. I asked him what he meant by that, but he wouldn't answer me. I better get going now, before he gets back." He finished putting on his clothes and bent down and kissed her as she sat on the edge of the bed, the blanket wrapped around her. "I guess we will just have to see where we go from here. All I know is that I love you and always have." He turned and left the room.

A Sense of Place

Chapter 16

In the morning, Wes woke to the rattle of wind driven snow on his window pane. He rose in darkness, slipped out of bed with a quilt around his shoulders and turned on the lights in the kitchen. He started water boiling for coffee and dressed hurriedly in long johns, thick socks, his work jeans and a flannel shirt. By then the water was ready and he made instant coffee, black and unsweetened. He sipped it on and off as he put on his top layer of a barn coat, rubber boots and a trapper style hat with fold down ear flaps made of rabbit fur. He took a couple more sips of the coffee and then set the cup on the drainboard, walked over and opened the door to the full fury of the December storm.

The wind swept down out of the northwest and pushed the snow before it. Snow hardly described it because the tiny particles of ice slashed at his exposed cheeks like knives. He pulled the door shut behind him and began the uphill trek to the main house. The first layer of snow had been wet but the flakes had been big and a substantial amount was already on the ground so the going was tough. By the time he got to the house he felt numbed to the bone. His eyebrows and eyelashes bore an icy film as did the long hairs of the rabbit fur hat where his breath had drifted up and congealed so that Wes looked like Boreas, the Greek god of winter. He burst through the door to the kitchen and was surprised to find Pat at the table and Nora heating up the griddle for pancakes.

"How you doin', li'l brother?" The effort to speak brought on another coughing fit and Wes stood just inside the door until Pat could calm the outburst.

"Surprised to see you up and around. Are you feeling any better? What did the doctor say?"

"Just peachy. He said I just need to get back to work, that's all." He leaned back in his chair, tilting on two legs, coughed slightly and then rocked forward and took a sip of the coffee in front of him.

Wes took off his coat and hat and pulled a chair up to the table. Nora hadn't looked at him or said anything still. Finally, she turned and brought a cup of coffee for him.

"How many pancakes do you want, Wes? I figured today we were going to have to get a real meal before we tackle the milking. We'll have to do some shoveling to get into the barn." She turned back to the stove and began to ladle out large dollops of batter onto the hot griddle.

"Works for me, I guess. I'll have three of those and get started while you feed Pat and yourself."

"No, you won't. We're all workin' together." Pat slapped the table for emphasis.

"No way, old man. You need to get that cough under control before you do anything." Nora said nothing.

"I ain't arguin' with you, Wes. I'm fine. Just need a little fresh air is all, so eat your pancakes and just you shut up."

Nora kept the pancakes coming until nobody wanted any more. She turned the stove off, slid the griddle aside and left the room. Wes and Pat had already put on their jackets when she came back in a set of coveralls. She slipped into her jacket and pulled on a knit hat and leather gloves.

Pat opened the door and stepped out into the wind. Wes glanced at Nora and saw the concern on her face. She caught Wes' eye and shook her head. She mouthed, "Stubborn as an old mule," and followed her husband out.

They took shovels from the equipment shed and began to clear a path from the house to the barn. Pat worked at the front of the group and cleared the initial path. Wes waded through the deep snow to the barn and began clearing the barn doors so they could get in and so that they would be able to get out after the milking. They were late today for the milking and he could hear the cattle inside lowing their discomfort and unhappiness. Suddenly, he heard Pat go into a severe coughing fit and then Nora yelling for him to come help. When he turned, he saw Pat crumpled in the snow face down and Nora on her knees beside him. Wes ran awkwardly through the drifts until he stood over them. Nora looked up at him, a stricken look on her face and then he noticed the blood on the snow.

"We need to get him to the hospital." Tears streaked her cheeks now.

"Ok. I'll get him to the Jeep. You go get it running and the heater on." Nora stood up and ran toward the house. Wes stooped and took Pat in his arms., picked him up and began to make his way slowly toward the house. Pat weighed so little now that he seemed but a hollow shell and Wes carried him easily. Nora had started the Jeep and run to the house for a blanket. She got back just as Wes reached the car.

"I'm going to put him on the front seat with you. I think it is better if he sits up. He is hardly breathing right now." He slid his brother onto the seat and Nora threw the blanket over him and then tucked it around him. Finally, she took a bandana from her pocket and wiped at the blood around his mouth.

A Sense of Place

"I'll stay here and do the milking. When I am finished, I'll come to the hospital. Be careful. Those roads are going to be treacherous today."

Nora was in the driver's seat now and looked across at him with a mixture of fear and sadness in her eyes. He shut the door and she put the Jeep in gear and pulled away. He watched her go until the taillights were out of sight. He looked toward the barn and its massive shape seemed to blur and shift like a hologram in the driving snow.

...

The summer of the trial, heat descended on Lapeer County like an oven. The fields wilted in white-hot sun; corn leaves, thin and pointed, hung limply from the stalks like bird tongues. At night Wes lay in his room naked on the sweaty sheets and tried to make some sense of something that made no sense.

The farm work fell squarely on Pat and him now, and it absorbed his time and helped to numb him through the daylight hours, but the night tormented him for long periods until exhaustion won out. He never knew what Pat thought during that time. Pat just seemed angry and sullen most of the time, and talk between them, which had almost disappeared once Wes got to high school, now seemed to evaporate entirely. He figured anything Pat thought now he only shared with Nora.

Dennis Hurley

For a while Wes' friends wanted to ask him about the murder, but they soon grew tired of the few facts that he knew, and so they fell into the more interesting arena of speculation and gossip. He welcomed the break. What he did know had come in bits and pieces. The basic story that had come out was that on the morning of the murder, Grandpa had asked the boys to help with killing rats in the loft, something they did every spring before they put up the first cutting of hay. He said he would get Cassie to help too. Grandpa and Wes had gone out to get everything ready and when Cassie didn't seem to be around, he sent Wes to go look for him at his cabin. While he was gone, Pat and John had heard a commotion as they were coming into the barn, then a scream from their grandfather. Pat and John had climbed immediately up to the loft and found Cassie standing over their grandfather, a bloody club in his hands. Pat and John had wrestled him to the floor and Pat had held him while John ran to call the sheriff. What had been the cause, no one seemed to know, but according to the sheriff Pat thought he had heard their grandfather complaining about Cassie's work, talked of firing him. Also, Cassie had been drinking. Without much thought the sheriff settled on that as the cause of the fight, and the prosecution started to build its case.

All this was hearsay as far as Wes was concerned. He personally didn't know what to believe. He had no one to share his thoughts with. Nora spent all her free time with Pat, and so Wes was left to figure things out on his own. All he knew was that the Cassie that he knew could never do such a thing. Oh, he had seen his violent side; there was no question about that. He also knew the side of Cassie that had helped him time after time, been there in a way that no other adult had been for him, not even his grandpa.

He wanted to go down to the jail and visit with him, but he didn't know what he would say nor how he felt, so he spent late June and July waiting for the trial to begin. He had never been really close to his grandma. She had always seemed somewhat distant and sad, more a figure in the background of his life, and so he had turned more to his grandpa and Cassie. Now her moods swung back and forth between crying and a sad, steady acceptance. She was as alone as he was, yet he couldn't reach out to her and comfort her in any way nor share her grief and take comfort from her strength. They walked their grief paths separately.

August 15th the trial began. Wes started the day as usual in the barn before dawn. The humidity in the air gave a hint of the rain that would make its appearance by noon. The barn seemed to sweat on days like that, great beads of moisture clinging to the whitewashed bark of the beams, and he felt its heaviness settle over him, press him down, as he went about the chores.

Pat fed while Wes milked, but no talk passed between them. They had worked together so long that there was no need for talk, and they each went about their chores in studied silence. When he finished with the feeding, Pat left the barn without a word. Wes knew that Pat might have to testify that day, so he said nothing to him as he left. Wes finished the milking and made his way from stanchion to stanchion, lifting the flip bars and letting the cows out one by one.

When the barn cleared, he stepped out into the hazy sunshine and began the task of moving the herd to the pasture they were using for the week. The cattle moved slowly, and he didn't hurry them. He knew that he had to go down to the trial eventually, but he had agreed to ride down with Michael Mulvaney, a classmate who had called to make the offer the night before. He didn't really like Mulvaney, nevertheless it seemed a better choice than riding down with his grandma and Pat. He couldn't face either of them at that point.

When he got the cattle back to the pasture overlooking the mill pond, he broke off from herding them and lay down on his stomach in the tall grass. He lay still for a long time just listening to the insects moving methodically amongst the weeds and grass stems. The sun rose steadily in the sky and the heat of it finally made him uncomfortable. He rolled over and stared up into the bright sky for a minute until the light became painful, and then he stood up and started back to the house.

He changed into a clean shirt and pants and went down to the kitchen and ate a snack of peanut butter and crackers. As he wiped off his plate and put it into the sink, he heard the sound of Mulvaney's old Chevy in the

A Sense of Place

drive and so he went outside to meet him. A skinny six-footer, Mulvaney looked awkward and out of place behind the wheel, but he handled the car well and said little as they took the back roads into Lapeer.

Lapeer bustled with activity as they drove along the main street and found a place to park. There were small family restaurants where farmers came to have breakfast and talk grain prices and milk production and they were filled with people this morning planning to attend the trial.

Mulvaney found a place several blocks away and he parked the car and they walked along past the Pix theater, the D and C Store, McClellands and finally to the county courthouse, an imposing Greek revival building with massive pillars and a golden domed cupola that added another story and a half to the two-story main building.

By ten thirty they were in the courtroom sitting in the back row along with what seemed like half the county. In the front row were Pat and his Grandma and John waiting to be called as witnesses. Nora sat directly behind Pat. She never once turned to look at Wes.

The rain hadn't yet arrived, but the humid air wrapped the courtroom tightly and seemed to absorb every breathable bit of air. Wes began to sweat instantly, his dress shirt soaked through at the armpits and along his spine. Mulvaney had on some kind of cheap after shave and the thick aroma added to the palpable heaviness of the air. The proceedings were a blur to Wes. There were no actual witnesses to the murder, only Pat and John and what they had come upon. The defense attorney had hired a signing interpreter to ask the questions of Cassie and interpret his responses. Hardly a necessity though because Cassie would say nothing to defend himself. Wes could hardly look at him, but when he finally did, he saw Cassie staring at him, a hurt look in his eyes that tore at Wes' heart. He looked away and couldn't look back at Cassie again.

It figured to be a short trial. The prosecutor called John to the stand first, and he seemed confused and fumbling, but he got through it and when he sat down, Wes saw him glance first at Cassie and then at Pat before he took out a bandana and wiped the sweat from is face and neck. Pat was next, and he went through his testimony methodically, dully as if he was drugged. He never really looked up when he talked, and Wes couldn't begin to guess what he was thinking. He could hardly believe it was the brother he knew, and the most puzzling part was that he and Grampa hadn't really gotten on that well ever, yet he seemed truly grief stricken.

As Wes watched him, it began to sink in. Pat's life was changed forever. Actually, both of their lives were changed whether they liked it or not. They had just been moved forcibly from boyhood to manhood in one brief moment. It wasn't grief at all, just sadness at his personal loss. Wes felt angry. Grampa deserved better than that. Cassie deserved better. Wes stood up, stumbled past the knees of the people in his row and left the courtroom.

A Sense of Place

He couldn't go back. The trial finished in just short of forty-eight hours. The jury stayed out an hour and a half. Hay needed to be cut. Fields needed tilling. Cassie would disappear into another kind of wilderness that day and never returned until they put him in the ground. For two days after the trial Wes quietly selected tools to take with him and packed a duffle bag with some clean shirts and jeans and two of the books Cassie had given him. Days before he was to start his sophomore year of high school Wes rose before sunrise, slipped quietly out the back door and never looked back. until he got word that Cassie had passed   .

•••

The snow didn't want to quit and its weight muffled the barn as he did the milking. The silence got him thinking about his grandma. He thought about how after she had greeted them on that first day, she had all but disappeared from his life. He remembered talking with his grandfather about it one day while they were taking a break from the haying. They were sitting in the cut stubble in the shade of an oak at the edge of the hay field. He couldn't remember now exactly how it came up, but somehow, he asked his grandfather why grandma was always so quiet and so sad. His grandfather looked at him with a pained look in his eyes, a look that said I don't really want to answer this. Finally, he turned away and gazed vacantly across the field.

Dennis Hurley

"You know, Wes, your daddy was your grandma's only son, her pride and joy. She was happy when he married your mom, but it made her sad when they moved down to Cleveland. She never got to see him after that. You know how hard it was when you lost your parents. I see it in you sometimes, but with Grandma, it was like she died when her son died. She has never recovered from that. She does what she can for you and Pat, but the life really went out of her the day she got the news." He hesitated for a minute. Finally, "She loves you very much, but she is so bound up with grief, there just doesn't seem to be much room for anything else. Maybe someday she'll come around, but I guess I wouldn't count on it."

His grandfather's voice filled with the same sadness that he saw in his grandma, and suddenly now in this snow muffled barn, Wes felt the hollowness inside himself more than he had ever felt it before.

Chapter 17

Two days came and went with the snow still piled high and the road still blocked. Wes began working on the county road whenever he had free time and gradually cleared a 16-foot lane down the middle all the way into Partridge Creek. On the third day Nora followed the milk truck in and arrived mid-morning looking worn out. Wes met her as she was about to get out of the Jeep. When she saw him standing there beside the door, she leaned her head forward onto the steering wheel, her eyes closed. When she opened them, she looked up at Wes who had opened the door and stood waiting to help her out of the car.

"Wes, I don't know if I can go back there tonight. I need to clean up and get some rest."

"You should do that, Nora. I'll do the chores and head in to be there for him. You get some rest and I'll get back early tomorrow to do the milking."

Dennis Hurley

Tears streaked her face now. "Oh, Wes. I don't even know how I feel about him. In some ways I just want this to be over. At the same time, I feel like a terrible person for even feeling that way."

"You are just tired, Nora. You get some rest and it will all be clearer for you. I'll keep things together. You just concentrate on getting him back and healthy. You have had a lot put on you lately and," he hesitated, "I don't know. Maybe my being here has added to that." He reached out his hand and she took it as he helped her out of the Jeep.

"They won't even tell me what's wrong with him. They say he told his doctor not to discuss it with anybody. What's that supposed to mean? Why would he do that?"

"I guess you'll have to ask him when he gets out of the ICU. He must not want to worry you."

"Yeah. That's sure the way to do it. Keeping me in the dark." She leaned against him as they made their way to the house.

In the kitchen Wes put on a pot of coffee and then went up to the bathroom to fill the tub with hot water. When he came down, Nora had put some eggs in a fry pan and scrambled them with a fork.

"Do you want me to make anything for you? I can mix up some more egg if you want."

A Sense of Place

Wes shook his head. "I'll do that while you go take a bath. It is ready for you now, so when you finish eating, go on up and take a bath and then get ready for bed. I'll see you in the morning."

She gave a tired nod and then flipped the eggs onto a plate and sat down to eat and drink her coffee. Wes sat across from her, hands clasped in front of him. "I should probably stay away from you right now. You have enough going on and I don't want to confuse things."

"No, Wes. I need you more than anything now. You steady me, help me make sense of everything. Please don't feel that way."

She ate quietly for a while and then looked up at him. "I had better go up and take that bath before I fall asleep right here. Thank you, Wes."

She stood, came around the table and wrapped her arms around his neck. She kissed him on the cheek and turned to go. At the kitchen door, she turned and smiled at him and then she disappeared into the darkened living room.

Wes sat at the table for a while, morning sunlight pouring through the window and resting across his scarred and tanned hands. He looked out the window at the brilliance of sunlight reflecting off the snow and its beauty moved him. No artwork he had ever seen could match Nature in its power to touch the spirit. He rose now and headed out to the barn to clean the manure gutters. He would rest for a while before the evening milking and then he would be headed to Lapeer to spend the night with Pat. He had really come to enjoy the daily farm rhythms, remembered from so long ago and now active once again in his life. The quiet of the barn gave him time to think about the past as he slid the shovel down the gutters and loaded manure into the spreader.

•••

He had never really confronted Pat about taking Nora from him. She had made her choice and after the injury, Pat seemed to be hardly there and only Nora seemed able to reach him. Wes just couldn't take that from him even though seeing her with him tore his soul apart. He spent the winter of that year trapping with Cassie and staying away from the house as much as he possibly could.

One icy morning in late February, he met Cassie along the banks of the little creek that fed the millpond. The marsh grass poked through the snow in broken clumps, twisted and brown and it crackled as he walked through it. A heavy grey overcast sky hung low over them. At first, they didn't talk, just went about their business, setting and re-setting the steel jaw traps along the banks and in the shallow water along the shore. Suddenly, they came upon an unusual catch, a dark furred mink, its long, slender body twisting and thrashing as it saw them approaching.

A Sense of Place

"Beautiful," Wes signed. A feeling of sadness came over him like he had never experienced before. "Hard to see such a beautiful, wild thing trapped like this."

"Just an animal, Wes. Just like all animals we trap."

"Maybe, but different for me. I don't know if I could kill it."

"Bring lots of money." Cassie smiled. "Bottle of the best whiskey."

"Ok, but I am going ahead. I can't watch." He moved past the mink and on down along the creek to his next set. He turned and looked back and the mink, teeth bared, defied Cassie as he maneuvered to get a clear shot to bring the ax down on its skull. He felt sick to his stomach. Suddenly, he decided he couldn't let it happen. He ran toward Cassie waving to get his attention.

"Wait," he signed. "How much for that mink? I buy it from you. Don't kill."

Cassie hesitated, unsure of what Wes meant. "You want to buy this pelt?"

"No. I want to let it loose. Set it free."

Cassie shook his head. "You sure? Beautiful pelt. Lots of cash."

"How much? I pay it."

"You don't pay, but how you let it loose? "

Dennis Hurley

Wes took off his canvas barn coat as he approached the mink. With a quick move he threw it over the mink and then stepped on the spring bar so that the jaws opened. Under the coat the mink squirmed loose and Wes and Cassie stepped back. The mink's head appeared from the edge of the coat and then it slid completely free and, limping slightly, ran to the edge of the stream. Suddenly, it stopped and turned and its dark eyes riveted on Wes for a moment and then instantly it disappeared over the bank. Moments later they saw it moving along the far side, its long, dark body moving in an undulating flow as it made its way into a thicket of red dogwood and disappeared.

As they followed the rest of the trapline, Wes collected his traps one by one and put them into his pack basket. Cassie watched him. Finally, he signed, "You not trapping anymore?"

"I think I am done with it, Cassie. I make my money with the carpentry now. Let the animals stay free."

Cassie shook his head in disbelief but signed nothing. They finished the trapline together and when they got back to the barn, Wes hung his traps from a nail on the wall.

...

As Wes finished loading the spreader, he glanced toward the spot where he had hung the traps so many years ago. Two of them still hung there, rusted beyond functioning. That trapline run had become a turning point for him. He had made a judgement about Cassie without realizing it then, and it had changed their relationship forever. He searched his memories, had since he came back, to understand who Cassie was. He had thought he knew him, but now the pieces he remembered seemed fragmented and confusing, mere shadows that he tried to piece together.

After a rest, Wes started on the milking. The now familiar routine went quickly and by seven he had finished and cleaned up. He changed his clothes and headed to his truck. He had decided not to bother Nora in case she still needed to sleep, but as he started the truck, she appeared at the kitchen door with her coat on. He waited for her to come out to the truck. As she got closer, he could see that she carried a paper bag. He opened the door and stepped out to meet her.

"When you didn't come in for supper, I was worried you hadn't eaten today. I made you up a couple of sandwiches to take with you. Wes, thanks for doing this. I needed a break and some rest. I feel better already and I am sure I will be back to normal tomorrow. You be careful. The roads are still pretty bad."

"Thanks, Nora. I appreciate it. Hadn't even thought about eating until now." She smiled and gave him a hug. The clean scent of her almost overwhelmed him. He kissed her hair and then slid back into the truck.

Dennis Hurley

"I'll be back before morning milking," and he slammed the truck door and pulled away. The drive took longer than usual with snow blowing off the tops of the snowbanks in long feathered streaks that obscured the road and made it difficult to see which way it went. By the time he arrived most of the entrances were closed so he slipped in through the Emergency entrance and made his way up to the second floor. At the nurse's station, he stopped to ask directions to the ICU.

"Who are you looking for?" The nurse, a middle-aged woman with short, brown hair, had a no nonsense look about her.

"Patrick Callaghan."

"He's no longer in ICU. They moved him to a room this afternoon. Let's see. It's 217. Down the hall to your left. Don't disturb him though. He is still pretty weak."

Wes assured her that he wouldn't and then walked down to 217. The room had just a low light, the glow from a machine set up next to the bed. Wes hesitated for a moment and then as quietly as possible, slipped in and sat on a chair in the corner. Although the room held a second bed, Pat was the only occupant. The smell of medications and disinfectant permeated the air and carried with it a feeling of thickness as if you could actually portion off parts of it. He stood now to look at Pat lying in the bed by the window. A tube ran out of his nose and off to some unseen connection. Another tube ran from his arm to a bag hanging from a pole next to the bed. He looked so small that Wes hardly recognized him. Suddenly, Pat opened his eyes.

"That you little brother?" The voice soft and weak

"Yep. It's me, Pat. Nora was exhausted when she finally got home. She has been here non-stop for the past three days. I told her I'd watch your sorry ass for her tonight so she could get a good rest. How are you doing?"

"Just peachy." The words labored, weak.

"Well you better get yourself healthy and get back home. We got lots of work to be done this spring and this little vacation you're on isn't going to get you out of it, you know." He smiled down at his brother and then leaned in and adjusted his pillow.

"I am going to sit right over there tonight and if you need anything, you call me."

Pat licked his lips. "There's some ice in that cup there. Could you give me a couple pieces of that? Dry as a bone."

Wes took the ice chip cup and tilted it toward Wes' lips until a couple of pieces slid out and into his mouth. He nodded his thanks and Wes went back to his chair. Pat closed his eyes and the room went silent again except for the rhythmic machine noise.

Dennis Hurley

Wes slept fitfully in the chair and awoke to the sound of voices as a group of doctors entered the room and began to talk with Pat. They glanced at Wes and then asked him to step outside. A short time later, the group moved past him and on to the next room. Wes walked back in and went to the side of the bed.

"I have to go now, Pat. Milking time again. Nora will be back later to be with you. You take care and get healed up so we can get you home."

Pat opened his eyes and reached out his hand and took Wes' hand and squeezed it.

"Thanks, little brother. I guess you were meant to come home when you did. Don't know what we would have done without you."

Wes squeezed Pat's hand back. A tremendous feeling of guilt washed over him as he stepped back and turned to leave the room.

The roads were clearer now and the trip back to the farm went quickly in the half light of morning. By 6:00 he had started the feeding. The radio played quietly in the background and the DJ announced that it was 6:15. Just then, Nora came into the barn, a thermos and a paper bag in hand.

"Good morning, Wes. I brought you some coffee and a fried egg sandwich. I know you probably didn't eat last night or this morning. Take a minute. You can't work on an empty stomach."

Wes smiled. "Always thinking of somebody else, Nora. I'm fine but I will take you up on that. Always loved those fried egg sandwiches."

"How was Pat? Any better?"

"They moved him to a room. He still looks pretty weak but he did talk a little. He's tough, Nora. Whatever it is, he'll beat it and be back to himself in no time." He said it with more confidence than he felt.

Nora nodded." I'll leave soon to spend the day with him, but I'll finish the feeding first while you start the milking."

They worked silently until Nora finished. Wes had just finished with a round of milking and ushered the cows out of the parlor and back to their stanchions when Nora appeared beside him.

"Time for me to go, Wes. I don't think I will stay the night tonight, so I will see you later. Take care of yourself and get some rest yourself." She wrapped her arms around him and looked up at him. For the first time Wes felt uncomfortable. He squeezed her once and then stepped away. "You be careful driving. I am sure the roads are better now, but they are still slippery. I'll see you later,"

Nora stepped back, a puzzled look on her face.

"Everything ok?"

"Yeah. Fine," he lied. "You better get going. I am sure he misses you."

Nora shook her head.

"I doubt that," and turned and left.

Wes couldn't get over the feeling of guilt he had felt earlier. No matter how poor their relationship had been as kids, Pat was different now, needier somehow and Wes couldn't get over the feeling he was taking advantage of that weakness. Was the love making just his way of getting back at Pat for all the abuse he had handed out when they were kids? It made him uncomfortable and confused. Part of him wanted to run, to disappear like he had always done when he found himself in a situation that confused or scared him, but this time was different. They still needed him here. If he ran now, the farm would for sure go under and he couldn't let that happen. He knew now that the farm meant more to him than he had ever realized. He didn't want to jeopardize that. When he left the barn, he felt more confused than ever.

Chapter 18

Wes finished the evening chores and made his way to the house to check and see if there were any messages on the phone. As he reached the house, headlights appeared on the road, brilliant pinpoints rising out of the darkness. Nora. He waited until she swung into the drive, the lights flashing across his body and then settling on the garage straight ahead. She pulled up to the garage and got out of the jeep and walked toward him.

"How is he doing today?"

"Much better. He talked up a storm most of the day. Still coughing some and really short of breath, but much stronger. He even got up and went to the bathroom by himself. He is a tough old bird."

Wes shook his head. "He always was tough. He'll be home and working around here in nothing flat." He meant it to reassure Nora, but he wasn't sure how he felt about it really. Wasn't sure if he really wanted him to come home. In the almost two months he had been back, they still hadn't really connected on anything but a superficial level. He had more than once wanted to ask him about the day of the murder, to try to clear up some of the things that had been haunting him for all these years, and yet, each time he tried, he had come up short. So, yes, he wanted him to come home. He needed more time with his brother, time to have Pat help him with some of the ghosts of the past that he hadn't been able to shed on his own.

When they got into the house, Nora turned to him and pulled him to her. She wrapped her arms around him and laid her head on his chest. Wes leaned down, felt the softness of her hair against his cheek and felt overwhelmed by his desire for her. He helped her out of her coat and then picked her up in his arms and carried her upstairs to the bedroom.

He stayed with her for the night and in the morning rose quietly before the alarm went off so he wouldn't wake her. He dressed in the bathroom and went down to the kitchen to start the coffee. As he did, he felt the immense silence of the early morning. No wind outside to disturb things; dawn just beginning to quietly crack the dark horizon. The only sound the gentle percolating of the coffee, its scent filling the air with its dark aroma, and he felt at peace.

Nora didn't come out to do the milking with him and he felt happy that she could get some rest. This whole thing had to be incredibly stressful for her. The sun broke through a light cloud cover and warmed the barn wall. He threw hay out for the cattle and then let them out for the first time in a week.

When he got to the house, Nora had a large breakfast prepared. She turned and smiled at him as he entered. He took off his coat and boots and sat down at the table.

"Good morning, Wes. I am sorry I didn't get out to help you this morning. I don't know how you got out of here without waking me, but I really appreciated the sleep. I have been exhausted almost every day since this happened."

"I am glad, Nora. I wanted you to sleep. Are you going back today?"

"I planned on it." She smiled at him coyly. "Unless of course, you wanted to do something else."

He grinned back at her. "I think we probably need to take our time with that. Eventually he is going to be back and this is going to probably have to stop." He shook his head. "Can't even imagine that now, but I don't see how we can continue."

Nora didn't say anything. She toyed with her food and ate very little. Finally, she looked up at him. "We'll see."

Dennis Hurley

Nora left at nine and Wes decided to spend the day at the home place cleaning up and starting some of the repair projects he had let go. He had drywall for the upstairs ceiling where it had gotten damaged from the leak and decided that had to be the first priority. He worked steadily through the morning, stopped for a quick lunch and then laid on the tape and first coat of drywall compound by midafternoon.

...

One night after the trapping season ended, Wes decided to go over to Cassie's cabin. They hadn't really talked since he had quit trapping and Wes missed their connection. After supper, Wes set out across the fields. A full moon lit the way and cast the world in stark contrasts of darkness and light. The ice on the pond had melted away earlier in the week and now the moonlight caught wave tops and sent back pin pricks of light. A light glowed through Cassie's window and Wes knocked on the door hard enough that it shook on its hinges so that Cassie could see/hear him. Wes heard a chair scrape across the floor and then the door opened.

"Come in," Cassie signed.

Wes could see a bottle of whiskey on the table that had been opened but with only a glass full gone. They sat down at the table. Wes didn't know exactly where to start but decided to ask Cassie about himself.

A Sense of Place

"You lived Flint when you were a boy? What did you do there?"

"My mother move us there so I could go to Michigan School for the Deaf." He spelled it out.

"Is that where you learn to sign?"

"Yes. I have many friends there. We talked all the time. My mother teach me too."

"What else did they teach you there? Did you learn carpentry there?"

"Yes. They teach all kinds of things, but I learn carpentry."

"Do you miss your friends from there?

"I see them sometimes. Now I have you to talk with." He smiled. "So, I still have a friend to talk with."

Wes smiled back at him. "We are friends. You are my best friend."

Cassie looked surprised. "What about Nora? She is not your best friend?"

"Not anymore. She's with Pat now."

Cassie shook his head. "They are not a good pair. She come back to you sometime."

...

Dennis Hurley

Now as Wes cleaned up the drywall tools, he thought back to that conversation so long ago. Had she come back or had he. It all seemed mixed up now. He had loved her intensely back then and had never felt such pain as he felt when she left him. He couldn't be sure if what he felt for her now didn't contain some element of revenge for Pat taking her away from him so many years ago. Did he still love her? He had suppressed his feelings for so many years that he couldn't really recognize what he felt now. He did know that he felt passion like he hadn't felt in a really long time and maybe that was good enough.

Nora returned before milking time. Wes saw her Jeep out the kitchen window as it passed by the old homestead. He had finished cleaning up his tools and so he headed up to the house to check with her. He found her sitting in the kitchen drinking coffee.

She smiled as he came through the door. "Hey, Wes. What have you been up to all day?"

"Just doing a little drywall repair at the old house. What do you know? Anything new with him?"

"He's coming home. Day after tomorrow, Friday." She looked disappointed.

"Ok. Do we have to do anything to prepare? Special bed or anything? "

A Sense of Place

"They haven't said anything about that. I think probably he'll need a few extra pillows to prop him up, but I have those. He is doing well. Stronger and feistier every day. I don't think he is going to stay in bed very long." She stood up and came around the table and wrapped her arms around him. They stood that way for a minute and then she leaned back and looked up at him. "I need to take a shower. Come with me."

"Why? You think I need a shower?" he teased.

"You definitely need a shower!" She took his hand and they climbed the stairs together.

They made love in the shower and then lay together on the bed until chore time. Wes rose and stood over her. "I'll do the milking if you'll make supper. I am pretty near starved." He laughed. "Whenever I have to cook for myself, I pretty much just don't bother to eat. Not really worth the trouble."

Nora, laughed. "Oh, I have seen your version of cooking, and I can see why. Sure. You go ahead. I'll make us something special tonight."

Wes hurried through the milking and when he came back in, the smell of steak and baked potatoes and beans and carrots filled the kitchen. They ate in silence, Wes eating like someone would take it away from him if he didn't get it eaten as fast as possible. Nora watched him, a half smile on her face. As he scraped the last of the beans off the plate, she laughed. "I guess you were hungry, weren't you, bud. I take it you liked the meal?"

"You might say that. It tasted mighty good, Nora. Thanks for that. Sure needed it." He got up and took his plate to the sink and rinsed it. "You know, you need a dog here. I am surprised you don't have one. What's a farm without a good dog to clean up the table scraps, and here we have two perfectly good steak bones and nobody to eat them?"

Nora turned away. "Pat won't have one. Same reason, I'm guessing, he didn't seem to want to have kids. He said he doesn't want to get attached to anything. Sure made me feel useless when he said that, like I didn't matter because he wasn't going to get attached to me."

Wes turned and grabbed her hand and drew her to him. "How could anybody not get attached to you? You are the most beautiful creature in this world both inside and out. I love you, Nora Callaghan."It was out there before he had a chance to think about it, and in that moment, he realized that it was the truth.

"Oh, Wes. I love you too. I think I always have. I wish you had taken me with you when you left. We would have had thirty years of being together and seeing the world. I can't believe we wasted so much of our lives apart."

Wes took her hands in his and looked into her eyes. "I am here now and I don't know how this is all going to work out, but we will figure it out, Nora. We will figure it out."

Friday came and, in the morning, Wes helped Nora get the bedroom ready before he went out to do the milking.

"Wait for me to finish the chores and I'll go in to help you get him home."

"No. I better do this myself, Wes. If we are there together, I am not sure that I won't give us away."

"Are you sure, Nora. He may be a bit of a handful." She shook her head.

"You can give me a hand when I get him home."

"If you're sure. Ok. I'll see you later." He kissed her and headed to the barn. He felt some relief at the reprieve. He wouldn't have to face Pat until later and maybe he could get himself together to not reveal his feelings when he saw him.

They were back by midafternoon. Wes heard the jeep as it pulled into the drive and labored through the now melting snow. He had been working in the machine shed and so he wiped his hands and went out to greet them. As Nora got out of the jeep, Wes caught a glimpse of Pat in the passenger seat. The first word that came to mind was gaunt. Pat's face had thinned out and his cheeks had deep hollows. He raised a hand and waved to Wes, a smile splitting his face.

Dennis Hurley

Wes opened the door to help him out.

"How you doin', li'l brother? You been keepin' this place alive for me while I been on my little vacation?"

"Doing my best, Pat. Good to have you home though. I am getting tired of working out there by myself with nobody to criticize every little thing I do." He smiled and reached in to help his brother out of the car.

"Well, I'm here now so I'll get warmed up and get right on your ass." He took Wes' hand and swung his legs out and stood unsteadily. Wes took his arm and they slowly made their way to the house. Nora had already gone up to the bedroom and was turning back the sheet and blankets as they entered. The climb, even though Wes had taken it slowly, had left Pat breathless and he stumbled to the bed and sat, head down on the edge.

"Are you alright to finish up here, Nora? If so, I'm going to head back out to the machine shed and finish up what I started out there."

"You go ahead, Wes. I'll get him to bed and then go down and start an early supper for us." She turned to Pat. "I think you could use a good home cooked meal after all that hospital food I would imagine."

Pat looked up at her. "You know that, Nora. Been lookin' forward to it since I got out of that ICU unit. They don't have a damned clue how to cook in that place." He turned to Wes. "Don't you be screwin' anything up out there, boy. See you at supper."

Wes shook his head and headed back out to work.

The days faded into a standard routine. Wes and Nora did the chores together most days and Pat eventually left the bed and sat in front of the television for a part of the day. By the second week, Pat had started to develop his own exercise routine. He would climb the stairs and come back down and repeat. By the beginning of the third week, he had added pushups to the routine and his strength had really started to return. By the end of a month, he had joined Wes for the milking and fallen back into the daily routine like he had never left it.

Wes and Nora said little to each other during the day, but their exchanged looks didn't go unnoticed by Pat. In mid-February, when they had finished the milking, Pat cornered Wes as he cleaned the milking parlor. "You got your eye on Nora, don't you?"

Wes turned and shut off the hose. "What are you talking about?"

"I see how you look at her. You still have a thing for her, don't you? I mean you two were an item before I took her from you."

Wes hung up the hose and then turned to face him. "So, what if I do. Yeah, you took her from me a long time ago. It was a shitty thing to do to a brother and

you know it. It makes no difference now. She is your
wife, not mine." He could feel the anger rising up in him,
wanted to grab Pat and punch his lights out. All the hurt
he had felt thirty years before flooded back over him, and
then he looked at the pathetic, withered man his brother
had become and it all fell away. There would be no
satisfaction in it and they would have only switched
places with Wes becoming the bully instead of Pat. He
pushed past Pat and left the barn.

He went straight to the old homestead, changed
clothes, climbed into his truck and headed into Lapeer.
He ate supper at a little restaurant at the edge of town and
sat for a while with endless cups of coffee listening to the
cook and waitress bantering back and forth as customers
came and went. He once again had that old urge to just go
back, pack his things and disappear. Finally, he rose,
went to the counter and paid his bill, with a large tip for
the waitress, and headed back home.

He flicked on the lights when he entered the
kitchen and was startled to find Nora sitting at his kitchen
table. "What are you doing here? You scared the hell out
of me."

She rose and crossed the kitchen to him. She had
been crying and now she wrapped him in an embrace and
rested her head against his chest.

"I was so worried you had left for good. I begged
Pat to tell me what had happened and he finally said you

had an argument. Wouldn't say what it was about but he went right up to bed. Oh, Wes. I can't deal with this anymore. I need you." She kissed him and pulled him closer.

"He knows, Nora. He cornered me tonight and wanted to know what was going on with us."

"What did you tell him?"

"I just said that I was attracted to you and then told him what a shit he had been for taking you from me. What's he going to do? He was in the wrong and he knows it. I wanted to beat the shit out of him, but what would be the point? He'll get over it."

He bent his head to kiss her hair and at that moment she looked up and they kissed. Wes pushed her away.

"You should get back. No use giving him any more reason to get all pissed about this."

Nora took both his hands in hers and drew him closer.

"What's the difference. If he knows, then what is keeping us from being together?" She pulled him toward the single bed still in the kitchen. He felt the pent-up passion of the past few weeks surge through him and he picked her up and laid her on the bed. They made love in the glare of an overhead light and then lay in each other's arms. Wes traced the curves of her face and neck with his hand, stared into her eyes until he lost himself. They fell asleep. In the middle of the night, Nora awoke, rose quietly and kissed him lightly on the cheek before slipping into her clothes and jacket and heading out into the darkness.

Chapter 19

Pat was silent about the encounter and the days
once again took on a steady rhythm again. The difference
now: Pat said nothing but the most directly necessary
instructions for what to do. They moved like characters in
a shadow play, seemingly passing through each other
without disturbing one another. For Nora, the coolness
hardly changed what she had felt for years.

"It is nothing new, Wes. It has been this way
practically since we got married-long periods of silence
and distance and then a glimpse of the old Pat every now
and then just to let you know he was still in there. Just
wait. He'll come around."

But nothing changed and the intense February
days melted into the warmer but still harsh beginning of
March. The one difference evident became the frequency
with which, Pat took to the bottle. Often, he would
disappear midday and head into Lapeer. When he came
back, he smelled of liquor and as he started the milking,

he had to be watched carefully by one or the other of them so that he didn't do anything that would cause a problem. Mostly though, his routine, so well-remembered, carried him through without difficulty. By mid-March he had developed a pattern and when the liquor finally began to break down his defenses and he would take a verbal swipe at Wes whenever he could.

"You son-of-a-bitch! Why'd you ever come home?" Long emphasis on 'ever.'

"You were the one who wanted me to stay. You want me to go now? How are you and Nora going to manage this place? You can't stay sober long enough to till a field or plant a straight row. You need to give it up. Quit hitting the bottle. If you do that, and I feel like you are able to handle the work again, I'll leave if that's what you want."

Finally, one night, practically falling down drunk, he took a swing at Wes. Wes, ducked the blow and caught him as he started to fall.

He laid him down on the barn floor and called to Nora. "Can you take over for me in here? I am going to carry him up to the house and put him to bed. He's going to hurt himself if he keeps this up."

Nora came into the milking parlor, shaking her head. "Wes, what are we going to do about him? I have never seen him like this before. He used to get drunk sometimes, but now it seems like he is trying to kill himself."

"I don't know, Nora. Maybe I should leave now. He seems pretty focused on me. I think he isn't going to get better until I get out of your life. We'll talk after I get him up to the house."

Wes bent and scooped up the limp body and draped Pat over his shoulder like a child. When he got to the house, he carried him up to the bedroom, pulled back the covers and laid him on the bed. He took off Pat's boots and slipped his pants off and hung them over a chair and then rolled the covers back up over him. He went to the bathroom and wetted a washcloth with some warm water and wiped Pat's face, turned off the light and went back out to the barn.

The night stretched infinitely above him as the Milky Way, like a windswept field of light, lit the southern sky. In many ways he felt trapped now and there seemed no solution to it. In the past, when this feeling had come over him, his solution had been to run, to find a new place, a new situation. Now he didn't feel he had that option. He had committed himself, mostly to Nora, but also, strangely enough, to Pat as well. The other factor that weighed on him now, his connection with this place and its location in the universe, in his own geographical and social history. In all the places he had lived and traveled to over the past thirty years, he had never felt that connection before. He felt torn. To save

Pat, maybe he needed to leave; to save himself he felt he needed to stay.

Nora had finished the milking and was just starting to turn out the herd as Wes entered the barn. She looked up as he crossed by her, a flash of concern swept over her face.

"Everything OK?"

"Yeah. I put him to bed. He'll likely not feel very good in the morning, but maybe it will be a wake up call for him. Somehow, we have to get him past this drinking thing. It's going to kill him one way or another."

"The question is, how do we do that? You know him. There is no changing him once he starts down a road. Believe me, I have been trying our whole married life. Look where that's gotten me; exactly nowhere." She flipped up the two by four lock on the stanchion and released a large Holstein.

Wes, continued freeing the cattle. "I don't know, Nora. Maybe I need to get out of here. Or at least get off the property, live in town and just come out to do chores. That way we aren't together and so it isn't so much in his face. I am pretty sure I am the source of his anger. He may not be saying anything, but it has to be eating him up to see you drifting toward me, maybe leaving him."

He had never said that aloud before. He had thought about it plenty over the past few weeks, but hardly admitted the possibility of it to himself. Nora had shut the barn door as the last of the cows had left. She walked up to him now.

"What are you saying, Wes? You want me to leave him? Go with you? You know I would do that in a minute. There is so much world to see and to see it with you? Well that would be perfect. You could do what you were doing before. Work one place or another for a while and then move on. Let's do it, Wes! I don't think I can go on here much longer. I could deal with it when I had no other choice, but now, you being here, it has opened up possibilities, feelings that I thought were long since dead."

"Oh, Nora. You know we can't leave him like this. I know you wouldn't do that to him. Let's get him healthy whatever that looks like and then see where it takes us."

Nora wrapped her arms around his waist. "Ok. But think about it, Wes. We have both waited all this time to be together. I don't want to waste another minute without you." She reached up and touched his cheek and then stepped back.

They ate dinner quietly so as not to disturb Pat, each lost in their own thoughts. After they cleaned up, Wes, took her in his arms and kissed her. "I am going to head back down to the house now. I'll see you in the morning."

Dennis Hurley

"I'll go with you. He's going to sleep the whole night."

"No. I think it would be best if I just go alone. I have a lot to think about and I think at the very least we should take it easy for a while. Maybe that will be enough to make him feel more secure, bring him back to himself again."

Nora made a pouty face but she nodded her head. "Ok. For now, but I am not going to stay away from you forever. You hear me, Wes Callaghan?" She smiled and gave him a peck on the cheek. "You get a good night's sleep, my love. I'll be thinking about you down there all by yourself."

He smiled back at her. "You too, Nora. We'll work this out."

Morning broke grey and windy, a fine mist shifted and swirling around the buildings. Wes headed up to the house for coffee and a snack before going out to the barn. When he stepped into the kitchen, he found Nora standing at the sink, staring out the window toward the barn.

"Everything ok, Nora? Where's Pat? Too sick to work today?"

Nora turned, her face betraying the concern she obviously felt. "I don't know where he is. I thought maybe he had headed out to the barn early, but there's no sign of a light or anything out there. Did you see his car in the drive when you came in?"

"Come to think of it, I didn't. You think he just took off? "

"I don't know, Wes. It's not like him to not do the chores." She shook her head. "Of course, nothing about him makes any real sense right now. He says nothing to me. I feel like I am in Limbo right now. I wish I knew what to do to help him out of this."

"You still care for him, don't you. I mean after all these years, no matter how difficult they have been for you, you still have feelings for him."

"I don't know, Wes. I mean we have shared a lot over the years. It has been both our struggle to keep this farm going, to make some kind of a living off of it, so I guess we have shared that at least. I have seen his good side at times over the years. He has always been one to help out a neighbor when they were in trouble. Always there for those who needed him. He just never was really there for me. It has been like I am invisible to him. I mean maybe it is just that he has taken me for granted, but somehow, I have never felt that was it. It is almost like I remind him of something that he wants to forget and so he tries to mostly ignore me."

Wes wrapped his arms around her neck and shoulders. "How could that be possible? How could anyone want to ignore you, Nora? It must be something else, something that doesn't involve you at all."

Nora turned, put her arms around his neck and reached up to kiss him, and then leaned back to look at his face.

"You see me, don't you, Wes? I'm not invisible to you? Because sometimes I almost feel like I have disappeared."

"I see you, Nora. You are as real as anyone could be."

She rested her head on his chest for a moment and then, "We had better get you some coffee and there are fresh oatmeal cookies in the jar. Let's get the chores done and then we may have to go and look for him."

After breakfast and still no Pat, Wes brought his pickup to the house and Nora got in. They toured the back roads around Partridge Creek first to see if he had just gotten a bottle and pulled over some place to get drunk, but they found nothing. Shortly before noon they headed into Lapeer to check the bars. They worked methodically street by street until they came to a little bar on a side street near the courthouse. Outside, they found Pat's car parked awkwardly along the curb.

Wes pulled over and backed into a parking place two spots back.

A Sense of Place

"Maybe you should wait out here. It might just make him mad to see us together."

"No way. I didn't come this far to hide in a corner. He needs to just deal with it."

Wes shook his head but he could see there would be no way to dissuade her so they got out of the truck and walked into the bar. The bar was dimly lit and smelled of spilled beer and maybe a few less savory things. It took a minute for their eyes to adjust to the dark interior and then they saw him, head on the bar, a full glass of beer in front of him. Wes approached and softly laid his hand on Pat's back. Pat sprang up like he had been shot and spun to meet Wes. He swung a hard right to Wes' jaw and Wes rocked back and then stepped in as the next punch came at him and slid his arm over Pat's, locked his hand behind Pat's neck and threw him to the floor. Pat tried to rise, but Wes pinned him down and twisted Pat's arm behind his back and held him in place. Pat labored for breath and saliva rolled out the corner of his mouth and onto the barroom floor. Nora had raced across the room and now knelt on the floor next to Pat.

"Pat. Enough. What's wrong with you? This is your brother. He's just trying to help you. Come on. We need to get you home."

Pat went limp. No resistance now and he nodded as best he could. Wes eased his hold on him and Pat rose unsteadily to his feet.

Dennis Hurley

Tears ran down Pat's cheeks and Nora took him in her arms and held him. She tossed a set of keys to Wes. "Could you go and bring his car up in front of the door? I'll drive him home and you can follow me."

Wes nodded and disappeared through the doors. Nora stroked Pat's hair as if he were a baby. "It'll be ok. You just need to get home and get some rest."

After they got him into the car and Nora drove away, Wes went back into the bar and paid Pat's tab- a surprisingly small one.

"How long has he been here?"

"Since I started my shift anyway. That was at 6 a.m. He had been here from before that though. The night guy said he had been there since at least 2 a.m. Never seemed to really get drunk though. Just sat there nursing a couple of beers not saying anything. I usually make conversation with these lone drinkers, but it was pretty obvious he just wanted to be alone with his own thoughts so I left him alone."

"Okay. Thanks." Wes asked for a pen and a piece of paper and wrote his name and the house phone number down and handed it to the bartender. "Could you give us a call if he ever shows up here again? It'd save us a lot of trouble looking for him. Thanks again." The bartender nodded and put the slip of paper into a lower corner of the bar mirror edge.

A Sense of Place

When Wes got back, Nora had gotten Pat up to the bedroom and into bed. Wes poured himself some coffee and waited in the kitchen. A half hour later Nora came into the kitchen and sat down across from him and stared at him.

"There's something seriously wrong with him. It isn't just you. He seemed really weak and he definitely has trouble catching his breath. I don't think he ever recovered from whatever put him in the hospital the first time. Maybe we should try to get him back in there tomorrow. Oh, Wes. I don't know what to do." She leaned forward until her forehead rested on the table. Wes reached across and stroked her hair.

"Let's see how he is doing in the morning. He and I are going to have to talk one way or another because we can't go on this way anymore. One of us is going to get hurt and it is pretty likely going to be him. We need to get it out into the open anyway so we can deal with it." He turned and headed out the door into a day that had turned uncharacteristically warm and sunny.

Wes worked on the Massey and finished with the engine re-build he had started and then went back down to his place to clean up. Afterwards he picked up a canvas bag in a corner that he had never unpacked since he had been there. He opened it to see what it contained and there on top of some T shirts were the two books he had taken so many years ago from Cassie's collection: The Republic by Plato and Shakespeare's Tragedies, an

Dennis Hurley

Anthology. He thought back to the first time he had discovered these books and his reading of The Cave from The Republic and it made him think about his situation now. What had been real in his life and what had been a perception limited illusion? Was his time on the road his reality or was it what he was seeing and feeling now, here in this place? Both places and times had a certain surreal quality for him. He still felt untethered, like he was drifting with no real understanding of anything either past or present, no answers to the questions that had haunted him all these years.

After the chores, Wes headed through the early evening darkness to the lights from the house. The sunset had been brilliant and had colored the sky in vibrant hues of red and yellow. A good sign for tomorrow. March had been dry so far and the frost had been gone from the ground for two weeks now so the fields were far drier than they would normally be at this time of year. Maybe he could get some plowing done tomorrow. He smiled at the thought. He loved the smell of the newly turned earth. Loved the sight of the furrow opening up behind him as he turned the soil with his plow. When he came into the kitchen, it surprised him that Pat wasn't sitting at the table, wasn't in the kitchen at all. He looked questioningly at Nora.

"He said he didn't feel like coming down to eat. I took him some food up to our room. I think maybe he is just embarrassed by what happened today." She turned back to the stove and picked up a large cast iron fry pan that she brought to the table.

"Steak and fried potatoes. I hope that is ok with you." She smiled at him.

"Couldn't be better. Thanks, Nora. I guess I am going to have to talk with him about this."

"Let it wait until tomorrow. I think he needs some time to just mull it over. Let's let him be tonight and we'll start fresh tomorrow,"

Wes nodded. "Ok. In the morning then." They ate the rest of the meal in silence and when they were done, Wes helped clear the table and filled the dishpan with hot water. They washed and dried the dishes and pans together and Wes felt her warmth at his side and felt a sense of contentment that somehow, he didn't think he deserved.

"I'll see you in the morning, Nora. I hope you get a good night's sleep. I think we are both going to need it to be able to get anything out of him."

Chapter 20

The next morning Wes once again felt a strong sense of Spring as he made his way from the house to the equipment shed. Pat hadn't come out to help with the chores or come down for breakfast either and Wes had begun to wonder how they were going to possibly get through this, but now the warm breeze that blew over his face brought rich earth scents and old, pleasant memories carried him away. He had longed for this without ever realizing it until now, and he was excited

Wes backed the tractor up to a three-bottom plow and lowered the hydraulics so that the lift arms lined up with the hitch pins on the plow. He had just gotten off the tractor to connect everything when he heard Nora calling to him, her voice tinged with an urgency he hadn't heard before. He stood up and turned toward the door just as she came running up to it.

"Wes. Pat's gone again. He hasn't left the farm, because his car is still here but he has disappeared. I found an empty whiskey bottle in the bedroom. He must have had it hidden someplace. Oh, Wes. I am really worried about him. I have never seen anything like this from him."

"Ok. Calm down, Nora. We'll find him and try to get this straightened out today. Do you have any idea where he would go on the farm?"

"Not really. He doesn't just wander the farm. He always has a purpose when he goes out to do something. Where should we start?"

"How about the loft? Cassie used to go up there to drink sometimes, remember? Maybe Pat keeps a bottle up there too. I'll climb up there and check."

"No, I'll do that. I know how much you hate heights. You go check down around your place. He used to go down there and sit on the porch every now and then when things were going badly for him."

They separated and Wes jogged down the hill to the home place to look for Pat. When he got there, he found no sign of him. He checked all the way around the house and went inside, but it was clear that he hadn't been there. Everything remained as Wes had left it that morning. He shut the door and started back up the hill to look for Nora when he saw her standing at the top of the hill waving frantically for him to come. He broke into a run and covered the distance quickly. When he got to her, he could see the tears running down her cheeks.

Dennis Hurley

"He's on top of the silo."

"What do you mean? On top of the silo?"

"He climbed up there somehow. I don't know. He's just sitting on the edge, his feet dangling down the side. He won't talk with me, just keeps staring off across the fields."

"Ok. I'll climb up there and talk with him, tell him he is scaring you. He'll come down. I am sure of it, Nora. You keep an eye on him outside. I'll climb up the chute inside and get up there with him."

"Wes, you can't do that. You are deathly afraid of heights. There is no way you can climb up there and get near him."

"I have to try, Nora. He'll fall if I don't get him off there. Hang in there."

Wes turned and entered the barn. There was an eerie silence to it with no cattle inside. Sunlight came faintly through the wavy glass of cobweb covered windows. He made his way to the access chute for the silo. The chute with its laddered side, rose up darkly for forty feet with only a crescent of sky at the top. Wes shuddered. Despite the coolness of the barn, he could feel his hands beginning to sweat. He closed his eyes for a moment and then stepped onto the first rung. He inched his way up, but by the fifth rung he already felt light headed, a little dizzy. He stopped for a while to try to clear his head. The darkness completely engulfed him now, his body blocking out any of the ambient light from below. He felt afraid to look up to the sliver of light above.

He began to climb again, each rung like a purgatory to be endured. Four more times he had to stop, to remind himself to breathe, to regather himself for the next step. Finally, his arm slid over the top of the silo and light poured down over him as he pulled himself onto the rim. On the far edge, Pat sat like he might just be sitting on a fence rail. Wes could hear him humming something to himself, swaying slightly to the rhythm of his tune.

Totally focused now, Wes began to inch his way around the rim, straddling it like a horse, his legs hanging one inside and one outside the silo, his outside foot trying to maintain purchase on the steel band that circled the outside. He didn't want to call to Pat, didn't want to startle him. He wanted to just gradually appear in his peripheral vision. He could think of nothing else but getting to his brother, wrapping his arms around him and holding him, protecting him. Finally, Pat turned his head, looked at Wes but registered no surprise, like this was just an everyday occurrence for them to be sitting at the top of a silo this way, but as Wes started to move closer, Pat held up a hand.

"No. Don't come any closer. I don't want you near me."

Dennis Hurley

"Pat. Why don't you come down with me now? Nora is worried sick about you. You're scaring her."

"Oh, I don't think it's me she's worried about, Wes. You're the one she doesn't want to see fall."

"You're wrong about that. She cares for you and wants the best for you."

Pat laughed slightly. "She might have felt that way before you came, but not so much now. I was never really good for her anyway. She'll be better off with you. I haven't been good for anybody for a really long time and now..." He hesitated as if considering whether to go on or not. "Now, I've run out of time."

"What are you talking about? You're still a young man, Pat. You have a lot of life ahead of you, time to do or be whatever you want."

Pat shook his head. "No, Wes. That's where you're wrong, but there are some things I need to tell you before I go. Some things that probably matter only to you and that you have the right to know."

"Ok. Let's go down and talk about them then, have a cup of coffee and get things out in the open."

"No, Wes. I won't be comin' down from here. Not that way anyway."

"What are you saying? I'm not going to let you do that. You can't do that to Nora and ...you can't do that to me. We have thirty years to make up, thirty years of carrying whatever hurt we each have and now we have the chance to make that up, to help each other heal. Don't do this, Pat!"

The wind had picked up and now Pat swayed alarmingly back and forth on his perch. He shook his head and then broke into a coughing fit. Finally, he got it under control, his voice weaker now. "You don't understand, Wes. One way or another this is the end for me." He closed his eyes and teetered a little as another gust of wind struck him. "Do you know what the doctor told me when I went in that second time?" He shook his head, opened his eyes and looked at Wes. "He told me that I had lung cancer. Told me that I had maybe a year if I was lucky. Lucky…Funny thing to say in a situation like that,ain't it?" He struggled for breath for a moment and then weakly, "I don't feel any too lucky. It took everything I had to climb up here. My lungs are already shot. Whatever time I have left will just be miserable for me, and Nora and you, if you stay. So, I am up here now to spare us all that pain."

"No, Pat. There has to be a way! I don't believe they can't do anything for you."

"Whatever they do ain't going to stop it. Oh, it might give me a month or two more, but at what cost? And I don't just mean money. The treatments are brutal and Nora would just have to watch me die slowly. Not worth it."

Dennis Hurley

Wes, looked down for the first time. Nora stood on the hay wagon below them. Her tear stained face looked up at him, and he could barely endure the pain of it. She obviously had heard everything, and, so far away, he couldn't even comfort her. He turned his attention back to Pat.

"She needs to have some input into this, don't you think? She's the one who will have to live with this, this image of you killing yourself, for the rest of her life. How's that fair to her?"

"I don't want to cause her no pain. She has hung in there with me even though I haven't really been there for her. I know that. I'd say I've never been really fair to her when you come right to it. She'll be glad she doesn't have to deal with the nursing shit that would go into this."

"You're wrong about that, but that should be between the two of you. Give her the chance to at least let you know how she feels."

"I know how she feels, Wes. She was never mine. I took her from you because I could, but she never stopped lovin' you. You oughta know that by now."

Wes inched forward slightly, closing the gap between them.

"You need to stay right there. I don't wanna have to go before I'm ready. I got some things I need to get off my chest first."

A Sense of Place

"Like what?"

"Like things I been carryin' with me all these years that have weighed me down and dragged the heart right out of me. There's been times I think I can escape 'em and Nora and me have had some successes here on the farm, but the shadows always come back."

"What are you talking about?"

Pat closed his eyes and a gust of wind rippled his shirt and then went still. He opened his eyes now. "You know the day Grandpa died? Didn't happen like John and me said it did."

Wes felt a cold shiver run along his spine.

"We was all up in the loft; me and John and Grandpa and Cassie. You see, Cassie was sleepin' back behind the stack of hay in the corner, the place he always kept his bottle so nobody seen him there. That's why Grandpa sent you to look for him. Grandpa had gotten on a kick about me and started tellin' me how lazy I was and since my injury, you know I was full of anger most of the time. Well, we all was standing there with them pitchfork handle clubs we used for rats and when I turned away from him, Grandpa gave me a swat on my ass. I turned real fast and caught him hard on the side of the head with my club. He went down like a sack of grain. About that time, Cassie stood up and seen what was goin' on and runs over to help grandpa, but it was too late. Grandpa was gone and Cassie just sat and cradled his head and started rockin' Grandpa back and forth. That's how he come to have all the blood all over him. John was the one thought to make up the story to blame Cassie, and I went along with it." He gasped for breath, gathered himself and started again. "So, a good man died in prison and here I am. The thing is, I've been in my own prison all these years. Nothin' I did or said was ever goin' to free me. So maybe this will." He started to edge further forward.

"No, you son of a bitch! You don't get off that easy! You aren't the only one walked away with a burden from that day. I knew Cassie couldn't do that. Cassie was my friend and I probably knew him better than anyone and I still didn't stick up for him, didn't at least get his story. I let down the best friend I ever had, and I've carried that with me all these years too. So, don't go thinking you were the only one hurt from that day, from that lie. Not only that, but I walked away from Nora all those years ago because I thought you two were in love, and I couldn't get in the way of that. So, thirty years wasted. Thirty years alone living mainly out of a suitcase and now I find out the truth and you want to take the easy way out? Not a chance."

Wes slid quickly across the rim, the concrete edges biting into his inner thighs, and wrapped his arms around Pat as he started to push himself forward. They struggled on the edge and suddenly, Wes saw the fear in Pat's eyes. Pat didn't want to die, was afraid of death, and

A Sense of Place

Wes held him tighter. They balanced there for what seemed like forever and then, Pat started crying and Wes gripped him even tighter. "It's going to be all right, brother. We just need to get you down from here so we can sit and talk this through. I'm going to hold you while you scoot your left leg back over the rim so you can sit like I am. That way I can help you get back to the chute and we can get you down. There's a lot more to be said, but not up here."

Pat nodded and then struggled to throw his leg back over the silo top so that they sat facing each other straddling the rim. When he had positioned himself, Wes began to pull him along with him as he inched backward along the rim. Very carefully Wes inched him along the rim and made his way back to the chute.

"Nora. Would you get me that mow rope that's loose up there? I think you can probably bring it up to me if you climb up the chute. I want a safety line on him as he makes his way down." Nora ran to the barn. Minutes later she brought the rope up to him and went back down to help from the ground. Pat no longer struggled and now clung, shivering to Wes as he rigged a harness in the end of the rope and fitted it on his brother.

"I want you to climb down the way you always do, but take your time. If you are having trouble breathing or get too tired, stop and get yourself together. I am going to have you on this rope so you don't fall. Just take your time."

Dennis Hurley

Wes wrapped the rope twice around the top rung of the ladder and then paid it out as Pat started his descent. When he was on the ground, Wes slumped down and lay along the rim of the silo on his stomach, a wave of nausea swept through him and only when Nora called up to him to ask if he was ok, did he sit up again and start to make his way slowly down the ladder.

A Sense of Place

Chapter 21

The wind had picked up while Wes and Nora
helped Pat into the house. Clouds thickened and the sun
contracted to a pinpoint of light as a cloud curtain drifted
across it. Wes stood in the doorway and stared at the sky
for a moment while Nora helped Pat up the stairs to the
bedroom. Definitely, rain in those clouds, he thought. A
change of plans, but then everything about today
represented a change of plans. He just wasn't sure what
that meant yet.

Nora came down and stood beside him, her arm
circled his waist and she held him close.

"What are you thinking, Wes? That was a lot for
you to take in all at once."

He turned to face her. "You didn't seem very
disturbed by what he said. Did you know any of this,
Nora?"

She looked at him and then slipped her arm away
and went over to the kitchen table.

Dennis Hurley

"Come sit down with me, Wes. We need to talk."

"You knew, didn't you. Why didn't you tell me? You knew how important it was for me to know the truth."

"Come, sit down. It's more complicated than that."

Wes paced back and forth. "How long have you known?"

Nora hesitated, looked down at her hands on the table. "I have known since about a year after the trial. It happened at about the same time that my dad died. It had gnawed at him and Pat felt so guilty that he wanted to turn himself in. He always thought he would be found out and that Cassie would get off, but Cassie not testifying for himself pretty well sealed his fate I guess. There was never any follow up investigation. After Pat told me, I didn't know what to do. I wanted him to confess to it, but then you had left and with my dad dying, all I had was him and I didn't .." She hesitated again. "I guess I was only thinking of myself. I was afraid. I didn't see any future for myself and so I didn't say anything. I am really sorry, Wes." When she looked up, tears were running down her cheeks. "I know how much Cassie meant to you and I didn't stand up for him when I had the chance. I can never forgive myself so I don't expect you will be able to forgive me either."

A Sense of Place

Wes slumped into a chair across from her, elbows on the table and covered his face with his hands. He stayed that way for several minutes and then took his hands away and looked across the table at her quietly crying there in the dim kitchen light. He reached across the table and touched her hand.

"I can be no madder at you than I am at myself, Nora. Why do you think I came back here? I paid for the funeral, the burial. I thought somehow it would help me shed the past, my betrayal of Cassie. He sacrificed himself because he thought it would be easier on the family if everybody thought it was him. I knew him and I knew he wouldn't kill Grandpa, but I let him die in prison rather than face what it meant and for that I will forever be haunted. So, no, I can't be mad at you without being equally mad at myself. The question now is what are we going to do for Pat?"

"I guess I am going to end up being his nurse until he passes." Nora stopped, stared out the window. The rain had started now and the wind drove it horizontally across the yard like a blowing curtain. "I am not sure I can do that, Wes. I have hung in there all these years with nothing to show for it but a wasted life with a man who never really loved me, but somehow needed me. Now I just don't know if I can sit there and watch the only meaning I ever had just slowly fade away. I am not sure that he even wants me here anymore."

Dennis Hurley

"I think we are going to have to see what he wants, Nora. He is the one who will have to make this journey now. I won't let him take his own life though. He needs to use this time to come to terms with what he did and maybe he and I need to come to terms with each other. So, I'll be here with him if you would rather not."

"What are you saying, Wes? Where else would I be? I am tied here no matter what. I would feel guilty if I left, and there is really no way for me to leave anyway." I don't have any money that isn't tied up in the farm."

"If you need to leave, if you can't be there at the end, I'll make it happen for you. When I came through that door the first time and saw you walk into the kitchen, I knew then that you had been through something tough. You've already been through enough it seems to me. You've done your part protecting him and taking care of him all these years. You think about it. I'll do whatever you need to give you some happiness."

Nora's face said it all to him. Her tears flowed freely now as she stood and came around the table to him. He stood and took her into his arms and held her close until the sobs subsided and then held her at arm's length.

"I have always cared for you, Nora, and I really want to be with you, but let's get Pat squared away and find out what we are facing. Then we can see what the future holds for you and me."

A Sense of Place

She nodded her head and stepped away. "I am going to get him to sign something so we can find out what the doctor told him. I am sure he is going to need medicine or something to help him through until the end. We need to know how to take care of him. I'll take care of that today and you make an appointment to see his doctor."

Wes nodded, reached into his back pocket and took out a bandana and wiped her face, drying the tears. "I'll call and then I am going to take off for a while. I need to spend some time letting this all sink in, try to get my head straight. I'll take care of the chores and I'll see you at supper."

Nora nodded, turned and left to go up to the bedroom to see to Pat. Wes made the call and then stepped outside. The sudden shower had stopped now, but the wind still gusted across the yard and the branches of the young elm outside the door bent and wove in response. Wes walked slowly back down the hill to the home place and got into his pickup. He knew where he had to go now and was anxious to get there.

Dennis Hurley

Chapter 22

He parked the truck at the closed wrought iron
gates of the cemetery. The sun battled the clouds, found a
crack here and there and intermittently lighted the
gravestones. He swung open the gate and made his way
up the hill to Cassie's gravesite. The dirt mound had sunk
some over the winter, but the fresh, rawness filled his
senses, brought unfamiliar tears to his eyes. He stood
still, the wind tousling his hair and he looked out across
the mill pond, little waves rippling from west to east
across its surface, catching the occasional flash of
sunlight, and reflecting it back in pin pricks of light. He
could still picture Cassie moving along the shoreline,
bending to a trap, moving with a certain animal grace that
set him apart from others even more than did his
deafness.

"What can I say, old friend but that I am forever
sorry. You were there for me so many times over the
years that we were friends and, in the end, I walked away

A Sense of Place

from you. I left you when you finally needed me, and I can never forgive myself for that. My one wish is that somehow you can forgive me."

He sat on the brown grass next to the grave, his back against a maple tree and closed his eyes. The sun had won the battle now and shone down on him and warmed him. A thousand thoughts raced through his mind. He remembered the sudden deaths of his parents and the loneliness he had felt right afterwards. That had eased some with Cassie and especially with Nora, but then those years traveling and working so many places had only intensified the feeling until he now realized that it had become the essence of who he was. The sun had descended almost to the horizon when he finally got up.

He did the milking and feeding alone that night and felt a familiar comfort in the cattle sounds and the rich scents that permeated every corner of the barn. It surprised him that somehow here, he could live in the moment where the past wasn't constantly resting on his shoulder. When he finished, he stood in the barn door and looked out at the open fields stretching uphill toward the east. Soon the barn swallows would be returning, their flights darting and skimming high and low had fascinated him as a boy and their yearly return had then given him a sense of permanence. He longed for that now as he felt balanced on a tipping point where he didn't know for sure what he would do or where he would be after this was all over.

Dennis Hurley

After he was finished, he closed up the barn and climbed once again into his truck and drove away. At first, he wasn't sure where to go and so he just drove the back roads trying to sort everything out, but before long his hunger got the best of him and he turned toward Lapeer and finally stopped at a little mom and pop restaurant along M 24. On the side a faded sign said Good Eats. He parked his truck on the shoulder and went in. A farm family sat at a table in the corner and looked up as he came in then turned back to their meal. Another group of men in bib overalls sat along the counter and talked quietly back and forth, talked of crops and spring planting and the weather and at once, Wes felt both a part of it all and as separated as he had always been. He took a small table by the front window and waited for the waitress.

Eventually, she finished with another order and came to his table. "What'll it be, Hon?

Wes eyed the board over the counter and quickly settled on the Special, creamed chipped beef on toast. She brought him a water, asked if he wanted anything else to drink, but he just shook his head and turned to stare out the window. Eventually his order came and he ate slowly, listening to the background chatter and glancing out the window as if he thought the answers he sought might appear out there at any time.

He returned to the farm at midnight and pulled in alongside the old farm house, shut off the truck, walked to the porch, sat on the step and looked up at the star filled sky ranging above him. A silhouette appeared on the horizon by Pat's place and then disappeared into the hillside darkness. A few minutes later, Nora appeared out of that darkness and came across the yard and stood in front of him. She had been crying and tears still streaked her face. She made no attempt to wipe them away.

"I was so worried you had left. When you didn't come in for supper, I went looking for you. I came down here and waited for a long time, but I finally had to go back and check on Pat, and so, when I finally saw your headlights, I had to come back down and see if you are alright."

"You don't have to worry about me, Nora. You have enough to worry about with Pat. I have my own set of problems to deal with, and I have just been trying to sort out my feelings today, and figure out what I need to do. I am not sure about a lot of things, but I am not going to leave here now. For one thing I have some penance to do for my past failures. I let you down once when I left without knowing what you were thinking. I am not going to let you down now going into the spring planting. You'll have to decide what you are going to do after this is all over, but I at least owe you and Pat my time now to keep this place running."

Nora sat down beside him and laid her head on his shoulder, slid her arm around his waist. She was crying again. "Thank you, Wes. I really need you right now. I am really sorry I didn't tell you right off what I knew about Cassie. You caught me off guard coming home like that out of the blue and all. All I could think about was being with you and how right it felt. I was selfish and didn't want to spoil it."

"It's what it is, Nora. We all made our mistakes. How is Pat doing?"

"He is having a hard time with his breathing. It is like he has given up. He is much worse than he was just yesterday. I don't know how long he is going to last. I want to take him to the hospital tomorrow, but he isn't having any of that. Says he wants to die right here on this piece of land."

"I can understand that. He and I might not be alike in a lot of ways, but we are definitely alike in that. Maybe go into talk with the doctor in the morning and see what we need to take care of him here. I'll do the chores so you can get an early start."

Nora left at eight the next morning leaving a note for Wes that there were pancakes in the oven, that she had already fed Pat and asking him to check on his brother a couple times while she was away. After eating, Wes climbed up to his brother's room. He pushed open the half-closed door and looked across at the hardly recognizable figure propped up with pillows in the bed across the way.

"Hey, young man." The voice weak and raspy.

A Sense of Place

Wes crossed the room and stood next to the bed. "How're you doing, Pat? Is there anything you need? Anything I can get for you?"

"No, I think I got just what I deserve now." Pat broke out in a weak coughing fit, gasping for air between coughs. Wes stood helplessly by the bed. He reached for the pitcher of water on the bedside table and poured a half glass and offered it to Pat when the coughing subsided. Pat sipped tentatively and then waved it away.

"I think I'm about done, Wes." A whisper now.

"You've got more time, old man. That iron constitution you have isn't going to give up that easy. You just take it easy now. I have some things I need to do outside, but I'll be back to check on you in a little while."

Pat nodded. "Don't be long. Might miss the big event." He closed his eyes and sank back against the pillows.

Nora pulled into the drive again at eleven. Wes had just checked on Pat and came out to greet her. "I have some supplies in the trunk, if you wouldn't mind bringing them in," she said.

Wes unloaded an oxygen tank, masks and hoses and a paper bag of pill bottles and carried all of it into the house. Nora had already gone up to check on Pat. Wes hauled the oxygen equipment up to the room and Nora helped him set it all up.

They worked quietly as Pat looked on. Finally, he wheezed out a response to all the activity. "Not goin' to need that, Nora. I just want you to let me go. Won't be long now. I can feel it." He gasped and started to cough again, this time rolling over so that he was half out of the bed, his head and torso hanging down the side, and then he was spitting blood. Nora, cried out and then quickly grabbed a towel and wiped at his face as she tried to help him back into the bed.

Wes lifted his brother back into the bed and drew the covers back. There was blood all over Pat's T shirt and Wes dabbed at it with the towel and then went to the dresser and got out a clean one. Nora turned away crying quietly. Wes helped Pat out of the bloody shirt, wiped the blood from his chest and helped him into the clean shirt. Pat gasped for breath now and Nora drew herself together to assemble the oxygen set up and fastened the mask over Pat's nose and mouth. In a short time, he was able to breathe more easily and, exhausted, he leaned back against the pillow and closed his eyes. Nora drew a chair up next to him and sat holding his hand, tears till running down her cheeks. Wes stood watching for a while and then backed out of the room and went downstairs to the kitchen and put on some coffee.

An hour later, Nora joined him and he poured her a cup of coffee and they sat across the table from one another. "I don't know if he will make it through the night, Wes. I think he has completely given up." She was crying again. Wes sat staring beyond her out the kitchen window.

"He is still tough, Nora. Don't count him out just yet." The words came out less convincing than he had hoped. She sat with her hands over her face, her shoulders heaving slightly with her tears. They sat that way, saying nothing more until Wes stood and walked to the door.

"I'll do the chores and then tonight I'll sleep on the floor in his room so if he needs anything, I can give you a little rest." She nodded and Wes turned and left.

The night drew its cloak over the house and Wes rolled up in a blanket on the floor next to Pat's bed. He listened as Pat moved restlessly back and forth, sometimes appearing to sleep but then awakening as if from a nightmare, strange garbled words spilling out between gasps for air. During those times, Wes sat next to him and held his hand, rubbed his shoulder to let him know he was there for him. When sleep would overtake him, Wes would once again lie down on the floor and try to escape into a restless sleep of his own. In the half light of early dawn, Nora came in and knelt next to Wes and ran her hand over his cheek. He woke with a start, saw her there and sat up, the blankets all around him in a jumbled pile.

Dennis Hurley

"I'll take over, Wes. There is breakfast for you downstairs. Eat before you go out to do the milking. How did he do last night?"

"Ok. Pretty restless, but I think he got some sleep. I'll check back after I am done." She nodded, the strain showing in her eyes as he stood over her. You take care of yourself too, Nora."

Two nights later as Wes arranged the blankets to take his turn at night duty, Pat once again burst into a severe coughing spell that ended in a rush of blood from his nose and mouth.

Wes cleaned him up and helped him put on a clean shirt again and then, put the oxygen mask on Pat and propped him up with pillows for a while. He sat that way, eyes closed, his breathing labored despite the oxygen. Finally, he took off the mask and opened his eyes. "Wes," the sound more like a weak puff of air than a voice. "I am really sorry." A long pause and then a gasp for air followed by the soft, hollow sound of Pat's words. "I couldn't of made a worse mess of my life. Or yours. Or hers." Tears formed along the lower rims of his eyes, broke over the edge like they were flowing over a dam and slid softly down his cheeks. He put the mask to his face and breathed the oxygen for several breaths. Finally, he took the mask away. "I know I don't deserve it. Do you think you could find it in your heart to forgive me? It'd mean the world to me." His breath came in painful gasps now and he pushed the mask onto his face again.

A Sense of Place

A picture of those boys that they had been so many years ago flashed through Wes' mind. The Pat who had lay quietly crying on his bed back then on that first day they had come to the farm and himself so empty he couldn't find a way to cry. He took Pat's free hand and squeezed it tight.

"We both are in need of forgiveness, brother. I walked away and left the burden on you. I left Cassie to rot in jail all those years when I could have defended him, helped him. Whatever your mistakes, they aren't for me to forgive. You need to find a way to forgive yourself." He hesitated for a minute now, looked out the window at the hay field that stretched away up the hill behind the barn, now bathed in sunlight. "No matter our differences all these years, you are still my brother and I will always love you."

Wes wiped at his own eyes now as unfamiliar tears filled them. He gave a last squeeze to Pat's hand, released it and stood up. "You get some rest now. Nora will be up to check on you soon. I have to get some work done if I am going to get started on the plowing in the next few days."

Pat nodded, rolled over on his side so that his back was to Wes. Wes saw him remove the mask. "I love you too, little brother."

Wes had just torqued a bolt on the plowshare he had replaced when he heard Nora calling to him from the house. He heard the urgency in it and took off running. Nora stood in the yard, shoulders slumped, face tear stained. Wes wrapped his arms around her. "He's gone, Wes. When I went up there to check on him, he looked so peaceful, I didn't want to disturb him, but I went to tuck the blanket up around him and I realized that he was no longer breathing. Oh, Wes. I never even got a chance to say goodbye." Sobs wracked her body now, and Wes held her tight there in the yard.

Five days later they stood on the same hill in the same cemetery where they had so recently buried Cassie. Sunshine warmed the backs of those in attendance and Wes had been surprised at how many had come. Whatever his past transgressions, Pat had been important in Partridge Creek. One after another, people came up to Wes and told him how his brother had helped them when they were in need and how sorry they were to lose him. It surprised Wes that he found himself crying again and blew his nose to try to hide it. Nora squeezed his arm and rubbed his back as they sat on the folding chairs and listened to the preacher talk about Pat. The difference this time was that the preacher actually knew Pat and had himself been helped by him once. Nothing impersonal about this sermon. Nora quietly cried throughout it. And in the end got up and went back to the car and sat there her hands over her face while the final words were said.

Back at the farm, she went up to her room and lay on the bed. Wes made coffee and sat drinking it in the

A Sense of Place

kitchen. They had been so busy for the past few days that he hadn't really had a chance to consciously think about the way forward, but now, as he sat there, he realized that he had known what he needed to do all along.

Nora came down and joined him in midafternoon. He poured a fresh cup of coffee for her and they sat in silence for a while. Finally, Nora looked up at him. "What are we going to do, Wes? What are you thinking?"

"I guess the more important question is what do you want to do, Nora? This part of the farm is yours to do with as you want. I guess the old homestead is mine according to the will that Pat left."

"Let's sell them both and travel, Wes. I have always wanted to see the country and now we have the chance to do that. You can work wherever you are and we should never have to worry about money. Let's do it, Wes. I don't know if I could stay here right now with the sadness and the memories."

"Nora, I've thought a lot about this over the past few days. I have been on the road for thirty years. I have been so many places during that time and the common denominator for all of them is that I never felt comfortable, never felt at home." He stood and walked to the window and stood there looking out at the fields. When he spoke, it was more of a whisper.

"I don't know that I ever really wanted to come back here, but when I did, I immediately felt at home. I felt this land, this farm, like it was part of me. I didn't even think that was possible anymore, but despite the mistakes I made, the memories that will haunt me all the rest of my days, I had pretty well decided this is the place I want to be." He turned back to her, walked back to the table and sat down across from her.

He reached across the table and took her hands in his. "You know I once told you about Cassie's theory about everybody having a place and a sense of that place when they were there? I have felt more comfortable here these past few months than I have in years, and I thought it was the farm that made me feel that way, the old memories and the happiness that I had felt most of the time here. You know what I have come to realize? What makes me happy? It's you, Nora. You are my sense of place. When I am near you, I feel grounded, safe somehow. So, if you want to travel, I will be there with you. I don't want to be separated from you ever again."

"Oh, Wes. I feel the same way. I have loved you since eighth grade, since I saw your hurt that day on the playground. When you walked into the kitchen with Pat that night last fall, it immediately felt like a second chance had miraculously come my way, and I couldn't really believe that I could be that lucky. I love you Wes, Callaghan. I always want to be with you too."

"Nora, we don't need to sell the farms right now. I have saved enough for us to do our traveling without that money and I think we both need to take some time to see what life holds for us. I am thinking that for now, we hold onto the farms, sell the dairy herd and lease the land for crops. Then we have the option to come back if that ends up being what we both want. We both have history here, some sad, but a lot of it is important. Your dad is buried here and what was left of my family and Cassie. I guess I would like to hold onto this place for now while I sort out those memories and try to understand the trajectory of my life."

Nora stood and came around the table and Wes rose to meet her. They stood face to face and she took his hands and looked deeply into his eyes. "We both have a journey to make and I just want to start it together. We'll keep the farms. They are our touchstone and you are right. We don't know where our lives will go in the future and this gives us an anchor."

Wes let go of her hands and took her face in his hands and bent down and kissed her tenderly.

By the end of May they had sold the herd. It had been hard for Wes to watch as the last of the Holsteins were loaded into the stock truck to head to a farm near Imlay City. Cattle and the farm had been so intimately entwined in his life as a boy and now after his return, that the farm felt empty without them. He had tilled and fitted the fields for planting while the final arrangements were made and a young farmer contracted to lease the land and live in the home place to keep it up. Wes boarded up John's family's homestead except for the kitchen door and they prepared to spend their last night there. A new truck sat waiting in the drive and after eating out at a restaurant in Lapeer, they came back and packed everything into it. When they were done, Wes turned to Nora. "Why don't you go in and get ready for bed. I'll be in after a little while. There's one last thing I want to do before we leave." She looked up at him searchingly and then nodded and went inside.

Wes got into their truck and drove to the cemetery once again. The sun had already set and a glow of half-light lingered along the horizon. He climbed up the hill to Pat's grave and stood looking at the still fresh mound of earth rising up from the ground around it. "Well, brother, it's done. I have tried to release as many as I could of the difficult memories that have haunted me through my life. Whatever is left now, I will have to carry with me. I hope you are at peace finally, that your burdens have been lifted in whatever world you have entered." He took off his hat and rubbed his fingers through his hair, put the cap back on. "Our lives sure didn't turn out the way we figured, did they, Pat. Rest in peace, brother."

He turned to the east and looked down on the mill pond. From a cluster of cattails, a Great Blue Heron rose, its massive wings beating against gravity until it soared above the trees, turned and glided away into the southern darkness.

A Sense of Place

Made in the USA
Monee, IL
03 October 2021

79272018R00166